Acclaim for Caitlin Kittredge's Black London series

"Takes supernatural shadows to the next level. Kittredge knows how to create a belie— —han fans will enjoy the mix of magic and

"Crackles with conflict ar who love their urban fan this book's for you!"

"*Street Magic* jumps right in to nonstop supernatural action, taking urban fantasy fans on a wild ride."
—*Darque Reviews*

"This is a dark, visceral read that sucks you in and doesn't let you up for air. That is part of my intense love for this series . . . It hit all my buttons: ghosts, magic, demons, cemeteries, England, moors, fog, supernatural creatures, ancient deities. The way things ended, I am seriously anxious to see what is happening next. Go out and get this!"   —*Night Owl Romance*

. . . and the Nocturne City novels

"*Pure Blood* pounds along hard on the heels of *Night Life*, and is every bit as much fun as the first in the series. With a gutsy, likable protagonist and a well-made fantasy world, *Pure Blood* is real enough to make you think twice about locking your doors at night. A swiftly paced plot, a growing cast of solid supporting characters, and a lead character you can actually care about—Kittredge is a winner."   —*Jim Butcher*

"I loved the mystery and the smart, gutsy heroine."
　　　　—Karen Chance, *New York Times* bestselling author
　　　　　　　　　　　　　　　　of *Claimed by Shadow*

"A nonstop thriller laced with a ferociously deadly menace. Count on Kittredge's heroine to never say die!"
　　　　　　　　　　　　　　　　　　—*RT Book Reviews*

"Kittredge takes readers on a dark adventure complete with thrills, chills, and a touch of romance. Well written . . . and impossible to set down."　　　　—*Darque Reviews*

"Fast-paced, sexy, and witty with many more interesting characters than I have time to mention. I'm looking forward to reading more stories in the exciting Nocturne City series."　　　　　　　—*Fresh Fiction*

"Wow, I am still thinking about this book. The last time I reacted to a book this way, it was the first Mercy Thompson book by Patricia Briggs. If you are looking for a book that seamlessly blends a police procedural with a paranormal, go out and get this book."　　　　—*Night Owl Romance*

"A tense, gritty urban fantasy that grips the audience from the onset."　　　　　　　　　—*Mystery Gazette*

"Caitlin Kittredge just keeps honing her craft with each new book. *Second Skin* has some pretty creepy elements and page-turning action. Readers who enjoy good solid urban fantasy will enjoy this installment."
　　　　　　　　　　　　　　　　　—*A Romance Review*

"*Night Life* dived right into the action, and carried me along for the ride . . . If the following books are written with the same care and interest as *Night Life*, they will be a welcome addition to this fantasy genre."

—*Armchair Interviews*

"Kittredge's amazing writing ability shines through in this wonderful tale of murder, magic, and mayhem . . . The intriguing plot grips you from the very first page and takes you on a roller-coaster thrill ride with an ending that will leave you gasping for more." —*Romance Junkies*

"If you're looking for a good paranormal mystery and enjoy reading about shapeshifters, give Caitlin Kittredge's work a try!" —*Bitten by Books*

"Hot, hip, and fast-paced, I couldn't put [*Night Life*] down. Don't go to bed with this book—it will keep you up all night. It's that good."

—Lilith Saintcrow, national bestselling author of *Working for the Devil*

"Luna is tough, smart, and fierce, hiding a conflicted and insecure nature behind her drive for justice and independence, without falling into cliché . . . A lot of fun to read."

—Kat Richardson, national bestselling author of *Poltergeist*

Also by
Caitlin Kittredge

BLACK LONDON SERIES

Street Magic
Demon Bound
Bone Gods
Devil's Business

NOCTURNE CITY SERIES

Night Life
Pure Blood
Second Skin
Witch Craft
Daemon's Mark

SOUL
TRADE

CAITLIN KITTREDGE

St. Martin's Paperbacks

NOTE: If you purchased this book without a cover you should be aware that this book is stolen property. It was reported as "unsold and destroyed" to the publisher, and neither the author nor the publisher has received any payment for this "stripped book."

This is a work of fiction. All of the characters, organizations, and events portrayed in this novel are either products of the author's imagination or are used fictitiously.

SOUL TRADE

Copyright © 2012 by Caitlin Kittredge.

All rights reserved.

For information address St. Martin's Press, 175 Fifth Avenue, New York, NY 10010.

ISBN: 978-0-312-38825-6

Printed in the United States of America

St. Martin's Paperbacks edition / September 2012

St. Martin's Paperbacks are published by St. Martin's Press, 175 Fifth Avenue, New York, NY 10010.

10 9 8 7 6 5 4 3 2 1

Part One

Paradise

With impetuous recoil, and jarring sound,
Th' infernal doors, and on their hinges grate
Harsh thunder, that the lowest bottom shook
Of Erebus. She open'd, but to shut
Excell'd her pow'r; the gates wide open stood.
—John Milton
Paradise Lost

1.

Pete Caldecott sat on a tombstone, watching fog curl soft fingers against the graveyard earth and waiting for Mickey Martin's ghost to appear.

Mickey Martin hadn't always been a ghost, and before a hail of constable's bullets had snuffed out his life in the winter of 1844, he'd managed to slit the throats of thirteen women.

Murderers weren't supposed to be buried on consecrated ground, but with a bribe to the right vicar, Mickey Martin's admirers made sure he got a proper burial. Even razor-wielding serial killers had their fans.

Mickey Martin professed to be a man of God, ridding the earth of wickedness, and in the poverty-stricken world of Victorian London, a bloke who went about slashing prostitutes and charwomen was looked on not as a monster, but as an avenging angel, cleaning the mud-choked streets of the East End of their filth.

Pete wasn't usually the one who sat in chilly graveyards, waiting for the dead. Usually, that was Jack's job. But Jack, the one who could see the dead with his second sight, the one who had all the talent when it came to disposing of the unnatural that crawled under cover of night in London, wanted nothing to do with the Mickey Martin business. Or, if Pete was honest, with much of anything lately.

She could have put her foot down, demanded that Jack be the one to take this on, but that would bring on a row, and she'd had her fill of those for this lifetime and possibly the next. Sitting alone in a graveyard at nearly midnight didn't bother her overmuch. It wasn't like she'd be getting any sleep at home, between Lily's erratic schedule and Jack's ever-present foul mood.

Still, she wished she could chuck it in and go home, sit down in front of the telly with Lily and Jack, and pretend just for the span of a program or two that they were a regular sort of family. The sort where Mum and Dad occasionally got along, and neither of them had any special connection to the ghosts and magic that wound around the city as surely as the river and the rail lines.

Jack had said this job wasn't worth their time when it had come in, but he said that about every routine exorcism. They weren't flashy, but they usually paid, the victims too terrified to even consider stiffing the person who had made the big bad ghost go poof. And something had to put food on Pete and Jack's table, to pay for Lily's nappies and the expenses involved with living in London, which were considerable. If that was boring, shopworn exorcisms, so be it.

It wasn't as if this particular ghost job had come from a disreputable source. PC Brandi Wolcott was a member of Pete's old squad when she'd been on the Met, smart and hardworking, ambitious and driven. And now terrified, after a routine call had turned into a brush with Mickey Martin.

Pete had a reputation with such matters, whether she liked it or not. Everyone at her old squad in Camden knew she'd quit to go chase spooks and vapors. Or at least those were the rumors. The truth was a little more complicated. But trying to explain to coppers like PC Wolcott that if they just cared to look, from the corner of their eye, a part of London would reveal itself—a part made of magic and shadows, harboring creatures like Mickey Martin and far, far worse—would end with leather straps and lithium, and that wouldn't help anyone.

"Caldecott." Pete's Bluetooth headset came to life, and she jumped. She cleared her throat before fishing her mobile from her overcoat. She didn't want PC Wolcott to know she'd been drifting and not holding up her end of their two-person search team.

"Yeah, I'm here."

"I've finished my perimeter sweep. Heading back your way." Wolcott was out here on her own time, which Pete gave her credit for—though not more credit than she gave PC Wolcott for calling her in the first place. Ghost attacks against the living were rare and could usually be written off as muggings or bad trips, but something about this one had shaken Brandi Wolcott badly enough that she quietly went searching for an exorcist, and found Pete. Beyond that, she hadn't said all that much, and Pete got the sense she was having second thoughts about the whole thing. You didn't want to be the only PC who believed in ghosts.

Pete shoved her mobile back into her pocket and let her hands follow. October nights brought on the chill and the threat of winter to come, and the damp crept through her hair and her clothes, all the way to her skin. She could feel the gentle pulse of the Black, the other side that people like Wolcott chose not to see, like the vibration of a subterranean train under her feet. She was mostly used to it by now, but on nights like tonight, when it was silent and the hum of the city seemed miles away, it seeped in and knocked around her skull, almost as palpable as the fog.

Wolcott's blonde head appeared, bobbing between the monuments. The churchyard was only a hundred meters from end to end, but it was crammed full of headstones and obelisks, with far more bodies than there were stones below Pete's boots. London suffered from too many dead and too little space, and before great swaths of green were cordoned off for burying by the later Victorians, the dead resided wherever there was room—in churchyards, under the church floorboards, in shallow pits that fouled the air and drew in the Black like a magnetic field.

"Christ, this weather," Wolcott said. Her bronze skin, painted on rather than earned under the sun, was as brassy as her hair. In her off-hours, Wolcott favored skintight satin pants, loud prints, earrings large enough to use as handcuffs, and makeup by the pound. But she was bright and had nerves of steel, and Pete was glad she'd agreed to come.

"It's going to piss down rain any moment," Pete agreed. She gestured toward a large winged angel, the biggest monument in the churchyard. "Can you take me through it again? What happened the other night?"

"Sure." Wolcott shrugged. "Station got a call from the vicar about half-twelve and I came around. Said there were lights out in the churchyard. Figured it was some hoodies pissing about, thought nothing of it." She walked a few paces, staring up at the angel. Its stone eyes were blacked over with moss, and the ghostly marks of old graffiti wrapped like white vines around its base.

"I got about halfway into the yard when I heard this sound," Wolcott said softly. "This low sound, like a moaning. Still thought it were kids, so I pulled out my light and gave the order to show their smart little faces."

The wind picked up, pushing leaves against Pete's feet, and the fog flowed and rippled across the uneven ground as if it were alive and making a mad dash for the safety of the church. "But it wasn't," Pete encouraged the other woman. Wolcott flinched, as if she expected Pete to accuse her of making it all up, or simply laugh in her face.

"Brandi," Pete said. She laid a hand on Wolcott's nylon-clad arm. "I believe you. The more I know, the easier it'll be for us to make sure this doesn't happen again."

The PC hunched inside her navy blue windcheater, and Pete saw then, up close under the sodium lights, that what she'd taken for reluctance was actually fear. Wolcott's entire body was strung with it, as if she were a puppet on wires. Pete sucked in a deep lungful of damp, cold air. Whatever had happened here, it had been a lot worse than a ghost popping out of a mirror or a poltergeist flinging crockery.

Not for the first time that night, she cursed Jack and his stubborn refusal to do anything that wasn't exactly in line with what he wanted.

Wolcott spoke again in a rush, voice rattling like the dead leaves all around. "I seen this shape hunched on the ground, and he were mumbling, over and over. It were Bible talk, I don't know. I never did pay attention in church."

" 'Behold, I am coming soon. I have my reward with me and I shall give to everyone according to what he has done,' " Pete said. That had been Mickey Martin's favorite passage to quote in his letters to the various tabloids and one-sheets of the day.

Wolcott's nose wrinkled. "Yeah, that. Street-corner nutter ramblings, I thought."

"It's Revelation," Pete said. "The handbook of all street-corner nutters."

"You some kind of brain, then?" Wolcott asked, clearly glad to have the subject diverted from what she'd seen.

"No," Pete said. "Just a very poor sort of Catholic."

"Was about to ask," said Wolcott. "Don't see many Catholics mucking about with the dark arts."

"You saw the man and then what?" Pete prompted,

deciding that the lecture on black magic versus exorcism could wait for another day.

"I told him the churchyard was closed and he'd have to move along," said Wolcott, "and then he just . . . he *looked* at me, and I can't describe it. Had dead black eyes, bleeding onto his face. Such deep holes. Felt like I was falling, and then the cold was all around, and he . . ." Wolcott swallowed, her voice trembling along with the rising energies of the Black.

Pete scratched at the back of her neck. The feelings picking at the part of her mind connected to magic were bloody active, even for a graveyard. Then again, not all graveyards boasted their very own serial killer.

"He came for me," Wolcott said. "Straight through the headstones, like he were made of smoke. And he grabbed for me, his hand went through my stab vest, and it was as if . . ." She shuddered. "He *knew* me. Could see every wicked thing I'd done, and was going to burn me up from the inside."

"I know it must have been terrible for you," Pete said. "If it makes you feel better—six other people have had the same thing happen over the last six months."

"Shit," Wolcott muttered, but her shoulders relaxed a fraction. Pete figured knowing it wasn't just her might help settle Wolcott's nerves—not that it did much for her own tingling hands and jumping heart. The churchyard had been silent for decades until the first terrified woman had called 999 from the pub across the road, and Pete had an idea why Mickey Martin was up and about again—when she and Jack had stopped the primordial demon, Nergal, from ripping his way into the daylight world, it had rippled out and touched everything in the city. Every ghost, every lesser demon, every scrap and snip of magic-having life in London had felt the effects. And now they were awake, and hungry.

At least Pete could put Mickey Martin in his place. The larger aftermath of Nergal and his brethren would just have to sort itself out.

"You're nicer about it than my DCI, but you still probably think I'm crazy," Wolcott mumbled, leaning against the monument. "Everybody else does."

"*Crazy*'s not the word I'd use," Pete said. Wolcott, too, represented a problem—when the Black echoed like a rung bell as Nergal and the other four primordial demons tried to break out of the prison the Princes of Hell had erected for them millennia ago, all of the citizens of both daylight London and the Black beneath with the slightest bit of sensitivity got a jolt like grabbing a high-tension cable.

For psychics like Jack it meant more sleepless nights, more waking visions, and more barrages from the dead and the living alike. For people like Wolcott, who would have never known she possessed the slightest bit of talent under normal circumstances, it led to nights like this.

It wasn't Pete's problem. Her problem was Mickey Martin and his recently reacquired hobby of murdering those he considered wicked.

"You don't seem so looney," Wolcott observed. "From

what they say around the station, I was expecting Stevie Nicks."

"I thought I'd leave my scarves and tarot at home, yeah," Pete agreed. She ignored the implication that apparently the longer she was gone from the Met, the more of a moony-eyed hippie type she became in common legend.

"Never liked stakeouts," Wolcott said. "Bloody boredom sets in quick, don't it?" She scraped a fingernail against the moss on the monument. "How'd you cope, when you was a DI?"

Pete's head started to throb, though she didn't know if it was from a lack of coffee, the cold, or Wolcott's persistent questions. She shouldn't be mad at the PC—Wolcott was just trying to distract herself from her nerves.

She did the same, counting headstones, listening to the faint thump of music from the far-off pub, feeling the droplets of fog collect on her face and hair. The whispers of the graveyard had stilled, and even the mist held its place, covering the ground, the headstones, and the dead beneath. For a moment, it was as if the entire city of London held its breath—no music, no cars, no trains, not even the heartbeat of the rushing Thames.

Then the pain in Pete's head spiked, and she knew the silence had only been a lull, not a finale.

From the stone behind Wolcott, the shadows began to seep and merge, moving of their own accord, against the light that gleamed from the vestry windows and the streetlamps beyond the confines of the churchyard. The monument gave birth to a dripping black shape that wavered from cohesive to vapor and back again, sliding through the pocked limestone like oil through water.

"Wolcott!" Pete shouted, but it was too late. The thing had Brandi by the throat and engulfed her, pouring into her eyes and nostrils and down her open gullet, choking her scream before it had a chance to be born.

"Shit," Pete said, only able to watch as the ghost of Mickey Martin poured itself like black, oily water into a brand-new body. She'd only met a few ghosts that could do that, and none of them had anyone's best interest in mind. Exorcisms were hard enough when you were only dealing with a vapor.

And yet, Pete thought as Brandi's eyes clouded over with silver and she let out a choked moan, her limbs jerking and spasming as the ghost took control, it didn't *feel* like a ghost. Pete wasn't a psychic—that was Jack's game—but ghosts felt like electricity, like lightning striking too close for comfort, like every ion in the room was awake and slamming against her skin. This was cold, and black, and bottomless, giving no sense that the thing inside Brandi Wolcott had ever been alive, never mind human.

The one thought pounding through her head over and over was that Jack would never have let this happen. He'd have known something was off, and been ready for this thing that was not a ghost.

Pete sidestepped as Brandi came for her, acrylic fingernails catching and ripping at the front of Pete's overcoat. Jack would never have let this happen, but he wasn't here, so she was just going to have to make do with her own wits. They'd served her well enough for thirty-one odd years; they'd do for a few more minutes.

Brandi came for her again. She was as fast and mean as a PCP addict, an inhuman sight with black energy spilling out of her eyes and her mouth, her face twisted in a grimace of perpetual agony.

Pete amended that. If she managed to survive the next few minutes, then she could figure out how to end this.

A headstone caught Pete at the knees and she fell, feeling her left arm twist under her, the ugly crunch of bone on stone resonating over Brandi's ragged breathing and Pete's own heartbeat.

"Aren't you pretty," Brandi growled in the guttural tones of East London. The voice of Mickey Martin, made rough and hot with hatred. "Pretty enough to turn heads." Brandi crouched over Pete, inhaling deeply at the nexus of Pete's neck and shoulder. "I can smell it on you," Brandi intoned. "Wickedness. Sin. The filth of the streets dripping off your skin." She grinned, black spilling over her tongue and down across Pete's cheek. "Going to enjoy slicing you open and watching it all bleed out."

Pete was glad Mickey Martin was a talker. It gave her time to plunge her hand into her opposite coat pocket and bring out her metal police baton. She tried to snap it open, but the bolt of lightning up her left arm told her that the plan was dead before it began. Her arm was sprained, at best. Shattered, at worst. Later. She could fix her arm later, when she was alive and away from here. Otherwise, they could arrange it in her casket so nobody would know. Either way, she had a more pressing problem.

Instead, she wrapped her good hand around Brandi Wolcott's neck and squeezed. Ghosts riding bodies needed life, breath. They weren't zombies, hunks of corpse revived by a necromancer. So Pete squeezed, with every ounce of strength left in her.

She expected that Mickey Martin would vacate Wolcott's skin, and then she'd have a fighting chance to send him back to the Bleak Gates and the land of the dead beyond. She never expected the smoke pouring from Wolcott to wrap itself around her wrist and begin the slow crawl up her own arm.

Not again, Pete's mind screamed. *Not this.*

She didn't allow herself to give voice to the scream she felt bubbling up in her throat. When a nasty from beyond the beyond was bent on her flesh, panic was a luxury she didn't have. She let the onslaught of the ghost's form come, because it was better for her to be Mickey Martin's victim than Wolcott. Wolcott didn't know how to save herself.

"You think this'll end well for you?" Brandi growled as the black smoke overtook Pete's hands, her arms, crept toward her mouth and throat.

"Better than it will for you," Pete rasped, as the first fingers of cold found their way over her tongue.

The ghost of Mickey Martin didn't feel right, as it bled out of Brandi Wolcott in a flood and rushed up at

Pete's consciousness. It didn't feel like a ghost; it just felt hungry, and cold.

This is wrong. Pete didn't have to be a psychic or a professional exorcist to know when things had gone pear-shaped. She'd had a ghost try to take up residence in her skin once before, and it hadn't felt like this, this . . . nothing, howling and trying to swallow her.

Brandi collapsed on top of Pete, choking, and Pete managed to wriggle out from under her and get herself upright. She was still tangled with Mickey Martin's ghost—or the thing that had been his ghost. Pete knew that the regular exorcism that she'd planned would do less than shit. It might tickle this thing that had grown out of the ghost, or ruffle a few hairs, but that would be about it.

Then it would just be a matter of how many pieces she and Wolcott were found in, once someone noticed they were missing.

What would Jack do? Something stupid, likely, but as Pete felt the chill air against her face, felt the smoke creeping into her nostrils, she decided stupid was better than nothing.

Rather than fight the smoke any longer, she let it come. She might not have the sort of talent that let her throw fireballs or read minds, but she did have one. She felt the thing trying to move into her flesh, overpower her mind, and she welcomed it. Let it in until it touched her talent, and reared back with a scream.

"Oh no," Pete told it, as the thing coalesced into a form, tall and skinnier than any man, with a mouth as wide as Pete's two hands put together. "You wanted me, you have me." She felt her talent wake up, begin to drain the cold from the thing, the malice and the hunger. It thrashed like a fish on a line, screaming now in pain rather than anticipation.

Pete recognized the thing now—a wraith, a personification of the hunger and the rage that were the dregs of a spirit. Wraiths consumed ghosts, fed until they'd burned through the spirit's energy like a bad battery, and then moved on. Any humans that happened along would be found by an unfortunate passerby after they'd been wholly consumed, desiccated and frozen from the inside out.

This wraith, though, would never escape to feed on any of the other spirits that haunted the churchyard. This wraith belonged to her now, and she felt its cold magic seeping into her, as her talent drank the wraith down. It gave one final spasm before it detached from the battered shell of Mickey Martin's ghost and scattered on the cold wind, wisps and faint trails and finally only the echo of its last howl against the headstones.

Pete felt her legs give out, and she sank to her knees in the rough dead grass at the base of the obelisk. Her fingers were blue, and her breath when she blew it out was frosty and opaque white. She could feel the wraith's magic fluttering inside her like a dying bird, and she let it go. If she held it in too long, her talent would burn her from the inside out. It hadn't been easy, to learn to let go of that dizzying high that came with sucking another being dry. That high was the ostensible upside of being a Weir, a channel for the darkest and oldest powers in the Black. Unlimited power, as much as you could steal—if you could hold it. Otherwise, you went insane when you hit the threshold and took too much of another's power. Or simply burst a blood vessel and keeled over dead, because magic was more powerful than any narcotic, and your lust for it had eaten you alive.

Weirs didn't usually last long. To make it to thirty-one was a feat, according to Jack. Most days, Pete wasn't sure it was something to be proud of.

"Fuck, my head," Brandi Wolcott groaned. "What happened, Pete? What *was* that?"

"Mickey Martin," Pete said quietly. "Or what was left of him." Wraiths were rare; it took a clever predator to survive by eating the innards out of ghosts, and London, while rife with spirits, was also rife with mages, exorcists, and psychics who ensured that predators like wraiths stayed where they belonged—in the vast screaming nothing where unfortunate lost souls could be consumed by any number of hungry things. They couldn't usually fight their way out to attempt to make a meal out of flesh-and-blood people.

Pete supposed she was just lucky she'd been the one to get the full brunt of this wraith, rather than poor Wolcott or some unsuspecting priest or church worker.

"So it's over?" Wolcott looked a bit mussed, but none the worse for wear. Most victims of possession never even knew it had happened. The mind glossed it over, a horror a regular person couldn't contemplate.

"Yeah," Pete said. Wolcott came and helped her up, and Pete bit down hard enough to draw blood when her arm spasmed again. "Fuck," she hissed. She simply couldn't be laid up right now—not only did she have more jobs booked over the coming weeks, but it was also going to be impossible to hold, feed, and change a baby with one working arm.

"You all right?" Wolcott's alarmingly orange brow furrowed.

"I'll manage," Pete said. Wolcott considered for a moment, and then nodded.

"Right. I'm parked up on the high street. Should get on home, probably." She started to walk away, then turned back. "He's . . . it's . . . that thing's not . . . coming back, is it?"

"No," Pete said. "That's done with."

"And those things he said to me . . . they're not true."

Pete shrugged, the last of her ability to sugarcoat gone. "I don't know what he said to you, Wolcott. I can't know if any of it was true."

The constable's mouth turned down at the edges, and she glared at Pete. "You know, them up in the squad was right about you."

"What, that I'm a nutter?" Pete shrugged and immediately regretted it, feeling the twinge of battered tendons.

"No," Wolcott said. "That you can be a bit of a bitch." She made her way through the churchyard and out the gate, not looking back.

"No argument from me on that score," Pete muttered, feeling for the keys to her battered red Mini Cooper. They'd fallen from her pocket in the struggle, along with her wallet and her mobile, scattered across the grass. Pete collected everything, and then gave a fresh yelp as she straightened up and almost bumped foreheads with a tall figure in a black coat and hat.

Her first thought was *Shit, shit, shit* as she braced herself to come face to face with a squad of witchfinders, the only sort of gits who favored the "Orson Welles circa *The Third Man*" look.

When the figures merely stood impassively, however, she got a second look. Their hat brims were pulled low, and what faces she could see had the corpselike pallor and waxy, unhealthy skin that normally only cropped up on zombies. Their mouths were free of red stitching, though, and the way they'd appeared out of thin air wasn't terribly zombielike. Zombies were brutes, and they were generally no good at sneaking about.

"Petunia Caldecott," said the leader. His voice didn't make her name a question. The other four stared at her, motionless as the headstones all around.

Pete figured there was no point in arguing. "Yeah?"

The figure extended a hand. His fingers were long, the nails nonexistent, pulled out by the root, gnarled scar tissue in their place. Pete gingerly took the black envelope offered, being careful not to touch the thing. Skin-to-skin contact in the Black was often worse than grabbing a live wire—and there was plenty of black magic that could be passed with only a touch. After the scene with the wraith that ate Mickey Martin, she wasn't about to take any more stupid chances tonight.

"You are cordially invited to attend the tenth full gathering of the Prometheus Club," said the figure. His voice was oddly high and reedy, as if he were on the verge of having his vocal cords wriggle their way out through his throat.

"I . . . have no clue what you're on about," Pete said, holding the envelope by the corner. In any other place, on any other night, this would smack of bad live theater, but she was rattled enough not to antagonize the waxen men. There was something about their mannerisms and the way they'd just *appeared* out of thin air that hinted to Pete that they were dead serious.

"The patrons of the Prometheus Club do hope you will choose to attend, Weir," said the lead figure.

"It took five of you to tell me that?" Pete asked, flicking her gaze quickly between the pale men. It wasn't exactly a secret that she was a Weir, but those in the Black were usually a bit more circumspect about saying it to her face. She scared people, and she wished she didn't, but the Weir was something to be afraid of. Hell, *she* was afraid of it.

"We are messengers," said the lead figure. "We have delivered our message."

"Yeah, well," Pete said. "Tell your club to shove it. I don't particularly cotton to shadowy errands, especially ones that come with an implied threat."

"That is a pity," said the figure, and he tilted his

head so that Pete caught a bit more of his face and a flash of his eyes. Or where his eyes should have been. The thing didn't have any sockets, just divots in the skull, covered over with that same waxy, unnatural flesh. Pete swallowed a roll of nausea. She'd seen worse. Crime scenes had been worse. She kept her face still. It wasn't as if she hadn't come face to face before with things that weren't strictly human. Or strictly alive.

"I never considered it a pity to miss a fancy party full of twats who think scenes like this are funny," she said.

"The penalty for refusing the Prometheus Club is dire," said the figure. He gestured woodenly at the envelope still pinched between Pete's fingers. "Would you care to reconsider?"

"No," Pete said instantly. The type who'd send heavies for a simple invite were the type you wanted to avoid. "No, I will not reconsider. And now I'm tired, so kindly fuck off and let me go on home."

"Your choice," said the figure, and all five turned and marched, single file, through the churchyard gate and into the inscrutable fog.

2.

The midnight streets were as deserted as they ever got in central London, and Pete made it home on autopilot, still trying to take off the chill engendered by the wraith. The church bells on Bow Street were tolling half-twelve when she parked the Mini in the alley behind Jack's flat.

Each step up the four flights to the flat hurt, and she leaned against the wall inside the door, collecting herself before she saw Jack and Lily. She didn't want him kicking up a fuss about her going on jobs alone. The prewar light fixture in the hall buzzed, and Pete made a mental note for the dozenth time that they needed to get the wiring in the place checked out.

Before she'd had to look at the flat through the eyes of a responsible parent, it had been more than fine. Now, though, she couldn't help but see the nicotine stains on the ceiling and the lead paint on the windowsills, the stove that emitted strange and dizzying odors anytime she or Jack tried to do more than heat up takeaway, and she realized that they'd never make enough money to move someplace more conducive to raising Lily. Not that Jack would go for it, if she suddenly found thousands of pounds lying in the street. He'd been living in Whitechapel since the eighties, and Pete couldn't imagine someone like him moving to the country, surrounded by flat motorways, flatter fields, Tesco superstores, and normal people.

The protection hexes that wrapped the flat like spider silk slithered away from her as she advanced into the sitting room. There might be a pile of clean clothes on the floor and a sink full of filthy dishes, but at least Jack hadn't let the hexes slide.

He sat on the sofa, Lily cradled in one arm, watching a film with no sound on Pete's laptop. He'd never kick in for a TV, but he'd finally given in to the allure of the internet. Lots of mages were technophobes—and lots tended to fry whatever electronics were in their range—so Pete counted herself lucky that she didn't live with a walking electromagnet, and that Jack had decided having an endless supply of Lucio Fulci films and spaghetti westerns was worth the extra bill.

"She's been asleep for a few hours," Jack said softly. He shifted, almost imperceptibly, and reached for his glass of whiskey. "I was afraid to move her."

Pete let herself drop down beside him, coat, bag and all. She was weary from top to bottom and still chilled to the bone. "I'll put her down in a few minutes."

Jack regarded her in the blue light of the screen. Clint Eastwood stalked across a dusty town square, merciless sun beating down on cheap plaster sets. "You look like shit," he said presently.

"I love you, too," Pete grumbled. Her attempt to pull herself together had been useless. Why did she even try to hide things from a psychic?

Jack tilted his head. "Did something happen?" he said. Pete scooped Lily into her arms.

"You might say that," she murmured. The baby grizzled a bit but settled down. Pete got up and put her in her cot in the corner of the sitting room near the disused fireplace, then switched on the baby monitor.

"You and Clint finishing up?" she asked Jack. Usually he stayed awake until near sunrise, which meant they rarely slept at the same time, but then again, it meant he was the one awake for Lily's dawn feedings. The part of Pete that wanted to spend time with Jack like they used to hated it, but the sleep-deprived mother in her thought it was a fantastic idea, and these days, sleep always won.

"Yeah, it's almost through with," he said. He caught her hand as she started for the bedroom. "You swear you're all right?"

"Sure," Pete said, fighting a grimace as her arm flared up. "Never better, luv."

Jack, at least, had the decency not to call out her lying.

Pete dropped her clothes on top of the ever-growing pile next to their bed, then collapsed on it in her jersey and underwear. She was tired—too tired to change, too tired to tuck herself under the duvet, too tired to do anything except stare at the ceiling, tracing the familiar stains, continents of cracks and water damage amid a plaster sea.

Still, she couldn't convince herself to shut her eyes and fall asleep. When Jack shuffled in from the bathroom and added his denim and his moth-chewed sweater to the pile of laundry, she sat up and decided she had to ask. "Jack, you ever hear of the Prometheus Club?"

He froze, for just a heartbeat, before he shrugged. "Might've heard some chatter, but nothing much." His glacial eyes focused on her with an intensity that made the cold in her bones return with a rush. "Why?"

Pete shrugged in turn. "No reason," she said. "Heard of them somewhere."

Jack got under the duvet and offered her half, and Pete curled on her side facing him. He wasn't telling her everything. After years of seeing him lie in every conceivable way, catching him was almost a reflex, an instinct for detecting the deception Jack used as an invisible shield. If you didn't know him, you couldn't hurt him. The first line of defense for paranoids everywhere.

Whether or not his paranoia was justified in this case, she could find out in the morning.

"Seen many wraiths around London lately?" she asked him, changing the subject. Trying to pry the truth out of Jack when he didn't want to give it was like trying to reroute the Thames—messy, difficult, and not happening.

"Wraiths? Not unless the sad old men are telling stories down the pub." Jack snorted. "Why, you see one?"

"Saw it, talked to it, felt it try to rip my soul out," Pete confirmed. She peeked under the duvet, checking out her injuries. Her leg was a solid parade of bruises on the side where she'd caught the gravestone, and she'd be feeling them even worse in the morning. If Lily weren't a consideration, she'd down a handful of the Vicodin Jack kept in the medicine cabinet, but instead she tried to shift the pillows around to support her sorest bits and switched off the light.

After a moment, Jack's arm snaked gingerly around her waist, and she let his warmth and smell of soap, leather, and tobacco envelop her. It was a scent that could smooth all her rough edges and calm her instantly, but it wasn't working tonight.

"Wraith moving into a churchyard around here's not a good sign," Jack muttered into her hair. "What'd it say to you?"

"Usual rot," Pete said. "It was riding Mickey Martin's ghost—what it hadn't already drained—trying its hand at the living. Almost turned poor Brandi Wolcott into a milkshake."

"Hmm," Jack said, but that was all. He didn't offer an opinion, didn't give voice to the fears knocking around Pete's brain since she'd gotten in her car at the churchyard. Pete listened as his breathing smoothed into sleep, but her own thoughts wouldn't quiet.

They whispered that she *should* be afraid, and if Jack had any sense he would be, too. That the talented—latent mages, unwitting psychics, and nascent sorcerers—were awake all over London because of what Jack had done.

That the incidents of ghosts and the Black spilling into daylight had multiplied by orders of magnitude since Nergal had tried to break free. They weren't stopping; they were increasing, like a flood tide rising to swallow everything in its path. Monsters thought to be only stories had once again appeared, and the fractious and scattered human magicians in London were no match for any of them.

The whisper of her own fears told Pete that the Black and the daylight world were wounded, ruptured and bleeding into one another, and nobody had the faintest idea what to do.

The thought kept Pete awake for what remained of the night, and her eyes were still open when the first gray whispers of dawn crept through the dirty panes and across the threadbare carpet of the bedroom.

3.

Neither Pete nor Jack had any jobs booked for the rest of the week—then again, Jack never had any jobs booked of late. Nobody in the Black trusted him, and nobody wanted him anywhere near them, especially after word had got round of what happened in Los Angeles. Personally, Pete thought that returning four of the worst things the Black had to offer to their iron prison in Hell was an accomplishment, not a liability, but mages were only human. They got scared, they got paranoid, they closed ranks. Jack might be more talented than most, and a damn good exorcist, but nobody in London would consider him worth the risk. Not for years to come.

Possibly not ever.

Pete herself, not being in direct contact with the four primordial demons or Nergal, was less of a risk, but nobody trusted her because she was the Weir. Only mundanes would hire her, and the work she'd done for Wolcott would barely cover their bills.

She scooped up dirty clothes from the bedroom floor, determined to do at least one thing today that would actually yield a tangible result. Lily was in her bounce chair watching children's programs on Pete's laptop. Jack was out on the fire stairs smoking. Pete figured she could take a few loads of clothes down to the wash, then do the sweeping and washing up before both Jack and Lily got bored and demanded her attention.

The black envelope given to her by the pale men fluttered to the floor from inside her jeans. Pete considered it for a moment, a square black stain on her floor, then decided she was being ridiculous. It was just paper—nobody was afraid of paper. She picked it up, sitting on the edge of the bed and sliding her thumbnail under the edge of the envelope.

She'd been inclined to ignore the sort of buffoonery that resulted in a bunch of gits accosting her in a graveyard, but Jack's reaction to her question hadn't been what she'd expected. If this Prometheus Club scared him so much, didn't she owe it to herself and Lily to at least see what they wanted from her? To be prepared for the worst?

The invitation was all one sheet, folded in on itself like a puzzle box, and Pete watched as black ink flowed across the white paper, spelling out a formal script before her eyes.

Miss Petunia Caldecott
The Prometheus Club requests your presence
10th full gathering of Members
Manchester, England
One week hence

Pete blinked, logically knowing that it was only a small enchantment on the paper, but transfixed all the same. How could they know she'd even open the envelope, not toss it in the bin?

Because they knew her, Pete realized, and knew she'd be too curious to not at least look.

She felt the same flash of worry and panic she'd caught in Jack's face take up residence in the pit of her stomach. She didn't like strangers knowing her this well. Where to find her, how to manipulate her.

She was about to crumple the thick paper and toss it into the bin when she felt a stab of pain in the hand not already aching from her tussle with the wraith.

"Shit!" Pete gasped, leaping up and dropping the invitation to the floor. Too late, she saw the ink had raced from the letters, through the paper, and into her hand, piercing her skin like a barb. The ink massed into a circle within a circle in the center of her palm, and Pete hissed, scraping at it but only making the pain worse. It burned and stung, like being tattooed with a hot iron.

On the floor, one final phrase bled across the thick white card.

Attend or die. The choice is yours.

"Shit," Pete said again, feeling her blood drain with all haste toward her feet. She swayed from the pain, catching the wall, which only made the mark hurt more.

"Luv?" Pete heard the sitting room window open and shut as Jack came in from his smoke.

"I'm fine," she managed. "Just . . . scraped a bit."

Her shaking voice gave her away, and Jack came running. "What's happened?"

Pete held out her palm wordlessly. The pain had largely ceased, but she still felt the intrusion of the ink under her skin, and foreign, unfriendly magic along with it.

Jack picked up her palm and turned it, brushing his finger over the ink.

"Stop!" Pete shouted through gritted teeth, as the hot poker feeling flared again. "Dammit, Jack, that hurts."

He whistled, removing his callused fingers from the ink. "That's a bloody strong one," he whispered.

"Strong *what*?" Pete demanded, trying to pull her hand from Jack's grasp. The ink was agitated at his touch, turning and twisting under her skin like a living serpent, trying to escape its confines. The pain made her a bit dizzy, the magic warring with her Weir as it tried to absorb the spell and was rebuffed. Pete coughed as a wave of nausea swept through her. That had never happened before, and it didn't improve her outlook on what might happen next.

"Strong geas," Jack said. "It's a compulsion spell. What did you *do*?"

"Why are you assuming I *did* anything?" Pete snapped. "All I did was open that stupid envelope." She stayed upright despite the vertigo and the sick feeling running all through her like a fever. She wasn't going to give whoever had cast the thing the satisfaction of passing out.

Jack cast his glance down at the envelope and then shut his eyes tight before meeting her gaze. "You didn't," he sighed. "You didn't get involved with the Prometheus Club."

"I *knew* you had more on them than you were telling," Pete said, pulling her hand free.

"'Course I did, but you didn't say you'd been *contacted* by them," Jack growled. He picked up the invitation between his thumb and forefinger and whispered a word of power.

Pete watched the paper curl up, eaten by blue flames. She hoped the ink on her hand would disappear with it, but it stayed under her skin, throbbing and hot. "Would it kill you not to snap at me?" she asked Jack. "I didn't exactly do this on purpose, you know."

He stayed silent, in his maddening Jack way, until the letter was only ash drifting to the carpet. Then he sat on the bed and gestured for Pete to sit next to him. She did it, mostly glad to have an excuse to sit down and quiet her spinning head.

"You better tell me, from beginning to end, what happened last night," he said. His voice was still harsh and clinical, and Pete flinched.

"I'd really appreciate it if you'd leave off behaving as if all of this were my fault. I didn't ask for them to show up and thrust that silly envelope at me."

Jack sighed and ran his hands through his hair, then put one around her. He was wiry but strong, and Pete leaned into the warmth of his chest.

After a moment he spoke, his voice vibrating through

her. "I'm sorry, luv. I just . . . I thought we'd be under their radar. The Prommies are a bunch of snobs, wouldn't deign to come down our level unless it was life or death."

"Is this gathering of theirs that?" Pete said, staring at her palm. "Life or death?"

Jack nodded, his angular jaw tightening. "They wouldn't have called you and made sure you'd come if there weren't something big on the horizon, big and bad enough to get them pissing themselves."

"What could that be? Who *are* these people?" Pete asked, rolling over some of the things she'd seen in her time with Jack. Demons, black magicians, the hungry ghost of Algernon Treadwell—even the first beings of Hell themselves, the veritable Horsemen of the Apocalypse. What could possibly be worse than that?

"To the first, I have no idea, and to the second, they're twats," Jack grumbled. "A secret society in the worst way you could imagine. Bunch of magicians more concerned with standing around patting each other on the back for being special than with actually doing anything useful. Holdover from the days of corsets, servants, and landed gentry."

"Like you said," Pete murmured. "Twats."

"Yeah," Jack said. He kissed the top of her head and covered her injured hand with his, softly this time. "Got no idea what they want with us. We're emphatically not Their Kind."

"I suppose we'll find out," Pete said. "When we go to Manchester."

Jack raised one eyebrow as if she'd lost her mind.

"We can't very well not go," she said. "I've got a compulsion spell on me, and I'm not chopping off my hand. We'll go, we'll be civil, and we'll figure out what they want from us, then find a way to graciously decline."

Jack sighed, then nodded. "Fucking Manchester. Could've been anywhere, and they chose Manchester."

Pete twined her fingers with Jack's. The pain had cooled some, and his touch soothed the burn of the ink. The back of his hand, pale as a corpse, was covered in his own black ink, feathers and thorns twining in a pattern that could make you dizzy if you stared at it long enough. Jack's tattoos used to be haphazard, but now they covered nearly his entire torso in the same pattern.

Something else she'd been ignoring—the change that Jack had undergone when he'd stopped Nergal. He'd had to make a bargain with the Morrigan, the patron goddess of his talent, and when Pete couldn't sleep, she often thought about how some day, the Hag would be back to collect.

But for now, there was this mess. Her mess. At least this time it was something she'd done herself and not something Jack had walked into. That was oddly comforting. Her problem, her solution, no collateral damage.

"How bad could it possibly be?" Pete whispered, turning to plant a kiss on Jack's jawline. His stubble rubbed her skin, and she concentrated for just a moment on the feel of him and not on all of the myriad shitstorms that swirled around them like a rotating crop of nightmares.

"You say that now," he said, with a laugh as dry as old bones, "but just you wait. It's the dirty North, luv, not a weekend in the country."

"Perhaps," Pete said, settling back against Jack's chest, listening to his heartbeat and Lily burbling in the other room. Jack was real, solid, the only thing she could count on to be real and solid now. "But it's not as if I have a choice."

Go to Manchester, into who knew what sort of situation with hostile mages, or stay in London and perish under the geas if she couldn't figure out a way to reverse it in time. It was the story of her life: shit choices, but the only ones available to her.

4.

As the train raced toward Manchester the next morning, Pete watched the fields and towns slip by, punctuated by trees and arials. She tried to keep her eyes open, but no sleep combined with the little she'd managed to snatch in the previous weeks meant the rocking of the train put her under.

It felt strange to be going somewhere without Lily. She'd gotten used to taking the pram, the diaper bag, and everything else any time she and Jack attempted anything more complicated than a quick trip downstairs to the small off-license next door.

"Don't you worry," Jack's friend Lawrence had said when Pete dropped off Lily at his doorstep earlier in the morning. "I got three little sisters, changed more diapers than I wanna remember. She and me, we'll have a good time." He bounced Lily in his massive arms and she cooed, trying to reach up and grab his dreadlocks. Lawrence chuckled, then fixed Pete with an unsmiling gaze. "What should I do if you don't come back?"

Pete felt as if somebody had kicked her legs out. "Excuse me?" she'd said, hating the wobble in her voice. Jack had disappeared on one of his errands to one of his many shady mates, saying there were things he needed before they went to Manchester, so she was on her own, the only one who could answer. She'd never wanted to smack Jack in the head more than at that moment.

"Clear you two are mixed up in some badness." Lawrence shrugged. "Don't think it's a crazy question."

"I . . ." Pete swallowed the hard stone that had grown in her throat. "My mum, I suppose," she said at last. "She's, um . . . she's prickly, but she'll look after Lily just fine."

That was more than she could say for her older sister MG, or any of Jack's crop of degenerate friends who weren't Lawrence. Her mother, the one person in her family who hated magic and those who had anything to do with it, was the only one she could trust. Pete swiped a hand over her face and tried to look at Lawrence like everything was all right.

"Right then," Lawrence said, and she saw from his expression she'd failed miserably. "See you in a week or so. And Pete?" He stopped her with his free hand on her arm. Pete chewed on her lip, which was as raw as her nerves at that moment.

"Yeah?" she said.

"Take care of Jack for me," Lawrence said. "He ain't been himself since, well. Since he got himself that new ink, and that new bargain with the dark lady."

"I always bloody take care of him, don't I?" Pete snapped. Lawrence didn't deserve being yelled at, but she didn't have the reserves to be civil any longer.

Take care of Jack. As if anyone else would want that thankless job. She'd been taking care of Jack since the moment they'd crossed back into each other's lives. *She'd* gotten him clean of drugs. *She'd* chased him into every godforsaken corner of the Black as the Morrigan's hold on him got tighter and tighter. And likely she'd chase him into the fire of Hell itself when he finally went down for good.

She could lie to herself and pretend that wouldn't happen, but she'd made her decision. Left her life, left everything normal, and thrown in her lot with Jack. Had a child with him, for fuck's sake.

That was as entwined as it got. And if she were honest, it wasn't as if he'd trapped her like a princess in a maze of thorns. She cared about Jack, and had for most of her life. She loved Jack, despite all his bad mistakes and bad choices. He was the only one who'd been there for her since her father died. Jack would walk through fire for her, and even when things were as bad as they were right now, she recognized the rarity of that.

When she'd met Jack at Victoria, they hadn't spoken much until they were on the train, and even less after they were in motion, rolling slowly through North London and picking up speed in the Midlands.

Lawrence's comment wouldn't leave her alone. She cared about Jack, knew he wasn't perfect and would never be. *She* wasn't perfect either. She had ghosts and scars. But the fact was, her ghosts didn't have teeth, and her scars weren't inflicted by a thing like the Morrigan. Those were facts, and much as she wanted to ignore them they remained, permanent as Jack's tattoos. He shouldn't be here. Shouldn't be drawing breath, shouldn't be walking around. He had died. Pete had watched it happen. The demon that Jack had bargained his soul to had collected and taken him to Hell. He should never have escaped, but he had, and when he'd died again, that should have been that. People died. Eight months visiting her da's cancer ward had drilled that home to Pete hard and fast.

But that hadn't been the end, either, and when he'd escaped the clutches of the Morrigan and sent Nergal back where the demon belonged, he'd come back different.

He wasn't her Jack. She could pretend everything had gone on as usual, but her Jack, the one she'd known since she was sixteen, the one with the devilish grin and the absolute disregard for anything after the next moment—that Jack had died when the demon collected his soul. When he'd returned to her after Nergal had been vanquished, he'd been different. Not someone else entirely, but as if he'd turned up with pieces missing. Part of Jack was still with the Morrigan, and part of the Hag rode his body in place of everything that had made him truly human.

Pete had tried to ask him about it, once, but she'd gotten such a look from him, of murderous rage and loss and grief and fear all at once, that she'd never brought it up again. Jack didn't remember what had happened with the Morrigan, or so he claimed, and Pete figured it was best for all if it stayed that way.

She felt the train grind to a halt, and her eyes popped open. Jack was snoring beside her, but when she turned back to the window nothing but green greeted her. The trees stretched away on either side, moss covered and ancient. She'd never seen trees like this, so gnarled and close in.

Pete waited for a moment for an announcement from the conductor, but none came. The tube lights in the ceiling of the car hummed, and she fidgeted until a flash of movement caught her eye.

The raven landed on the closest branch, impossibly large and stony-eyed. It tilted its head this way and that, and then it leaned toward her.

"You should go home, Weir," it croaked.

Pete started, but she didn't react otherwise. "Oh, really," she said. "And why is that?"

The raven hopped a bit closer, the moss-covered branch bending dangerously under its weight. *"You know this isn't going to end well. You are not a meddler, Weir. Leave the mages to their schemes and the gods to their plans."*

"I'm not," Pete agreed. "And for that reason, I don't appreciate the Hag sticking her nose in my business."

"The crow woman shares your sentiment," said the raven. *"This is no place for you, Weir. Your presence will only make matters worse. Destruction walks in your*

*wake, and you should stay away . . . for Jack's sake as
well as yours."*

"That's all very menacing and portentous," Pete said,
faking. "But I've got a better idea—how about you fuck
off, and I'll get on with my day?" Bravado was the only
thing that worked on things like the Morrigan's messengers. It was that or scream, and she would never give
the Hag the satisfaction.

The raven shifted, head tilting to the side. *"You are
not afraid of us."*

Pete snorted. "You think you're the first old god to
visit me in my dreams? I am the Weir. It's practically
commonplace."

She'd never get used to the dreams. Weirs had the
power to dream the truth, which also made them a handy
conduit for any entity that wanted to speak its piece to
the daylight world.

"The warning remains," the raven said. *"The Morrigan will not be denied. She is death, she is—"*

"She is eternal," Pete said. "Second verse, same as
the first. Here's a tip—if you want me to pay attention
to anything that raggedy old crow has to say, tell her to
change her fucking record."

The raven twitched, and then abruptly it took flight,
a black shadow flicking across the sun, gone in the
blink of an eye. Pete exhaled. Fucking gods and monsters were all the same, thinking they could just tune in
on you any time they liked.

The train window, rimed with a thin layer of rain-
drops, cracked in a spider web pattern directly in front

of Pete's face, with a force that pasted her back in her seat. This time, when Pete looked, it wasn't a raven staring back at her, but the glowing gold eyes of the Morrigan herself. Her face was pale, chased with black veins, and her hair was feathery and black, flying around her head as wind and rain lashed the train car.

Pete felt the vibration of the Black down to her bones as the Morrigan manifested herself, placing one taloned hand against the glass, leaving deep furrows as they screeched across the cracks she'd made.

Jack can't deny me, she hissed. *What makes you think you can?*

"I helped you," Pete said. She was quivering, and there was no hiding it, but she wasn't going to start having a fit. "I helped you put Nergal down. And you got what you wanted—you left your mark on Jack."

What I wanted *was my birthright,* the Morrigan screeched. Lightning split the nearest tree, and Pete was momentarily blinded. When she could see again the Morrigan was inside the train car, standing before her. Her dress was a tattered shroud, stained with the blood of a hundred dead, and black blood dribbled from her lips when she spoke.

You denied me my war, Weir. The march on the daylight world that my army will *have, at the end of all things. You think you've saved your pathetic little slice of the cosmos, but you've merely granted it a stay of execution.*

Cold took over Pete's body inch by inch—not the chill of outside air, but the final cold of death, as her body shut down and her heart ceased to beat. She could see her breath when she whispered, "You might have Jack, but you'll never have me. You'll never have the end of my world that you want. Not while I'm alive."

The Morrigan snarled. "Then perhaps we should do something about that, since you're Hell-bent on being the heroine of this story."

She reached for Pete, bloody talons wrapping around her throat, searing Pete with her cold touch, talons ripping through her skin, into her jugular vein. Pete felt hot blood gush forth, and the last thought she had was that she wouldn't even have time to scream, wouldn't have time to tell Lily one last time that she loved her . . .

She woke up with a thrash and a scream, and Jack turned to stare at her, taking off his padded headphones and narrowing his eyes. From his MP3 player, Pete heard the strains of the Runaways.

"Sorry," she said. Her heart thudded so violently that her breastbone ached. "Bad dream."

Jack grimaced. "That sounded like a little more than a nightmare."

People were staring, and Pete shrank back into her seat, looking out again at the low gray land passing all around them.

"You really can't tell me anything else about these Prometheus Club bastards?" she asked. Jack huffed at her abrupt change of subject, but there was no way in any Hell that Pete was telling him what she'd seen.

The Morrigan could try to scare her, but she could

only reach Pete in her dreams. In the daylight world, at least for now, she was powerless.

Jack shifted in his seat, and Pete caught sight of the tattoos along his wrist. She wondered just how long the Morrigan would remain in her dreams.

She realized she was glad for the more pressing problem of the geas. The Morrigan able to reach into the larger world via Jack was a horror that didn't bear contemplation.

"I'm not holding out on you, if that's what you mean to say," Jack said. "Nobody knows about the club except the members of the club, and nobody knows the members." He shoved his MP3 player back into his bag and leaned his head back against the seat, rubbing his forehead.

"*Supposedly,*" he said, "they're a sort of ruling council of the UK, all the big muckety-mucks from this side of the Black and the other gathering together to rule from the shadows, punish the little people who get out of line, all sorts of fun activities for the rich and wanky." He played with the cord of his headphones. "I could tell you the exact weight and measure of the load of bollocks I think that is, but I bet you can guess."

It sounded like a load to Pete, too. Nobody could hope to control the Black. Nobody could even hope to control the mages and other magic-workers of the UK, never mind the demons, Fae, and other, less visible creatures skulking around the Black.

If the Prometheus Club thought they were going to control her, they were in for a rude surprise.

5.

The train ride to Manchester was only a bit over two hours, but when Pete stepped off the carriage she felt as if she'd stepped onto the surface of another planet. The ever-present tide of the Black was gone, replaced by something that felt more akin to a brick wall, something you could scrape the back of your knuckles against and leave skin behind.

Jack massaged the spot between his eyes. "Fucking hate this place," he grumbled.

Pete hefted her bag and joined the tide of people heading for the taxis and public transport. Jack lagged a few steps behind, squinting as if he'd just stepped into bright sun from total darkness. "I don't think we should check into a hotel," she said, falling back to walk with him. "Too easy to track us that way. Besides, we're broke."

"Yeah. If you're interested, I do know a couple of viaducts that are decent to sleep under," Jack said. He tried to smile, but the expression looked like it hurt, and Pete winced.

It was easy to forget, with the flat and Lily and the normal life they had when they weren't doing this sort of thing, that Jack had started life as a poor kid from a bad council estate in the worst part of Thatcher's Manchester. He'd slept rough, done drugs, and fought tooth and nail to survive on the streets before one of the Morrigan's other shadows, Seth McBride, had recognized what he was and trained him to be a mage.

Pete could have slapped herself for making Jack bring that part of his life up again. He never talked about it, beyond the vaguest generalities. What little Pete knew had all come from other people or the one dip she'd taken inside Jack's memories via her talent, which had been enough for ten lifetimes.

"I don't think we've resorted to a carboard box just yet," she said. Trying to keep up the smile, keep it light. Pretend it would all be fine. If she had no other skills, she had that one.

"I'll look up a few old friends, if they're still above-ground," Jack said. "'Least there are plenty of holes to crawl into in this town, if you need to stay low."

Pete nodded, deciding that even though Jack's "friends" usually turned out to be lowlifes of the highest order, staying unseen was definitely top of her list.

"I'll make a call," Jack said, heading for a bank of payphones.

While he fished for change and dialed, Pete scanned the crowd. She'd felt the prick of eyes on her back since they'd left the train. Not a magical feeling, a copper feeling. The crowds weren't as thick as they had been in Victoria, and her tail didn't have many places to hide.

A few likely suspects—a young kid with a backpacking kit, an Indian woman in a business suit—passed her by when she stopped in the center of the sidewalk and pretended to check out her mobile.

An older gent, chubby and balding, stumbled when she stopped short and cut an abrupt left to the newsagent's stand, pretending that had been his destination the entire time. Amateur hour, for sure. Probably not the Prometheans, then. They could at least afford a tail who wasn't fifty pounds overweight and wearing an eggplant purple windcheater, red-faced and panting with his attempt to keep her in sight.

Pete took a step toward him, and they locked eyes. Purple Coat surprised her then—rather than look away and pretend to be busy buying a newspaper, he nodded to her and then gestured with his chin for her to come over.

Pete cast a look back at Jack, who was chatting away on a pay telephone. She caught a snatch of conversation, including "Fuck off, you old bastard." He was within screaming distance if she needed him, so she cut through the new stream of people coming off a Cardiff train and approached the fat man.

"You're Petunia Caldecott," he said without preamble. "The Weir."

"On my better days," Pete agreed. "Nobody calls me Petunia, by the way. It's Pete."

"I need to ask you something," said Purple Coat. He

shifted, fists shoved into his pockets, and Pete tensed again. This gent could very well be a nutter. He certainly looked the part. She and Jack didn't have many fans in the UK these days, though assassins usually went directly for their target.

Mentally, she cataloged her options. She could run, thump him with her police baton, scream, or try to sling a hex, which was about as reliable as closing your eyes and hoping the other bloke missed. Physical magic was Jack's game. She was just a beginner.

Purple Coat drew out a crumpled object wrapped in newspaper, and Pete started breathing again. "Ask, then," she said. "Haven't got all day, have I? We've somewhere to be."

"I know," he said. "The Prometheus Club."

Of course you do, Pete thought, because nothing since those odd, pale creatures had shown up in the graveyard had been a coincidence.

"You going to warn me away?" she asked Purple Coat. "Threaten me? Whatever it is, kick on."

"From what I've heard, neither of those will have any discernible effect on you," said Purple Coat. "I just needed to reach you. To talk to you before you disappeared into that den of vipers."

Pete held up her hand, exposing the twin circles of the geas. "It's a little late for that, mate. They've got their hooks in good and tight." She cocked her head, taking his measure. He was dirty, up close, and had the sour smell of the infrequent bather. His eyes were bloodshot and even though he was still a fat bastard, his skin sagged from weight loss. He looked sick, and exhausted, and his eyes kept roaming the train station even as he bit back a yawn. "Who are you, anyway?" Pete asked him. "When was the last time you slept?"

"My name is Preston, Preston Mayflower," he said. "I used to be a Member." Pete could hear the capital letter in his voice. "I'm sorry for the state I'm in, Miss Caldecott, but I can't rest. They have members who can reach you in your dreams, get inside your head. I can't allow that to happen."

He twitched as a businessman passed too close and tucked himself inside his windcheater. Pete had dealt with plenty of paranoids as a copper, and she knew the difference between drug-induced insanity, genuine mental illness, and fear.

This was the latter. "What's wrong, Preston?" she asked, employing her best soothing tone. "What's so important that you came here?"

"Listen." Preston grabbed her wrist, abruptly, and Pete jerked in reflex. She didn't get much feedback from Preston, though, just a jumbled buzz of magic, like the last bit of static electricity when she brushed against metal in winter. The raw nerve of Manchester's Black was stifling her ability to sense anything more.

"Please don't touch me," she said gently, removing Preston's hand from her. "I don't want Jack to get the wrong idea."

The threat of Jack Winter made Preston recoil like a spring, which would have amused Pete if the poor man hadn't looked so terrified. "I'm sorry, it's just . . ." He swiped a hand across his eyes. "I used to have a normal life, Miss Caldecott. They're going to say things about me—that I'm a nutter, that I went off the rails and betrayed them, that I've always been crazy and unstable. But I'm *not*." He shuddered. "I was a geomancer—someone who could consecrate and bind the earth, find holy sites, tears between the Black and the daylight, that sort of thing. Made a nice living as an estate agent, when I wasn't searching out trouble spots and places of power for *them*."

"Okay," Pete said. "I believe you, Preston." She didn't know what she actually believed, but he needed to hear it and she needed him to get to the point.

"When I found it, they tried to take it, tried to lock me up," said Preston. "They tried to take it for themselves. I saw it then, what the tenth gathering was really about, and I'm here to warn you, Miss Caldecott. Break the geas. Don't get anywhere near the Prometheans, and if you must do so . . ." Preston shot a bug-eyed glance into the crowd, eyes roving over every face as his sallow cheeks flushed. "Don't take the crow-mage with you."

Pete started at that. "I don't know what you mean, Preston. I want to understand, but you're not making much sense, luv." To warn her away was one thing, but to suggest that the Prometheans had unsavory designs on Jack was much worse. Nobody who wanted to use him for their own ends was on the side of good, justice, and happy kittens.

"They'll pour honey in your ear," Preston whispered.

"They'll make me out to be the villain, and they'll send you in my stead. But they're ignorant at best, and liars at worst. They don't realize how things have changed because of what Nergal did." He swallowed and coughed—a wet, contagious sound that came from deep in his lungs.

"If I had a pound for every time somebody told me that," Pete said. She didn't mean to be flip, but Preston looked near tears at the thought that she wasn't taking his rant at face value. He thrust the bundle at her with a sharp, violent motion.

"I know you don't believe me, and I wouldn't either, but you have to take this. Take it and *don't show it to them*." When Pete took a step back, Preston snatched her hand and pressed the paper-wrapped object into it. "Take it," he said. "Keep it safe. Maybe it can help you where it couldn't help me."

Jack came up behind her, and Pete nearly jumped out of her skin when he spoke. "This fuckwit bothering you?"

"No . . ." Pete started, but Preston was already off and running toward the taxi line and the street beyond.

"Who was that?" Jack said.

"He was . . . I don't know. Random nutter, I think," Pete said, though the thought nagged at her that Preston had been entirely too frightened to have made what he said up out of the ether. "Told me the Prometheans weren't what they seem."

Jack snorted. "In other news, water is wet, Arsenal's defence is shit, and the Pope wears a silly hat."

"That's how I felt," Pete agreed. She told herself to shake the vague feeling of unease as they made their way to the end of the taxi line. Preston Mayflower didn't have to be a portent of certain doom. He could be crazy or, worse, he could have been sent by the Prometheans themselves as a test, to see if Pete would be a good little soldier if faced with an excuse to try to slip her geas and get away.

Whatever the reason, she didn't have the energy to play games with yet another set of shadowy intrigues. She barely had the energy to drag her bag along the curb.

The ache of exhaustion was the excuse she gave herself afterward for seeing a streak of purple from the corner of her eye but not realizing what was happening until it was far too late. Preston Mayflower shoved his way through the throng at the curb, broke through the taxi line ahead of them, and cast a frantic look over his shoulder. His face was nearly the same color as his windcheater, and sweat flew in a sparkling arc from his balding head.

Pete followed his line of sight, her mouth forming into a shout, and saw two people pressing through the crowd behind him, the sort of nondescript that usually lent itself to undercover cops. One man and one woman, beige coats, dark hair, nothing remarkable about them. Except the look of fear they elicited from Preston Mayflower.

A taxi slammed on its brakes, tires screeching, and the driver leaned out his window to scream a curse. The woman of the pair got nearly close enough to touch Preston as he dodged into traffic, but he took another loping step forward, eyes bugging out in terror and seeing nothing in front of him.

All of it happened in the space of two heartbeats, from her first view of Preston to the squeal of hydraulic brakes and the sickening, final impact of a body making contact with a Manchester city bus.

Cries went up from the taxi line and the bystanders. A transit copper came running, yelling into his radio, while the bus driver dismounted his vehicle, face ashen and hands shaking.

"He was just *there* . . ." the driver cried. "Nothing and then *there* . . ."

The woman of the pair reached Preston's body and bent down, rolling him onto his back. One leg and one arm were twisted behind him, and the body made a sound like a sack of apples being tossed about. To any casual observer, the woman was administering aid, checking a pulse and pulling at Preston's eyelid, but Pete watched her other hand creep across the windcheater, inside the pockets, and feel around the waistband of his stained trousers. She looked at her companion and shook her head imperceptibly, and by the time the copper reached the scene, they had melted into the crowd, two beige vapors gone on the wind.

Pete swallowed the scream that had never gotten further than the back of her throat as Jack stared at the body. He asked, "Holy Hell, did you see that bastard leap?" but she didn't really hear him.

She felt the weight of the wrapped parcel Preston had forced on her inside her own pocket, and a chill crept over her exposed skin, all the way down to her bones.

Whatever was inside the parcel, Preston Mayflower had just died to give it to her.

Jack gripped her arm before she could pull out the object and open the paper. His touch created a warm spot on her frozen skin. "Come on," he said in her ear. "Rest of the cavalry'll be here soon. No point in still hanging about when they show up."

Pete allowed herself to be led away, and soon the crowd had shut them off from the scene in the street. She could still hear the sick impact of the body and the squeal of tires, though, and see the panicked expression in Preston Mayflower's eyes. If that had even been his real name.

She hadn't felt good about coming to Manchester, but she had allowed herself to think it might work in her favor—clearly the Prometheans didn't want her dead, just obedient. If she did what they asked, or at least heard them out, she'd be able to get out clean.

Now, though, she wasn't sure. Not of her plan, or of anything, including the Prometheus Club's true intentions. But she couldn't break the geas, Jack couldn't break the geas, and she wasn't naive enough to think anyone they went to in Manchester about the problem wouldn't run straight to the Prometheus Club with the news that Pete Caldecott was trying to skip out on their invitation.

So she'd go. She'd be a good little soldier, at least for now. But she wouldn't trust the bastards who'd forced her to come here one bloody inch.

She let Jack hold on to her as they walked a block over and down, then hailed a cab. Nobody followed them, and Pete forced herself to relax until they were away from the center of the city and heading into Jack's old stomping grounds.

6.

Pete hadn't grown up on a council estate, but she'd had plenty of school friends who had, and she knew the drill. Suspicious of outsiders, and angry at their lot in life, and they didn't give a fuck about much of anything.

Council estates in London were mostly cut from the same cloth—tower blocks where her friends lived stacked on top of one another like past-date merchandise, filled with noise, cigarette smoke, and older boys who leered at them any time they had to pass by in the stairwells or the garden.

The cabbie who drove them sped away, his taillights smears of red in the pools of dark created by broken streetlamps. Pete looked up and down the street, but they were the only souls about. The sun was still setting over the Beetham Tower in the center of the city, but the shadows here were already long. Alexandra Park, Jack's old estate, contained squat brown semi-detached houses, rusty iron gates, and windows covered with tatty curtains that twitched in sequence as the residents of the estate scrutinized the outsiders. It was as if a child who

was shit at taking care of his toys had discarded a
model town and left it to moulder and rot.

"Feels like home already," Pete said, staring down a
particularly cheeky bitch who peered at her from her
front garden, glaring as if Pete had just kicked her pets.

"Lot better than it was," Jack muttered, lighting a
cigarette. "Back then, someone would've chucked a
bottle at you and someone else would've pulled a piece
and demanded all your worldly goods."

He pointed to a corner shop, windows bright with
fresh vegetables and hand-lettered signs in Farsi. "That
place burned down in eighty-eight or eighty-nine, 'cos
of some hooligans. Mum was too stoned to keep me
inside, so I watched the whole thing from the pavement
until the fire brigade shooed me away."

"Dare I ask what greasy friend of yours we're bunking with in this charming hamlet?" Pete said. Alexandra Park wasn't any worse than wandering down the
wrong street in Peckham, but there was an undercur-
rent of hostility that she'd never felt in her hometown.
They weren't wanted, and both the residents of the estate and the currents of the Black drifting through like
oily water made sure that Pete knew it.

Jack kicked his boot over the broken pavement, all at
once unable to meet her eyes. Pete pursed her lips.
"What? What about this am I not going to like?"

He sighed. "Tried a few numbers. One's dead, one's a
guest of Her Majesty for the next five to seven years, so
if we want to stay off the screen, this is our only choice."

Pete cocked her eyebrow, letting Jack know she didn't

appreciate the ultimatum. "Spit it out. What's wrong with the bloke?"

Jack stamped out his fag. "Nothing's wrong with *her*. Not all me friends have some inherent character flaw."

"Oh" was all Pete said. She'd been prepared for most anything, except that. It wasn't as if she shouldn't have guessed. It wasn't as if she could explode, stamp her foot, and demand to go home. Jack had slept with other women—she'd slept with other men, too. She'd just smile, be calm, and put up with whatever ex or former fling he'd dragged her to with the style and grace befitting a fucking grown-up.

"It's just up there," Jack said, sidling away from Pete as if she might bite him. She forced herself to put a smile on her face and pretend her stomach wasn't in a knot. It wasn't the woman—it was coming face to face with Jack's history, the part of his life he'd never spoken about for more than two sentences.

This woman would know it all, far more than Pete. She'd have memories that Pete could never share.

Which was far more of a reason to be flamingly jealous than sex. Pete breathed deep as Jack hopped the steps of one of the dingy council houses and pounded on the door with the flat of his hand. She could be gracious for however long they were stuck here.

The door burst open, and a blonde wearing a bright red top and fitted jeans exploded from within the house. "Jackie!" she cried, and threw her arms around Jack, nearly knocking him off his feet. "Come here, you bastard!" the woman cried. "Let me get a look at that mug!"

Or she could try not to kick the woman's teeth in, Pete revised. Graciousness might be a peak she couldn't summit.

"Fuck me," Jack said, patting the blonde on the back while trying to wriggle free. "'M not fifteen any longer. Be gentle with me."

"Can't believe you're still standing, much less walking and talking," the blonde said, slugging Jack on the arm. "The way we all went back then, thought you'd be six feet down for sure."

"What can I say?" Jack said. "The bad pennies always turn up." He stepped back and held the blonde at arm's length. "It's good to see you too, luv."

Before the blonde replied, she finally noticed Pete was there. Her expression narrowed, and Pete felt as if a bright and critical spotlight had been turned directly in her eyes. Jack's friend might be a chavvy blonde with a big grin on her face, but her eyes were the same as Jack's—those of a suvivor who'd seen and absorbed too much in their lifespan. Pete decided then and there that she wasn't turning her back on Jack's childhood sweetheart, not for a split second.

But it didn't mean she had to be a cunt, either, so she stepped up and extended her hand. "I'm Pete."

If the blonde thought the name was odd, she didn't let on, just crushed Pete's small fingers in a dockworker's grip. "Wendy."

"Good to meet someone Jack was mates with back

in the day," Pete said, leaving off the snide implication that they'd been far more than that. She didn't want to start up with the pissing contest before they were even in the door.

"Oh, Christ!" Wendy barked a laugh. "Mates from further back than I care to admit." She elbowed Jack. "You'd be a wanker to tell this cute little thing me real age."

Jack grinned back at her, the genuine smile he reserved for people and situations he trusted. "Your secret's safe with me, luv."

Pete removed the uncertainty from that equation. Wendy and Jack had definitely slept together. She might grit her teeth until they were nubs, but she wouldn't get territorial. Wendy was doing them a favor, and Pete was going to take the high road if it killed her.

"Should we step inside?" she suggested. "Lot of eyes around here."

"Good idea," Jack said. To Wendy, he flashed another charming grin. "Appreciate you helping us lie low, darling. We're in a bit of a spot."

"An' none of your noncey little mage friends would help you out?" Wendy clicked her tongue against her teeth. "For shame." She gestured them inside. "C'mon. Nosy old bint across the street's got nothing better to do than poke in my business, and the rest of them are just waiting to paint rude things on me front door when I'm not around."

Pete followed Jack, kicking the door shut behind her

with a hollow thump that she tried not to compare to a coffin lid.

Wendy's council flat crouched on the shoulders of an empty one below it. Narrow as the stairs were to the flat in London, these were half the size, shadowed and perfumed with decades of smoke, cooking oil, and stale piss. All council flats of a certain age smelled the same. Pete had been to enough of them on welfare visits for the Met to know what lay beyond the door—gray carpet, a rusty radiator, leaky windows, and a kitchen that smelled constantly of damp rot.

Wendy's flat didn't disappoint, although it was snug and dry, and rife with protection hexes. Pete felt them skitter across her face like a welter of tiny spiders when she stepped over the threshold. That was rude—one waited to be invited in when entering a mage's dwelling—but she wasn't in a polite sort of mood, so she shoved through the hexes, not particularly caring if she left the ends in tatters.

"Not a lot of room," Wendy said. "But what's mine is yours and all."

"Thank you, luv," Jack said, touching the back of her hand. "I mean it. Most mages aren't mad enough to take on the Prometheus Club."

Wendy laughed again, the husky bark endemic to chain smokers. "You could always convince a girl to be a bit mad, luv." She winked at Pete. "This one's got a touch of the devil about him. Drove me mum mad, us seeing one another."

"Where is your scary old hag of a mother?" Jack asked. "Terrorizing old men down the rest home?"

"Christ, no," Wendy said. "She kicked off near ten years ago. About time, too—if I'd had to see her into her twilight years, all her screeching about Jesus and his seven fucking dwarves or what have you, I'd've topped meself."

"And not a soul would blame you," Jack said, setting his bag down and looking about the place. "I'm going to wash up, luv," he said, and then left Pete alone in the sitting room with Wendy.

Pete stood in the center of Wendy's stained Ikea rug like a knob, waiting for an invitation to sit, smoke, or even fuck off, but Wendy went back to ignoring her until she'd lit a fresh fag from a pack lying on the sofa.

"Still the same old Jack," she said. Pete felt the sharp craving penetrate her skull at the hit of smoke, but she bit it back. She'd quit when she'd gotten pregnant, and she wasn't about to let Wendy and her sad little council flat drive her back into the habit.

"I wouldn't know," Pete said. "We met later on."

Wendy appraised Pete, with a good deal less friendliness than she'd displayed in front of Jack. "Oh yeah. You're just a little girl, aren't you?"

"I'm thirty-one," Pete said, keeping her voice low and calm. She wasn't going to do this—she wasn't going to play some silly game that had started between Jack and Wendy before she'd even been born.

"'Course you are, sweetheart," Wendy said. "But younger when you met, I'd wager." She grinned. Her teeth were the same color as her stained plaster walls. "Jack always did like to get 'em young and willing."

"All right, look," Pete said. "I appreciate that you're put out helping us like this, and that you might think you have some kind of claim to Jack, being there first and all, but I'm a grown woman, not a teenage girl, and seeing as he and I have a baby back in London, I really doubt he's going anywhere. Sweetheart."

Wendy glared at her through the fog of smoke, but she stayed quiet. Pete didn't feel any better—she actually felt worse. She hated the reminder that there was an entire life Jack had lived before her. Friends and enemies, love and heartbreak. She could know about it, but she'd never be part of it. She'd always be the one that came after, the younger woman, the one who'd sent Jack down a spiral he nearly hadn't climbed out of.

If she were being honest, she knew she wasn't Jack's first love, or even his second. Not by a long shot. Wendy might not be either, but she was a reminder of the Before, and the other Jack, the one Pete had never known and never would.

"Not like he ever made an effort to look me up after he took off," Wendy sighed at last. "Broke my heart one day when I went 'round to his flat and he was just gone. His mum was stoned off her arse, as usual, and I didn't hear from him for near ten years."

"That's Jack now, too," Pete said, feeling herself soften toward Wendy just a bit. "Good at flash, not big on follow-through."

Wendy sucked on her fag and gave Pete a wry smile.

"That's us." She gestured at a shabby photo in filmy glass sitting on her end table next to the ashtray. Pete extended her hand.

"May I?"

Wendy nodded, and Pete ran her thumb over the glass to clear the dust away. Jack, young and skinny, stood next to Wendy on the stoop of her council flat. They couldn't have been more than twelve, Wendy's hair in an eighties perm that looked like it could support its own weather system, and Jack slouched in a shirt and tie that both had clearly been borrowed from someone who was much larger and a fan of bold paisley prints.

"What was the occasion?" she asked Wendy.

"I had a part in the school play," Wendy murmured. "*The Music Man*. Jack and his da came to see me, since me mum was always at work."

Pete focused on the tall figure standing behind Jack and Wendy. Wendy squinted at her through the smoke from her fag. "What?"

"Nothing." Pete swallowed the dozen questions that exploded into her brain. "Jack never said much about his dad. I always thought he was dead."

Wendy shrugged. "Probably is, now. Showed up once in a blue moon, threw cash around, left. Never gave a fuck one way or the other what poor Jackie was actually going through at home."

Before Pete could contemplate the photo any further, Jack returned from the loo, swiping his hands across his jeans. "Everything all right, then?" he asked, darting a look between Pete and Wendy.

"Tip-top," Wendy said, stubbing out her cigarette. "I'll just go down and get something for tea, yeah?"

She left, and Jack paced the flat, four steps to each wall, until he finally scrubbed a hand over his face. "I can't take this," he muttered, heading for the door.

Pete ran after him, nearly falling down the broken front steps. "You can't just go running about Manchester by yourself," she said. "Not after what happened at the train station."

Jack ignored her, walking for a good minute in silence. "You'd think it'd be easier," he sighed at last.

"What?" Pete asked, though she knew.

"Coming back here," Jack said. "I haven't been back to Manchester since I was fifteen, Pete. I didn't even come back for me mum's funeral."

"I wouldn't worry over it," Pete said quietly. They walked another block, until they stopped in front of a flat, same as all the other flats in the row, with empty windows peering into a sad, floral-papered sitting room.

"I wouldn't have ever come back if I had it my way," Jack said. "But I'd do it for you, no question."

Pete opened her mouth, then shut it again. What the hell did you say to that? Jack might be the sort of fuckwit who'd look up an ex-girlfriend and expect everything to go swimmingly, but he had never left her. Never let her down, never done anything less than all he could to protect her. Even at the cost of his sanity and almost his life.

"I know," she said at last, reaching for his hand, but Jack wasn't beside her any longer.

"This is it," he said, stopping at the semi-detached on the corner. "Good old number seven. Every time the council was ready to kick my mum out for fighting and keeping her shady boyfriends here on the sly, she'd cry and make me come with her to the hearing, look sad and skinny and pathetic."

Pete thought back to the photo, to the small dark-haired boy who held only the barest hints of the Jack she knew. She would have felt sorry for that boy. She *did* feel sorry for that boy.

Jack conjured a cigarette and lit it, blowing smoke at the darkened windows. "Can't believe we ended up spending fourteen years here. No wonder my dad bolted as soon as he saw an opening."

"You ever see him after you lit out?" Pete asked cautiously. "Your dad?"

"Never since the day I packed a kit and shut the door behind me," Jack said. "He crops up, he's asking for a kick in both the teeth and the arse."

"Fair enough," Pete said. He didn't want to talk about it, and that was his choice. The questions she had were just going to have to keep waiting, as they always had.

She and Jack reached the end of the road, which ended abruptly in a pit of gravel, mud, and leftover rainwater, green scum floating on top. The residents had been using the place as a makeshift tip, and an icebox of some indeterminate vintage lay on its side, doors gaping open.

A number of small children ran in circles amid the garbage, shrieking and giggling. They weren't playing the cruel games that Pete remembered from the council kids around her neighborhood growing up, nor were they smashing things for the Hell of it. The game seemed to involve one kid who was a dragon, who shot the others with some kind of foam dart launcher, slowly turning each to his side when they got hit. It was an innocent game, without any sharp edges. They seemed happy.

"You think Lily will ever be that?" she said.

Jack snorted. "Raggedy little council rat? Not if I have anything to say about it."

"Come on," Pete said sharply. "It's not like they're running about setting small dogs on fire. I meant do you think she'll ever be like *that,* right this moment?" Her voice trailed off to a whisper. "Happy, with nothing troubling her?"

"'Course I do," Jack said, surprising Pete by twining his fingers with hers. "She's got you, doesn't she?"

Pete looked at her feet. Better modesty than letting Jack know she was hiding a prickle of tears in the corners of her eyes. "Right" was all she said.

"Pub's down the way, used to be decent," Jack said. "'Course, that was 1984. Care to chance it?"

"Would I ever," Pete said. She let Jack lead her back up the road and into the high street, the lights of Alexandra Park coming on around them one by one, like stars filling a darkened sky, remote and frozen as outer space.

7.

The residents of the Dodger's Arms—and Pete used the term on purpose, since the men at the bar looked as if they'd been sitting there since at least before Thatcher came to office—glared at her when she and Jack came in out of the twilight, but Jack ordered for them at the bar, and at the sound of his ever-thickening Manchester burr, the punters turned back to their sudsy pints and let Jack and Pete be.

The weight of the packet Preston Mayflower had given her knocked against her chair when she hung her jacket, and she pulled it out, turning it in her hands. Jack examined the dirty paper object over the lip of his pint glass. "What've you got there?"

"Mayflower slipped it to me," Pete said. She picked at the edge of the paper, which was greasy—she wagered from the many times Preston had performed this exact motion. "I'd really like to know what could possibly be enough to throw yourself into traffic over."

"Could be nothing," Jack said. "Bloke *did* fling himself in front of a bus for no fucking reason."

Pete thought about telling him what she'd seen, the two figures chasing Mayflower, the real fear driving the madness-tinged exchange they'd had.

But Jack had enough to worry about being back home, and she didn't *know* the figures came from the Prometheus Club. She had her suspicions, sure, but she wasn't going to get Jack up in arms until she was certain. The Proemetheans hadn't been after her, anyway. They wanted her with them.

Unless they know you have this grimy little trinket, her logic whispered. Preston had been scared enough to try and warn her away from the Gathering, and now he was dead for his trouble.

Then again, Preston could be a complete frothing nutter. The only thing Pete could figure was that she couldn't trust anyone in Manchester—not the Prometheans, not Wendy, and not Mayflower.

So decided, she took a long swig of her pint. Sooner or later, she'd tell Jack the whole story, but not tonight. Not with the ghosts of his past looming so large that he'd already downed a pint and a shot and ordered a repeat.

Though the pub was dingy, it had been a long time since she'd just been able to go out and relax—at least since before she left the Met. She and Ollie Heath, her partner, used to go out a few times a week with some other DIs from the squad, drink and laugh at horrible jokes and unwind. Take their minds off life on the murder squad, which was bleaker than most and less rewarding than nearly all.

She fingered the packet for a moment longer. "Suppose you're right," she told Jack. "It's probably nothing."

He extended his palm. "Let's see it, then. Strange men slip you gifts, I think I deserve to know."

As she unwound the soft, worn paper, Pete felt a frission of anticipation, the barest finger of the Black scraping over her talent, leaving the slightest bloody scratch. It vanished as the paper fell apart and the small, hard object Mayflower had passed her thunked onto the sticky pub table.

"Shit," Jack breathed, as the small stone caught the light. To Pete it looked rather ordinary—something like those crystals you bought in museum shops, leftover pieces of larger geodes—pretty and sharp-edged but ultimately unremarkable.

"I'm just glad it's not a severed ear, really," she said, mindful of Jack's ashen expression. The crystal was cool to her touch—too cold, as if it had been out in the void of space. She pulled back her fingers as the tips turned blue.

"An ear would be a fifty-quid note compared to what that is," Jack muttered. He grabbed his second shot and knocked it back with a shudder, making all the ink up and down his arms ripple.

"You all right?" Pete asked. She cast a quick look around the pub, but they were still relatively incognito. Nobody spared them a glance of more than a few seconds.

"Not really," Jack said. "You say the train station nutter *gave* you this?"

Pete rubbed the spot between her eyes where a fierce headache bloomed. "Just give me the bad news. What is it—a bomb? A cursed object? Am I going to start vomiting toads?"

"That's a soul cage," Jack said softly. When he was really worried, his voice dropped to just above a whisper, rough and tight as dragging his palm over gravel. "I've only seen a few, and ones this compact are extremely rare."

Pete flinched. She'd encountered a soul cage when she'd been attempting to undo their mistake with Nergal, and they were nasty pieces of work. "But don't they take up whole rooms?" she protested. "And aren't they used on the living?"

The soul cage as she knew it had been writ with magic sigils and used to trap the soul of a victim eternally, in the space between the Black and the Land of the Dead. At the base, they were torture chambers, and usually only necromancers could construct them. Nergal had deserved no less, but Pete had a feeling that whoever had their soul encased in the cold crystal was merely unlucky.

"Not this one," Jack said, gingerly taking the crystal and turning it in its cloth without touching it. "This one . . . this is a masterful piece of work, I'll tell you. Made with care, for somebody this mage really and truly hated."

Pete caught a flash from the crystal in the low light, and for just a moment it seemed something moved beneath the lava-glass surface, oily and alive. She drew back in her chair, as far from the soul cage as possible. She didn't even want to think about what it would be like, soul ripped from her body, trapped in a tiny sliver of the in-between caught in the cage. A miniature Purgatory for a single soul, entrapped for eternity.

"Can you tell what sort of thing is in there?" she asked in a whisper.

Jack laid his finger carefully against the side of the crystal. "Human," he said. "Beyond that, I'm not poking around." He swiped his fingers across his jeans, brushing off the invisible psychic residue of whomever the soul cage contained.

"So what do we do with this?" Pete asked. Jack's eyebrow went up.

"What d'you think?" he demanded. "We don't know what sort of sod is cooped up in there. At best, he'll be a mightily pissed off ghost when he comes out. At worst, he got his soul caged for all eternity for a reason. You do *not* mess with magic this strong." He lowered his voice, looking around. "Not to mention that whoever made that is mucking in dark stuff of the highest order. Not a bastard whose careful work you want to undo. So we're not doing a damn thing except wrapping it back up so it can't give me frostbite."

There's no doubt of that, Pete thought as she looked at the crystal, watching the soul within move beneath the surface. "Preston didn't exactly strike me as the type to work with necromancy and black magic," she said. "Though I admit he did come across as completely off the wall."

"The real question is, why you? Why pass on something so rare to a complete stranger?" He fixed his gaze on Pete. The full power of Jack's gaze, with blue fire magic dancing behind it, was something to behold. It could pin her to the spot, for good or for ill, and she knew without a doubt that she was being looked through, inside and out. He didn't use it often, but now Pete felt her breath catch. His eyes were one of the things that had made Pete fall for him in the first place. She'd been young and dumb, for sure, but even now she couldn't deny that Jack's gaze still mesmerized and drew her in.

"I don't know," she said in a whisper, and left it at that. She never understood why other people expected her to rescue them, to save the world and avert disaster. She was just Petunia Caldecott. An ordinary woman who happened to be able to do one extraordinary thing. She certainly wasn't a mage of Jack's caliber.

Jack sat back and sucked on his lower lip. "Damned if I know why, either."

"I know you didn't want to come back here," Pete said. "And I'm sorry about this stupid geas, and I'm so grateful that you're here with me."

The soul cage couldn't lead to anything good. Prometheus Club or not, why the fuck had Preston given it to her? How could he be sure she wouldn't simply flip it back to the Prometheans to get on their good side?

Not that she would. She didn't like people who assumed she'd toe the line just because they put on a good show of force. Her da had taught her better than to knuckle down to bullies.

And there was Jack to consider. Preston's own words were on a repeat she couldn't stop: *If you must go, don't take the crow-mage with you.*

But the Prometheus Club hadn't given her a choice. Attend or die. It didn't get more clear-cut than that.

So she'd have to do what she always did when life in the Black threatened to eat her alive—she'd keep her eyes open and her instincts sharp, and whoever wanted to do Jack harm or use him for their own ends would have to go through her.

She put the soul cage back into her coat, deep in a zippered pocket, and let Jack pay the check. "Let's go," he sighed. "Maybe Manchester will seem a little more hospitable now that 'm pissed."

He leaned on her on the way out of the bar, and Pete let them walk in silence, enjoying the closeness and the warmth of his body. It lasted for half a block, until Pete heard echoing footsteps and felt a prickle in the Black, one that wasn't hard to decipher.

"Someone's following us," she told Jack. "Keep walking, don't look back, don't act different."

He tensed, some of the muzziness disappearing from his expression. "Black's going crazy," he said. He gave a shiver, and Pete could only imagine what he was seeing.

"I know," she said as Jack gave a low grunt of pain, the assault on his sight making him shiver against the length of Pete's body. "I know, but just keep walking when I let go of you. Get back to Wendy's and I'll meet you there."

"Why?" Jack demanded, balking. "What are you going to do?"

Pete let go of him, taking advantage of his slowed reactions to shove him forward. She wheeled around. "I have no idea," she said, mostly to herself.

Jack, to his credit, didn't try to white-knight it. He just kept going, melting into the shadows quick as a black cat.

Alone in the street, Pete was only half surprised to see the man and woman from the train station. The woman pointed a crimson-nailed finger at her. "Petunia Caldecott," she said. "You've been avoiding us."

"I'm sorry, do I know you?" Pete said. She swiveled to the left and to the right. Alexandra Park had plenty of nooks and crannies for more assassins to hide in, but it appeared to be just the three of them.

"Not yet," said the woman, "but I know you. And I know what that ink stain on your hand means."

The geas flared, and the pain returned tenfold when the woman spoke. Pete forced herself to keep her expression neutral and not flinch. She was good at not flinching, no matter how much it hurt. The Prometheans looked far more ordinary than she would have expected, a bit posh, even. Magicians weren't supposed to be posh. The ones with actual talent usually looked more like either vagrants or escapees from an old Dracula film. Even Nicholas Naughton, the necromancer whose help nearly wiped London off the map with Nergal, had looked like a slightly scruffy country gent, all turtleneck sweaters and scuffed boots.

"I should have known you two were Prometheans, what with all the skulking and talking in circles," Pete told her. "Is this the part where you threaten me with car batteries and pliers?"

"Of course not!" The woman looked genuinely offended. "If you'd just alerted us you were reaching the gathering early, Miss Caldecott, we could have arranged rooms for you and Mr. Winter at our headquarters in the city center."

"Maybe I'm happy where I am." Pete folded her arms. The woman gave her a smile that suggested the very idea was adorable.

"Because a tip in Alexandra Park is your idea of a vacation?" The woman tsked. "Manchester is so much more, Miss Caldecott. You don't need to shack up with Wendy Macintosh and try to hide from us. We *want* you here."

"Yeah," Pete told her. "That's sort of the problem, isn't it?" She felt a complete lack of surprise that Wendy and the woman from the Prometheus Club had talked. Wendy was the type who'd look after her own arse. A survivor in all the ways that mattered.

Pete figured she'd been planning to meet the Prometheans eventually. But not like this, not when everything was on their terms. If she ever saw Wendy again, she was going to fetch the woman a smack that would shake those yellow teeth out of her head.

"You can try to keep running," said the woman, evidently seeing the flash in Pete's eyes. "But I'll have a leg locker hex on you before you can take two steps. I don't

want us to start off on this sort of ground, Miss Caldecott. I want us to get along." She stepped forward and
extended her hand, gesturing to a long black car that
pulled up to the curb.

Pete thought of Preston Mayflower, the expression of
panic and despair etched on his face just before the bus
hit.

"Fine," she said, pasting her best faux-civil smile on
her face. "We can be friends, if that's what you want."

The woman grinned back at her as she ushered Pete
into the car. "I'd like nothing better."

8.

The ride was, by Pete's count, less than five minutes, but it felt like an eternity. The woman touched one hand across the back of Pete's neck as soon as they sat down in the rear seat, and a veil of blackness dropped over Pete's eyes. She gave a start. "What the fuck is this?"

"Shh," said the woman. "Just a little obfuscation hex. Procedure for all visitors not formally inducted into the club."

"Well, I've already seen *you*," Pete snarled. "And what you did to Preston." She waited, hoping that she'd provoke something out of her companion other than smooth platitudes.

"Poor Preston," the woman purred. "He was a wayward soul. The type you really wish you could help, but alas, even we can't save everyone."

"And Wendy?" Pete asked. "You got a whole network of sad sacks keeping eyes on the city for you?"

"Wendy doesn't deserve any of your ire," she said. "Aside from her inability to keep her mouth shut the moment she clapped eyes on Mr. Winter, she didn't do a thing. We have our own ears on the . . . grittier side of things here in the city."

Pete felt a touch on her shoulder. "Hush, now," the woman said. "You'll get answers as soon as I'm allowed to give them."

Pete went quiet, not because the woman had ordered it but because she knew she wouldn't get anything else useful. She was talking to the Prometheus Club's PR— somebody who had a glib answer for everything, and who unpleasant truths slid off of like oil skated across water. If she wanted real answers, she was going to have to play.

She just hoped Jack had gotten out of trouble's way, although knowing him, it was more likely he'd run into it head first. To pass the time, Pete counted—turns the car took, seconds that ticked by. They circled the same route twice, and Pete knew she wouldn't be able to find the place by walking if she tried. So far, the Prometheans were beating her soundly at the game of being clever.

She didn't like it, not at all, but she swallowed her resentment as the car purred to a stop.

"Here we are," said the woman. "We'll get you and Mr. Winter settled in rooms, and then we can all have a chat."

"Jack?" Pete's voice sounded strangled, and she silently kicked herself for betraying her nerves. "He's here?"

"Mr. Winter is not as sneaky as he might like to

imagine." The woman's voice swelled with amusement. "He gave my partner quite a talking-to on the ride over, in language I would not repeat."

"Trust me," Pete said. "I've heard it all. I want to see him. And I want you to take off the magic blindfold—I'm through with cloak-and-dagger shite."

"I told you," said the woman. "Patience. You'll see Jack soon enough, and we'll be inside momentarily."

"If you've done anything to hurt Jack . . . ," Pete started, but the woman cut her off with laughter.

"*Hurt*? That's the absolute last thing on my mind, trust me." She leaned close enough so that Pete could feel her breath, smell the cloying orchid reek of her perfume. "Even if he is a degenerate demon follower with a black mark on his soul." She drew back, and the perky false note was back in her voice. "That's not my concern."

Pete felt the air change, dry and recycled against her face, and she was marched down a long hall—approximately fifty-seven steps—before going through a door and being sat on a bed.

"And here we are," the woman said. "You're free to come and go in the club, but know your geas is still active. It'll lay you flat if you try and cross the threshold to the outside." Her heels clacked, and Pete heard the moan of ancient hinges. "I am sorry about that," the woman said, after a moment. "But it's necessary. You must understand that we can't fully trust you."

The door slammed, shaking the floor under Pete's feet, and as she heard a latch click the hex cleared from her eyes. Pete screwed up her face in the wash of bright light from the chandelier above her head, before she fumbled at the switch to dim it.

"Of course," she grumbled as she checked out the room. "You toss me in the back of a car, threaten me, and on top of it force me to come to Manchester, and it's *me* who has the problem with trustworthiness."

The room wasn't new or nearly as posh as she would have expected from the fancy motor and the woman's outfit. Plaster cracked at all the edges of the windows and doors, and the floor was nearly black with old varnish and wear. The windows, leaded and wavy so she couldn't see out, were painted shut. Pete heard an echo of a car horn from far below—too far to drop, even if she could have gotten the casement to open.

Escape options rapidly dwindling, she forced herself to keep examining everything. Even if she wasn't going to bolt straightaway, she might as well figure out as much as she could about the Prometheus Club. It always paid to know exactly what sort of wankers you were dealing with, especially in the Black.

She touched the door and didn't sense any protection hexes. The door itself was hewn from heavy oak and iron, banded three times to keep out Fae. The door wasn't locked, and the hinges screeched again as Pete pulled it open, using small and cautious movements as she stepped into the hall. She checked for cameras, and found nothing obvious, but she figured a group like the Prometheans wouldn't need to nip out for a microphone and recorder if they wanted to listen in on her.

Still painfully aware of the geas, Pete moved slowly down the hall, trying to act as if she were just going for a stroll. No hexes snatched at her, no curses bit into her flesh.

The Prometheus Club wasn't just devoid of spells, it was devoid of magic, full stop. She'd rarely sensed a place that was such a dead space in the invisible tides of the Black. It felt like there was a tiny empty spot in her skull, setting up an echo and throb.

This would all be right in the end, she told herself. Lied, was more like it, but she needed to stop herself from doing anything rash while the Prometheans could still hurt her or, worse, hurt Jack. This wasn't the first time she'd been on the wrong side of magic, with just her wits and whatever she happened to have in her pockets.

She kept going, walking through hallway after hallway done in the same monastic dark wood and plaster. The Prometheus Club was kitted out with flourescent lights and ugly, dank carpeting, but otherwise was very much as it must have been when the mages took up residence. She navigated narrow hallways that doubled back on one another and locked doors that slowed her down every time she had to use her bank card to slip the antique latches. There was a complete absence of other people.

She hadn't thought this out before leaving her room to wander about like a simpleton trying to find Jack. And then what was she going to do? Stroll out the front door? There was no way that bint in the good suit was letting her go until she'd had her say.

Desperation breeds sloppiness, Connor Caldecott

would have told her. She'd learned that before she was even aware of it, watching her father get ready for work every day, double and triple check his gun and his kit, make sure his warrant card was in full view, the simple laminated slip displaying his narrow face and combed-back hair, raven black above a brow that she couldn't remember ever not being furrowed.

At last, Pete found a stairwell and felt her stomach unknot just a little. Stairs at least meant she was going somewhere. She took them two at a time, forcing herself to be slow and quiet as she opened the door at the bottom. A long, narrow hall greeted her, lit only by the flickering glow of candles set into notches in the wall. Pete reeled as all at once the magic absent from the upper floors launched at her like a flood tide. So much power it nearly took her feet out from under her, made her grab the wall to stay upright. Pete gagged. This wasn't right. The Black here was too strong, too overwhelming. She'd crossed a barrier and triggered some kind of terrible drowning trap made of magic.

Forcing herself to stand and move, Pete kept walking. She wasn't sure if it was the overwhelming pummeling of the Black on her talent or simply exhaustion and fear, but the hallway seemed to expand and narrow as she approached the far end. Though she knew it was only an optical illusion, Pete shivered. It was cold here, and damp, and the magic still howled and scraped at her talent, begging to be let in, be eaten up and absorbed and allowed to unleash whatever the Weir might desire.

Pete fell against the far door, which was mercifully

unlocked, and stumbled through it. On the other side, the darkness was absolute, except for a thin beam of light from somewhere that reached the surface of the earth. Pete stared. There was no way—no way she could have descended one staircase from an upper-floor and suddenly be meters below the earth, in a basement.

She heard the click of stiletto heels on the stone floor. The beam of light illuminated a pool of water lapping at the edge of slate tiles, a black plinth rising from the depths, covered in centuries of moss and grime, but little else. Pete stayed still, tracking the sound, until the woman came into view. She'd changed her clothes and wore a smart gray blazer, denim, and pumps that would have set Pete back five or six exorcism jobs—and that was just if every client paid.

"I did tell you if you decided to play the clever game, you'd lose," the woman said, cocking an eyebrow at Pete. She wasn't pretty, but she had the sort of face you couldn't look away from, and a few spun-copper curls had worked their way free from her pile of hair.

"Sorry," Pete said, acutely aware of her slept-in clothes and the mess of tarry black hair falling in her eyes. "That's a bit like asking water not to be wet."

"You're cute, aren't you?" the woman said, with a twist of a frown. "How's that worked out for you so far?"

Pete felt the hand with the geas prickle, cat claws scraping across her flesh, and forced a smile. "I've had better days."

"I know you don't believe me," said the woman. "But we did bring you here for something other than locking you up and then watching you try to escape." She closed the distance between them and extended her hand to Pete. "I'll make you a bargain—you stay and listen like we asked, and I'll take the geas off now. I'll extend my trust to you, because I see our usual methods just won't work, and I'm smart enough to adapt. Deal?"

Pete regarded the hand. Small and soft, nails done in a red just slightly more luminous than blood. Hands that had reached for Preston Mayflower as he flew into traffic, hands that had searched his pockets in the moments after, only to find nothing.

"Deal," she said, and grasped the woman's flesh. She got nothing. Not power, not an abscene of it. A brick wall—one, she was sure, carefully constructed to avoid the problem of skin contact with other mages. It was a good trick, one Pete freely admitted that she'd kick a sweet old pensioner to learn.

"I'm Morwenna," said the woman. "The fellow who was with me last night is Victor. You'll meet the others who've arrived tomorrow at supper."

"You all just got first names?" Pete asked. "That part of being a Promethean—you all go the Cher route?"

"Being a Promethean is many things," Morwenna said. "But no, I have a proper name." She turned Pete's palm over, caressing it with her fingers, and a hot pain seized Pete, making her gasp and grit her teeth. After a moment, the geas crawled up through the layers of her skin and into Morwenna's flesh, where it vanished.

"There," Morwenna said. "I'm a woman of my word. Are you a woman of yours?"

Pete regarded her. The Prometheans were rough in their methods, it was true, but her choice was to listen to Morwenna's spiel or get trapped in here again. And there was Jack to consider, who'd undoubtedly do something boneheaded and guaranteed to slag off the Prometheans if left to his own devices.

So she smiled, and nodded, and told Morwenna, "I always am."

"I'm relieved to know that," Morwenna. "Come with me, then. We've a lot to talk about."

9.

As Pete walked with Morwenna, halls straightened and doors appeared. When the two women reached a set of stairs, they behaved as they should, and Pete let out a deep breath when the pressure of the Black against her mind and body eased. Morwenna favored her with an amused glance. "Sorry about the hex. It's for everyone's protection."

"If you want to protect your floors from puke, you might reconsider that one," Pete muttered.

"We're very proud of it," Morwenna said. "The illusion will go on forever if you're not welcome here. Why have cameras and thugs when you have magic? Anyone we don't want to come in, or to leave . . ." She spread her hands. "They're stuck in the loop, forever."

Pete shivered, which Morwenna clearly mistook for awe. "I think it stands as a testament to the power of the Prometheans—each of us contributing our talent to keep our most sacred space safe."

On the main floor, she led Pete into a music room hung with musty silk drapes. A piano sat dust-covered in one corner, and an assortment of staring, stony-eyed mages sat on an assortment of sofas, all their glares trained on Pete.

The one bright spot was Jack, slumped against the arm of the nearest sofa, holding a glass of scotch as if he wanted to choke the life out of it.

"You see why I didn't want to come here?" he asked Pete. Morwenna went to a side table set with bottles and plates of tiny desserts and poured her own tumbler.

"You didn't have to convince me," she said. "Only here because they tricked me."

The man Morwenna had identified as Victor grunted.

"Why are we pretending this is a dinner party? Morwenna, did you speak to her about Preston?"

"I'm getting to it," Morwenna said, in a tone that could have formed ice across the top of her drink. "Miss Caldecott and Mr. Winter are not suspects that you are interrogating for the FSB, Victor. We do things differently here."

Victor glared at Pete and Jack in turn, but he retreated to the table of food and sank his teeth into an apple tart. Pete kept her eyes on Morwenna, but she didn't forget about Victor. He was definitely the one in the duo familiar with violence.

"How much do you both know about the Prometheus Club?" Morwenna asked, and Jack snorted.

"Is this where you tell the origin story and we get all wide-eyed and slack-jawed?"

"You know something, Mr. Winter," Morwenna said, fixing him with a glare. "If you'd just joined with us the first time we approached you, all of this would be far easier to explain."

"First time?" Pete's stomach dropped. Then again, she didn't know why she was so surprised. Jack wasn't forthcoming about anything in his youth—why should he throw out the small detail that the Prometheans had approached him before?

If you must go, don't take the crow-mage with you.

"Dammit, Jack," Pete mumbled so only she could hear. Morwenna and Jack were still engaged in a staring contest.

"We would have loved to have had Jack from the start, when he first came into his talent," Morwenna said. "But as it turns out, good things come to those who wait, because we were able to access Miss Caldecott as well."

Pete gritted her teeth and pointed at Morwenna. "You. Stop talking about me like I'm a piece of fucking furniture. You." She turned her finger on Jack. It shook a bit, the anger coursing through her like a fever. "How could you not tell me? I *asked* you, Jack, and you lied. To my face. That's low even for you."

"Luv," Jack said, holding up his hand. "Listen, I was fifteen, and my answer to them's going to be the same now as it was then: Fuck off and leave me alone."

"I wish we had that luxury, believe me," Morwenna sighed. She drained her coffee and set the cup down with a *clack*. "We're not in the habit of coercing those who don't carry the same values as the Prometheans."

Pete gave a small, involuntary snort. "Yeah, I see how not in the habit you are."

"I took the geas off," Morwenna said. "And I prom-ise you, this will be a lot easier for all of us to get through if we resolve to be civil."

"Sorry," Jack said, putting his feet on the table and knocking aside several small decorative figurines. "Civil's never really been my bent."

He was showing off, and in that moment Pete didn't know who she was more irritated with. Morwenna made her choice swiftly, though, and moved to Jack, standing over him like a teacher catching a pupil texting dirty notes. She stared him down until he looked up at her and moved his feet off the table with an elaborate sigh.

"We're wasting time," Victor spoke up. "If you can't lay it out, Morwenna, then I'm going to do what we should have done in the first place—compel them to do what needs to be done and dispose of them when it's over."

"Here's a tip," Pete said. "If you want my help, don't imply that'd you'd rather murder me, all right?"

"Both of you shut up," Morwenna snapped, never tak-ing her eyes from Jack. Pete had to admire her intensity—she never blinked, like a shark in expensive shoes. "You know that the Black is in turmoil, Mr. Winter."

He smiled up at her. "We're trading threats, might as well call me Jack, luv."

Pete watched the muscles of Morwenna's face tighten and relax. She was good at hiding things—almost as good as Pete herself.

"Hell," Morwenna continued, "most of it is turmoil you *caused*. Because of your inability to toe the line and play the role you're going to fill, one way or another. Instead you fight it, and the rest of us suffer."

"Got a question for you, luv," Jack said, lacing his fingers behind his head. Only Pete saw the wire tension in his limbs. "What makes you think I give a shit about anyone but meself?"

"If not us, very well," Morwenna shot back. "But somehow I think even a stone-hearted bastard like you might care when his daughter is a demon's slave and his wife is a corpse roasting on a spit in Hell."

Pete started to move, the reflexive rage at the mention of Lily moving her before her higher brain realized what was going on. The lizard one knew what it wanted to do, though—slap the smirk off Morwenna's face.

Victor had his hands on her before she could blink, and she gasped as his hand closed around her throat, bony fingers digging into her windpipe as his other hand pulled her left wrist into a submission hold common to cops and soliders. Pete could feel that he was faster and stronger than she was, and in a pure physical match he'd shred her. Though her animal instinct rebelled when she did it, she relaxed under Victor's grip.

"You're a cunt," she muttered.

"You have no idea," Victor murmured against her hair. "Be still now, girl. I'd hate to have to hurt you."

"Listen, miss," Jack drawled, crossing one booted foot over his thigh and looking up at Morwenna, seemingly ignorant of the struggle going on between Pete and Victor. "You seem to have forgotten that I was the one put Abbadon back in the box, and Nergal, too, if we're counting. Wasn't my fault they got prison-broke in the first place, was it?"

"If you're looking for a pat on the back, you're barking up the wrong fucking tree," Morwenna said. "You have a destiny, Jack, just like we all do, and the longer you fight it the more situations like Abbadon appear. You muck about with demons like they'll protect you, but they can't. Not from the Morrigan. Not from what you were born to do for her, and by extension for us."

Pete saw Jack's expression slip, just for a moment. If there was one thing he was afraid of, Morwenna had just ripped off the lid and exposed it to the light of day.

Jack met her eyes for a moment, and Pete raised her eyebrow. She'd toe up against Victor if he needed a distraction, odds be damned. But Jack shook his head minutely. He looked back at Morwenna and forced a smile that was as cheerful as rigor mortis.

"Don't know if your memory is shoddy or just selective, luv, but the Hag was the reason for that whole mess with Nergal. Biting off more than she could chew, like the bitch she is. Trying to throw her weight about and start a war with the daylight world. Typical of her, really. Always did have a bit of a one-track mind, that broad."

"I understand your reluctance, believe me," Morwenna said. "But ask yourself, Jack, what would be better for our world: an infestation of demons and creatures like Abbadon, or the Morrigan continuing as she always has, as the bride of war? Doing what she has always done to balance the Black and the daylight world—muster her army of the dead and winnow the world when it becomes too crowded?"

"'Cept this time she's going to cut down the whole world, not just the bits in the Black," Jack said. "Need I mention that she was all for Nergal pillaging his way through the daylight side, creating enough souls for her to march against anyone else who stood in her way on her crawl to the top of the corpse heap?"

"Need I mention that if you had performed your duty as your station requires, you could have influenced the Morrigan to stay her hand against innocents?" Morwenna asked, low. "You fight so hard to stay in the mud, Jack—one would almost think you liked it there." Piece said, she retreated to a wing chair, sitting and crossing her legs primly at the ankle.

Victor grunted a laugh at Jack's gobsmacked expression, and Pete felt her desire to hit him in the throat redouble. Morwenna shot him a glance.

"Victor, for fuck's sake. We're not the mafia—let go of her."

Victor released Pete, although his expression betrayed great disappointment. Pete rubbed her throat, feeling the tender lines where she'd sport bruises in a few hours. She owed Victor for that, but she filed it away for now. What would a dust-up accomplish, besides putting her in hospital? She could be patient.

"Next time," she told Victor, "you and I are going to have a discussion about why you don't put your hands on me."

"Like there will be a next time." He snorted and went back to the tray of pastries.

"So you actually think Jack can convince the Morrigan to flit around like a pet parakeet, doing just as you say?" Pete asked, turning her attention on Morwenna. That was pure mad talk. The Morrigan was a force, not a person, a thing that could not be bought or reasoned with.

"On the contrary," Morwenna said. "You aren't prisoners. You aren't subjugated. We want Jack to join us of his free will. There's a place for him at the head of our table." She tapped her fingers against the chair arm and smiled dreamily. "The crow-mage and the Prometheans were one and the same, until that insufferable lowlife Seth McBride broke the chain."

"Yeah," Jack said. "And every crow-mage before who died horribly because he couldn't serve two masters, that had nothing to do with you lot."

"Membership in the Prometheus Club offers great rewards, but those come with great risks," Morwenna said. "We all assume them when we accept membership, but together, we are protected. Alone, Jack . . ." She sighed. "Your skin tells the story. She's got your scent now. You know it's only a matter of time. If you'd just gone with her willingly, you'd be in a position of unimaginable power. No demonic price on your head. No primordial monsters sniffing after your blood." She stood and walked to a bell pull, yanking on it. Far away, a clang sounded. "Honestly, the fact that you've made it to forty is impressive," Morwenna said.

Much as she had grown to hate the woman in the short time she'd known her, Pete had to admit Morwenna was right. Jack had chosen to stay human, stay away from the Morrigan, and ignore the fate his very birth had marked for him. And because of that, their lives were shit and Pete was constantly checking over her shoulder, waiting for the next stone to drop on their heads.

Still, it was a better life than being the dead general at the head of the Morrigan's army of lost souls, devoid of any humanity, the puppet of the very thing that had brought forth war and death from primordial mud.

"This was inevitable, the moment you chose to turn your back on your purpose," Morwenna continued. "And now you've left us no choice. Things have been set in motion that require the full brunt of the Prometheans' intervention, and that includes you and Miss Caldecott."

A moment later a man in a black suit appeared, the sort of cheap, boxy number favored by private bodyguards. He was carrying Pete's and Jack's bags, and he dropped them unceremoniously in front of Morwenna.

"Thank you, Bruce," she said. To Pete, "Now that we've spoken and you understand that you *will* assist us, we'll put you in a suite and return your things." She held out Pete's bag to her and had the audacity to smile. Pete snatched it roughly. Morwenna had worn out her self control. She felt snappish and dangerous, ready to bite the head off the next bastard who crossed her.

Morwenna offered Jack's kit to him, but kept him at arm's length. Whatever else she was, Pete conceded, she wasn't stupid. "We don't want to be your adversaries, Jack. You're the one who set that dynamic, not us."

Pete did a cursory check of her bag. Everything appeared to be there, minus her mobile and all the cash and plastic from her wallet. The Prometheans left nothing to chance.

"Let me ask you something," she said to Morwenna, straightening up. Her baton was still in her bag, but if she was honest with herself, that wouldn't net her anything except the chance to go down swinging. "If I said fuck off and we both walked out of here now, can you honestly tell me there'd be no repercussions?"

"No," Morwenna said. "Honestly? The time for that passed when Jack turned us down the first time. You've seen it, Pete. The chaos, the wrongness of the Black when it whispers to you. Things are past the event horizon, and it's how we come out the other side that matters now. We need Jack, and you, to solve the problem that's cropped up before the ripples destroy everything you and I know."

"Why me?" Pete sighed. "I can't do anything useful. My talent just burns things down."

Morwenna closed her hand around Pete's shoulder. "Let's talk, you and I."

Jack moved closer to her, but Pete held him off with a glance. His jaw jumped, but he picked up his bag and turned to the guard. "All right, big'un," he said. "Let's see this suite you've got."

Morwenna led Pete back into the room with the rock, the soft dripping of the water making Pete's hair stand out in a frizzy halo. Morwenna appeared as polished as ever. "You really don't know, do you?" she asked. "You don't know the first thing about the Black, or about what you are."

Pete took a few steps toward the plinth rising from the water. She'd seen plenty of Roman ruins as a schoolkid, taken a weekend to Bath when she'd been engaged to her ex-boyfriend Terry and seen the steam rising off the hot springs. Back in her old life, when things were simple. This seemed different though, carved from the living rock as it was, with the building constructed around it much later.

"I know enough," she told Morwenna, but the other woman shook her head.

"You are a beginner, Pete, practically a white-robed virgin, offered up for sacrifice. It's criminal what Jack let slip through his fingers. Seth McBride, for all his failings, at least taught him to take care of himself in this harsh realm we inhabit. You didn't get any of that."

"You don't know him," Pete said. "So kindly shut up about it before I *do* walk out of here and leave you in the lurch."

Morwenna frowned, pretty face going pinched, but then she pointed at the rock. "Even you must know the story. The arm reaching from the lake, clutching the blade that would unite the warring tribes and give us England as we know it."

"You can't be serious," Pete said. The rock *could* have held something long and straight, long ago. The groove had been nearly worn away by time and moisture.

"That's just a story," she said. "And a silly one at that. Moist woman rises from lake, gives farmboy magic trinket, hijinks ensue? Please."

"King Arthur and his knights? Yes, that's a fairy tale," Morwenna said. "But there was a man, not Arthur, but a mage, who many centuries past united the Black. Who protected men from Fae and showed the demons that our world wasn't theirs for the taking. Who stopped the bloody battles between rival factions and made us see that we could work together, one man from each tribe, on a council that would protect all of us from the end times. He had no name anyone remembers, so Prometheans gave him the name of a hawk, both predator and guardian, watchman and warrior. The Merlin was the first one to shape the Black, Pete, and his is the only seat in the Prometheus Club that's remained empty since he disappeared. Conditions now are ripe for his return, for a mage of immense power to claim his seat."

"And you think *Jack* is this . . . person?" Pete said. It was a ludicrous idea. Jack wasn't a chosen one of any stripe. He'd find the very idea hilarious.

"I have no idea who the Merlin might be," Morwenna said. "Jack is filling his own seat, that of crow-mage. But our reliable texts say when the outlook is hopeless and the odds stand stacked against us, he will appear. Once in a thousand years, the Merlin will return to unite the Black against destruction. And I can tell you that this is the time, Pete. This is it." Morwenna touched the rock with her fingertips, and then drew back. "Our darkest hour."

Pete sighed. Morwenna might be well-dressed and not overtly insane, but she had delusions like members of the rest of the groups Pete and Jack had run across. "Fine, you're looking for your Luke Skywalker. What's this problem no one but Jack could possibly solve?"

"We'll brief you both when the rest of the Members arrive in the morning," Morwenna said. "I just wanted to impress on you how seriously we need Jack's involvement."

"And what about me?" Pete said, thinking that Morwenna had a lot of nerve acting as if Pete would take anything she said with any seriousness after that tale. She'd heard saner theories from deranged crack addicts on the streetcorners in Peckham.

"You're the Weir," Morwenna said, as if that explained everything. "We haven't had one for nearly a hundred years. Not since my great-great grandmother sat at the arm of Queen Victoria. It's a seat long empty, but trust me when I say you're desperately needed."

"I can't be what you need," Pete said. "You said it yourself—I'm a neophyte. My talent doesn't listen to me, and I couldn't care less about gods and monsters and how they want to end the world."

"You are, because you're the only one," Morwenna said, giving Pete a look as if she were very stupid. "You're the only Weir in Britain, Petunia. Maybe the world."

That stopped Pete in her tracks. She felt a curious sick sensation, as if she'd fallen and her body hadn't quite caught up with her plummeting stomach yet.

Of course she'd wondered, about all of it. Her gift, which seemed to be rare and peculiar. But she'd never thought she was the only one. Weirs were rare, but rare didn't mean unique. She couldn't be all alone with her talent. There had to be at least one other who knew the ever-present threat of the Black, the energy threatening to fill her and burn her from the inside out.

"I can't be," she whispered at last. She felt weak and fragile, out of control and dizzy, as if the floor had heaved under her feet.

"As far as we can tell, you are," Morwenna said. "And our resources are vast, Pete." She squeezed her shoulder, and this time Pete felt a pulse of power, deep and true as the blade of a broadsword. The kind of power that could cleave or heal with equal ease. Morwenna was easily the most powerful human mage she'd encountered, and would give some of the inhuman a run for their money. "You should be proud," Morwenna said softly. "It's a rare and wondrous gift you possess."

"Yeah," Pete said, as Morwenna walked away and left her staring at the plain gray rock. "*Gift*'s not the word I'd use."

10.

The suite was a far cry from the bare room they'd put Pete in, and Jack was sitting on the bed smoking when she came in. She favored him with her worst copper look. "Must you?"

"What?" he said. "Not like I care if I yellow the Prometheans' plaster."

Pete slumped on the bed next to him. She realized she was incalculably tired. She could run on adrenaline for a while, but eventually she'd hit the wall. She'd usually been good for about forty-eight hours on the Met before she'd crash and have to take a rest on the bunks in the nap room. And that was when she was poring over leads and collating evidence, not running for her life, smacking goons in the head, and listening to Morwenna's insane theories.

"You all right?" Jack asked. Pete laid her head on him as he leaned back against the pillow. She listened to his heartbeat, slow and thumping, a far-off train rolling over uneven track.

"No," she said at last, looking up into his face. He had dark stubble along his jaw, and the vertical scar he'd gotten from the business end of a beer bottle glowed in the low light. His face was familiar to her, gave her a feeling that things were all right, even when they really weren't. "Jack," she said, "have you ever heard of another Weir?"

"Well, 'course I'd heard of them," he said. "How else would I know what you were when you showed up?"

"I mean another person like me, alive as we speak," she said. "Have you ever even heard of one?"

Jack considered for a moment, exhaling a stream of smoke before setting his fag in a saucer. "Heard, sure. Rumors and the like. Heard there was one in India. Maybe China."

"Morwenna said I'm the only one," Pete blurted.

Jack chuffed. "Morwenna's a great idiot. She's so blinded to the real world, all she can do is parrot that musty old legend about how the Prometheans are going to unite the Black under their banner."

"What would it mean?" Pete said. "If I *was* the only person in the world who could do this?"

"It would make you very fucking sought after," Jack said. "But you know that. You're nobody's puppet, Pete. 'M not worried about you."

"They're not as bad as I thought, honestly," Pete murmured. "The Prometheans. Crazy, yeah, but I don't get the sense they'd murder us in our beds."

"You just say that because you didn't grow up watching them snatch your friends off the street and manipulate mages they felt were beneath them. For fuck's sake, Pete, they threw a bloke under a bus."

"He threw himself," Pete said softly, although the memory of Preston's terrified face did a lot to throw the smiles and polite words of Morwenna into relief.

"Don't tell me you're actually thinking of taking them up on this asinine offer to join their little glee club?" Jack said, raising his eyebrow.

"No," Pete said. "Of course not. We'll do what we have to to placate them and get back home. Like we planned."

"Good," Jack said. "No place for us with people like them, Pete. They don't have our best interest in mind. Whatever that ginger bitch Morwenna says, they just want to use us."

Pete sat up, irritation swelling in her. "Then why are *you* still here?"

"You heard them," Jack said. "Don't fancy spending the rest of my life ducking into alleys to avoid a Promethean death squad, is all. Had a hard enough time avoiding them when I was a kid."

"You don't talk about it much," Pete said. "Being a kid."

"'Cause I wasn't one," Jack said. "I had a miserable, shitty childhood, and I'd just as soon leave it behind. All right?"

"Fine," Pete said softly. She didn't know why she'd expected Jack to suddenly open up. Perhaps because with Lily, he'd have a chance at a do-over. Or maybe because she'd known him since she was sixteen, but still didn't really *know* him, beyond the moment they'd met. There were still gaping holes in Jack's life that were entirely dark to her.

Not that she thought he kept secrets. Jack's secrets were large and nasty and had teeth, and had a way of not staying secret for long. It was just that he knew nearly everything about her—her mother leaving, Connor dying, her engagement to her ex, Terry, everything in between. She knew Jack better than anyone, but his past was still almost wholly dark to her. It made for an odd relationship, the Jack she knew and the parts that remained hidden, an incomplete picture whose details she could never quite see.

"Luv, don't be mad," Jack said, and kissed the top of her head. "I just don't want to talk about it. And I don't want to be here, but I don't see as I have much of a choice. And that makes me itchy, and I'm sorry if I snapped at you."

Pete started to tell him to forget it, they had bigger things to worry about, but she found herself nodding off, and before she realized anything, it was light out and there was a knock on the door. She opened it and found another black-suited guard, a woman this time, who gestured Pete into the hall. "Breakfast is served, Miss Caldecott," she muttered.

Pete nodded and shut the door again, to find Jack slipping into his leather jacket. The thing was probably older than she was, and it was terribly battered, but Pete was glad Jack wore it. It was familiar and comforting. For her part, she felt for her mobile before she realized it was missing, then stepped out empty handed. It felt odd to be defenseless, but she wasn't. She had Jack with her, and she had her gift. Morwenna, at least, seemed to be in awe of it, so that gave her some currency, at least until they realized she was a screwup who could barely keep herself from being incinerated.

"Lovely little breakfast," Jack said as they walked. "Wonder how many babies they've roasted on spits."

Pete gave him a sharp elbow. "Try to be nice, all right?"

"'M always nice, me," Jack said. "You're the one who's not nice."

Pete didn't have time to retort. In the peculiar way of the club, they'd already arrived in a posh dining room replete with wood paneling, china cabinets, and a table long enough to seat a dozen more people than currently occupied it.

Everyone stopped talking and fixed their stares on Pete and Jack as they entered, and only Morwenna looked as if she didn't want to rip their heads off and serve them as entrées.

Jack was right—she wasn't particularly nice. But she could behave herself, a skill he sorely lacked. Social niceties would take one a long way. Suspects were much chattier when coppers got them a fag and a cuppa than when they began by shouting and beating them with telephone directories.

The guard gestured them into two seats at the end of the table, the farthest from Morwenna, who sat at the head. Pete was the buffer between Jack and the rest of the guests, even though the bloke next to her glared—or she thought it was a glare. She couldn't be sure under the layers of flesh that compressed his face like a deflated balloon. He was easily the largest person she'd seen up close, and he regarded her with a slow, heavy gaze.

"Little slip of a thing, aren't you?" he said. "I expected more from a Weir, especially one reputed to be such a great bloody bitch."

"I won't make any of the obvious retorts," Pete said. "Because they're all far too easy."

"All right," Morwenna said from the head of the table. "Let's at least pretend we're all adults for the duration of the meal. Make Miss Caldecott and Mr. Winter feel welcome."

"I'd be happy to," said the big bastard, grinning at Pete and brushing his finger over her forearm. "I'm a very welcoming sort."

"Touch me again and after I break that finger off, it's going up your arse," Pete told him, beaming her sweetest smile at the assembled gathering. A few chuckled, but the majority still looked like they'd rather murder her than welcome her.

Jack shifted in his chair and took a sip of tea. "Now I know what a custard cake at a fat camp feels like," he grumbled.

"I'd like to thank you all for coming," Morwenna raised her voice above the chatter. "It's always good to have everyone in the clubhouse."

The big bastard gestured at the ten empty chairs. "I'd hardly say we're fully assembled, Morwenna. If this is the showing you could get, I have to wonder if voting you into that seat was a hasty idea. You're far too pretty for such heavy duties."

"The gathering isn't for five days yet, *Gregor*," Morwenna shot back, cheeks heating and eyes shooting fire. "We've plenty of time to assemble the full complement of the club."

Gregor snorted, a sound that may have been either an attempt at a laugh or the first signal of a cardiac arrest. "Whatever you say, dear."

"I *do* say," Morwenna said. "And seeing as how I'm the head of the council, why don't you shut your fat fucking gob and show me a little bit of bloody respect?"

Pete worked hard to suppress the smile that bloomed on her face, but she did a poor job. Gregor snarled under his breath, the full-bodied growl of a bear or a lion rather than a human sound. Pete inched her chair away from him, closer to Jack.

"Shapeshifter," he said by way of explanation, under his breath. "Smelly, bad-tempered arseholes with no manners."

"And great hearing," Gregor snarled. "You're going to pay for that insult, crow-mage."

"What are you going to do, sweetheart?" Jack spread his hands. "Sit on me?"

Morwenna slammed her palms onto the tabletop hard enough to rattle silver and china. "I said *enough*."

The shapeshifter glared daggers at Pete, but she refused to look away, and after a moment he settled back, grumbling.

The breakfast proceeded in relative silence, Pete using the time to choke down poached eggs and toast and check out the other mages seated around her. They mostly regarded her as if she were something sticky on their shoe, and she finally pushed back when her stomach was in such a tight knot she couldn't swallow another mouthful. "It's been eventful," she said to Morwenna. "But unless you're going to tell me what we're doing here among all these bastards who clearly want to light us on fire, I think we're done."

There was a general murmur of unease along the table and Victor slid up behind her, putting a hard hand on her shoulder. "Sit down, Miss Caldecott," he growled.

Pete rotated her neck so their noses were almost touching. "Get your hand off me."

Everyone was staring at her, including Jack. Pete could tell from their expressions that whatever she did next would likely mean the difference between walking out of the Prometheus Club and the Manchester police finding her body months hence, if they found it at all.

"Morwenna, I've had enough of this," Victor said. "She's not Promethean material. You want the crow-mage, fine, but we don't need her."

"Victor," Morwenna said, narrowing her eyes. "Not now. Let Miss Caldecott alone." She left her seat and gestured to Pete and Jack. "Let's have a chat, the three of us." She gave the rest of the Prometheans a dazzling smile. "Please enjoy your meal. There will be a general business meeting at noon in the conservatory."

She took Pete by the elbow, smiling in a conciliatory

fashion until they cleared the dining room, and then her grip tightened and her expression became stony. "What is wrong with you? Do you want to get both of us into the shit?"

"Hey!" Pete jerked her arm from Morwenna's grasp. "You're the one who wanted us here so badly you had to force us."

"She doesn't just want us," Jack drawled. "She *needs* us." He regarded Morwenna with a lip curl. "Got yourself into a tight spot, didn't you, darling? Something you can't handle in house." He leaned past Pete and into Morwenna's space. "I can smell it on you. You're desperate."

Morwenna gave Jack a hard shove through the door into the conservatory and slammed it behind them. "I'm not so desperate I won't lay you on the floor if you cross me, Mr. Winter."

Pete inserted herself between the two before Jack could do something stupid like get into a hex-slinging contest with Morwenna and whatever Prometheans were on the other side of the door.

"All right, all right. It'd help a lot if you'd stop being vague and tell us what the fuck is going on." She felt jangled. The weight of so many mages who clearly wished her ill still pressed against her, making her heart beat faster and sweat trickle down the groove of her spine. "It's clear we don't fit in here, Morwenna, so I'm with Jack—what's happened to bring us all together?"

Morwenna flopped on one of the sofas, and though it was barely ten in the morning snagged a decanter and poured herself a drink. "This is my first time at the head of the table. The gathering of the club only happens, in full complement, every hundred years or so," Morwenna said. "The last time was during the early days of the Great War. My grandfather sat at the head, and he narrowly survived a poisoning attempt." She flinched. "My great-uncle, his brother, wasn't so lucky."

She fished around in her pockets for a moment, then turned to Pete. "You couldn't spare a cigarette, could you?"

Pete shrugged. "Gave it up. New mum and all."

"Here," Jack said, extending his pack of Parliaments. "Now tell us what somebody knocking off your relatives has to do with Pete and me."

"The Prometheans aren't perfect, but we do try to do right," Morwenna said. "Not always what people outside *think* is right, but what maintains balance, harmony. What keeps people safe." She lit the cigarette and inhaled, exhaling with a shudder. "There were, once upon a time, those who disagreed with our views. They formed a splinter group, and broke with us, around the time of the Hundred Years' War. They named themselves, in typical arsehole fashion, after Prospero."

"Bloke from *The Tempest*?" Jack muttered. "Cunts."

"You don't know half the story," Morwenna said. "The Prospero Society is everything we're not. They don't want balance. They want power. They want to tear us down, and they count demons among their number. When the Black falls, it will be because a Prosperian kicked the stilts out from under it." She leveled her gaze at Pete. "Preston Mayflower was a good man. He was invaluable to us."

She went to a painting hanging over the piano, a bland landscape showcasing a few crookedly painted cows, and took it off the wall. Behind it, Pete saw a digital screen, and when Morwenna brought it to life a map of the UK appeared, covered with different symbols and bands of color. "These are all the known trouble spots in the Black, all instances of mages going rogue, hautings or possessions, and uses of black magic. We track areas where the Black and the daylight world mingle, too."

"Thin spots," Pete whispered. The map was so rife with color that it appeared to be diseased, and she shivered looking at it. If ever there was tangible proof things were sliding over the edge into chaos, this was it.

"Preston was able to locate them for us," Morwenna said. "He was a geomancer—he detected unbalanced power in the earth, the Black poisoning the land, that sort of thing."

Pete took a seat so her posture wouldn't give her away. She kept her expression neutral, and thanked her lucky stars that Jack didn't know any more than he did. He couldn't trip her up.

"Preston was in Hereford, scouting out some unrest reported by the local mages. We thought it might be a case of a demon summoning gone wrong. But when Preston came back . . ."

Morwenna drained her glass and rolled it in her

hands. Her cheeks flushed from the drink, and she screwed her eyes shut. "He was different. Before, he was my friend. But something happened to him. He became erratic, and he refused to come back to Manchester. We dispatched another mage, Jeremy Crotherton, to bring him back and find out what the Hell was going on, but . . ."

She sighed and rubbed her fingers across her temples, carving vicious red indents in the skin. "We think the Prosperians got to Preston. He started threatening to go public, to reveal us to the daylight world, and we haven't heard from Jeremy since he went to Hereford. Poor Preston," she said softly. "He didn't deserve this."

Morwenna drew out her mobile and scrolled through her voice messages. "This was the last message from Jeremy," she said. "You can see why we're concerned."

A hiss of static emanated from Morwenna's phone, and then a reedy voice came through. "Morwenna, it's Jeremy. I can't . . . I mean, I can't keep this up for much longer. Preston's off the rails, he's . . ."

A scraping sound cut off the voice, and then there was a crash and a scream. Jeremy cut back in, panting so heavily Pete almost couldn't make out the words. "I'm sorry, Morwenna," he rasped. "I tried, but the soul cage is too strong. This *place* is too strong. For the love of all you hold dear, don't send anyone else to—" Jeremy's voice hitched, and then it was obvious he had dropped his mobile. "What are *you* doing here? You stay away from me! You stay—"

The message cut off with a screech of feedback.

Morwenna thumbed her voicemail off and tucked her phone back into her pocket, resuming her defeated posture. "The next time I saw Preston, he was in ruins. Raving, completely mad. The Prospero Society got to him and they twisted him and they made him do things for them."

She abruptly sat up and stared at Pete. Pete felt the gaze penetrate all the way to her core. This was the Morwenna she'd first seen—cold and devoid of feeling. "I know he reached out to you at the train station, Pete. It's very important that you tell me what the two of you talked about. Preston was not a well man and he'd become paranoid, convinced we were out to harm him."

Pete felt the weight of the soul cage in her pocket. If Morwenna knew she had it, there'd be no chance of her walking away from this. "What you said," she shrugged. "He told me to stay away from you, and he rambled a bit. I got away as quickly as possible."

"And the soul cage that Jeremy talked about," Morwenna said. Pete could see the vein jumping in her neck. It mirrored Pete's own heartbeat, and Jack's. He was sitting perfectly still, wire-strung, ready to run or fight at a moment's notice.

Pete met Morwenna's gaze and didn't blink. "I don't know what that is," she said evenly. "Sounds like a nasty bit of work, though. Preston's doing?"

"Just something Jeremy thought might be useful intelligence," Morwenna said, then sat back. Pete felt as if she might pass out. She looked at Jack instead, trying to reassure him silently that she had this under control.

"So Preston is on the side of the big bad evil and this Jeremy bloke is MIA?" she said. "After chasing demons in Hereford? What exactly are Jack and I supposed to do about all of that?"

"The Prospero society wants an insider among the Prometheans," Morwenna said. "They tried for Preston, but he couldn't stand up to their techniques and he went over, genuinely tried to help them get inside our organization. But you . . ." she smiled at Pete, and it was as if they hadn't been ready to go at each other's throat a moment ago. "You're more used to this sort of thing. Down and dirty, in the trenches. You'll be perfect."

Pete was learning quickly that she preferred the sort of bastard who let you know flat out they hated you. Morwenna's hot and cold act was going to give her a heart attack.

"Just hold up here," Jack said. "Your whole purpose was for us to be fucking bait?"

"Think of it as an opportunity to do some good," Morwenna said. "An actual insider would be far too dangerous—the Prospero Society clearly has no trouble reaching inside a mage's mind. But you and Pete can go to Hereford, find Jeremy, and figure out who the Prosperians' agent is. It's the best way."

"It's a shit way!" Jack exclaimed. "Why should we do your bloody grunt work?"

"Because you don't have a choice," Morwenna said. "And neither do we. For the good of everyone in the Black who doesn't want to see the world swallowed whole by something like Nergal, you'll do as I say."

Pete's first impulse was to tell Morwenna to bend over and cram it straight up her own arse, but logic dictated the woman was right. Even if they could fight their way out of here, she and Jack already had too many enemies. They didn't need a group as powerful as the Prometheans wanting a piece of their hides as well.

"Jack," she said. "Let it be. She's right." She went and sat next to him, putting a hand on his knee, and favored Morwenna with the sort of look she usually reserved for the killers and rapists she ran across on the murder squad. "If you try and fuck me over, and more importantly if you harm one hair on Jack or our daughter's head, there is going to be such fire rained down on you it will make the end of the world look like a chuch fete by comparison. You reading me, Morwenna?"

"The Prospero Society won't be able to resist the two of you," Morwenna said without missing a beat. "This isn't a game, a tug of war, any longer. This is stock your pantry and batten down the hatches before the war comes to your doorstep."

"So what, we swan around Hereford until a creepy bloke in a long coat makes overtures?" Pete said.

"Oh, didn't I mention?" Morwenna said. "You'll be among old friends in Hereford, Pete. When Jeremy arrived he found the place has become something of a mecca for those buffeted by the Black—ordinary folks who've seen things they don't understand. It's like they've got their own little social club, right there among the weekend Wiccans and those nutters who hunt the Loch Ness monster."

Pete felt an uncomfortable frisson of regret crawl up her spine. "I don't follow you," she said.

"There were quite a few traumatized families after the Algernon Treadwell business back in London, I heard," Morwenna said.

Pete tensed her hand on Jack's leg until he grunted in pain, and she felt the words grit out of her as if she'd swallowed a handful of stones. "What are you saying, Morwenna?"

"The children you saved—or failed to save—are in the village in Hereford where we last heard from Jeremy," Morwenna said. "He found it quite peculiar, so many survivors of a spirit attack in one place, but I imagine for you it'll be like a reunion."

"You knew," Pete spat. She wanted to slap Morwenna in the face. Jack was holding her in place now as her body vibrated with fury. "You knew this whole time that I'd run into those people."

"Consider it added incentive," Morwenna said. "We have no inkling what Preston found in Hereford, but it was bad enough to spread like a virus through the community and utterly corrupt him. So if you want to save those innocent babes, I suggest you get moving."

"I'll do it," Pete told her, standing. "Because I know when I'm beaten, and you've left me no choice. But don't think we're friends after this."

"I have enough friends," said Morwenna, also standing and smoothing her skirt. "What I need are allies." The fleeting moment of vulnerability was gone and she gripped Pete's hand, her fingers like warm iron bands around Pete's small bones.

"You've got them," Pete said, squeezing back, not wanting to be the first one to let go. "By dint of being a devious bitch."

"Welcome to the fold," Morwenna said with a thin, razor-sharp smile. "You're a Promethean now."

11.

Jack stayed quiet until the Prometheans had deposited them, their mobiles and IDs, and their luggage on the sidewalk, and he glowered as the cab wound back toward the train station. Pete sighed as they pulled to the curb and the taxi driver waved away her cash. "It's taken care of, luv."

"You going to pout much longer?" she asked Jack.

Jack's lip curled. "This is a little beyond pouting."

"Look," Pete said. "By rights, I should be the one in a snit. She tricked me, and she's a damned liar. At least we're out of there."

"Yeah, and thank Christ and his fleet of rowboats for that," Jack said. His whole frame twitched, unease evident with every breath. He looked like he had in the bad old days, when he was looking for his next fix of either magic or heroin. Pete felt the uncomfortable sensation of memories that she'd rather stayed drowned breaking the surface.

"I'm sorry," Pete said softly, hefting her suitcase. She felt uncomfortable looking back at the spot where

Preston had died. Was what Morwenna said true? Had he been dipping into black magic that drove him crazy?

Or would the Prometheans would have done worse to her if they'd found the soul cage? "I'm sorry, Jack," she said again. "I was trying to do what wouldn't get us killed or put on yet another hit list. Forgive me if I'm not sufficiently guns a-blazing for your taste."

"Petunia, it is not just you anymore!" Jack burst out, his voice echoing off the broken brick fronts of the nearby flats. "It's me, and it's Lily, too. You call me irresponsible, but you've never once thought about yourself in all this. You have an obligation to stay in one piece now. We need you." He gripped her by the hands, harder than Morwenna ever had, so hard she inhaled a sharp breath. "*I* need you."

Pete looked at her boots, willing her tears not to spill. "I know, Jack. I'm doing this *for* you." She looked at him. "How much longer do you think either of us can avoid the Hag? What will happen to Lily then?"

Jack wasn't given to demonstrations, so Pete was surprised when he wrapped his arms around her hard enough to drive the air from her lungs. She returned the gesture, patting his back, hands caressing the rough leather. "I'd never let that happen," he muttered against Pete's neck. "I'd never let her hurt you."

"Jack," Pete sighed. She drew back at arm's length. "You can't promise that. I can't promise that nothing will happen to me during this little stunt Morwenna cooked up, but I *can* promise that if I don't do it, eventually things *will* go past the point of no return, and that'll be in. End reel, roll credits. And seeing as I like things the way they are, I'm going to do my damndest to make sure the Morrigan never gets her Hell on earth." She squeezed Jack's hand. "I'm not afraid. Not of this. I'm more afraid you won't be with me."

Jack looked at the floor sighed heavily. "'Course I will," he said. "You're the only person I stick me neck out for. You know that. Anyone else would be shite out of luck."

"You're so romantic," Pete said.

"That's me," Jack agreed, pulling her close again. "Man of the fuckin' year."

The loudspeaker was blatting that their train was about to depart, so Pete bought two rushed and hideously expensive tickets from the machine and jogged onboard with Jack. Once she'd sat, the last thing Morwenna had said really hit her, almost pressing her physically into her seat.

It had been a long time since the Treadwell case—not in years, but certainly in experience. She hadn't kept in contact with the families of any of the children Algernon Treadwell had drained of soul and feeling to sustain his spirit, and she'd gotten the distinct feeling they wanted it that way.

Now, though, she was going in blind, and she didn't like it. She brought her mobile to life, flipping through numbers to find the only name from her days on the Met still in her directory. Though it was long after his shift ended, he answered on the second ring.

"This better be the world endin', Pete."

"Isn't it always, Ollie?" Pete said, steadied a bit at the sound of his thick Yorkshire accent. Ollie was from a time when none of it—ghosts, demons, the collateral damage of people like the children Treadwell had fed on—existed for her. Just the usual atrocities, wrought by and on plain old humans.

Ollie Heath groused, and she heard bedsprings creak. "Why do I know you're interrupting my beauty sleep for some illegal errand that'll probably get me sacked?" he said.

"Because you know me too well," Pete told him. "Look, Ollie, I don't have a lot of time. I need you to track down a bloke for me. And then an address."

Ollie sighed. One day, Pete knew, she was going to run out of credit, and he'd shut her account. She hoped not soon, though. She genuinely liked Ollie. He was a good copper and a decent bloke. Asking him to do something that could get him sacked wasn't exactly fun for Pete, but she needed real information, not the carefully edited load of shit Morwenna had fed her back in Manchester.

"Right," Ollie said. "Got a pen. Go ahead."

Pete rattled off Jeremy Crotherton's name and the details of his last known sighting. "An accident report, a John Doe turning up in a couple of pieces—according to his, uh, friends, he just vanished." She chewed on her lip, trying to keep the emotion out of her voice. Ollie wouldn't help her if he thought anything was hinky about this request. "And I need to find an address for Margaret Smythe."

Ollie sucked in a breath. "That kid what you helped out back in the day? What d'you need her for?"

"It's important, Ollie," Pete told him, her gut clenching with unease. If Margaret was in harm's way, Pete had to do something. Warn her somehow.

"'Course it is," Ollie said. "Even if it wasn't, you know I'd do it. Call you back when I find something."

He rang off, and Pete pressed her forehead against the cool train window as the twilight land sped by in a blur of fog, shadow and bursts of light. She wanted a fag, so badly she could already taste the harsh, dry filter paper on her tongue. Wanted a drink, wanted to scream. Wanted to go home.

But none of those things would help in the moment. Nothing she could do until she knew what she was really getting into.

"You know, I could throttle that bloody Wendy," Jack said, snapping her out of the vast circle of rage and self pity in which she'd found herself rotating. "Everything we've been through, and she flips on me for a few quid and pat on the head from some bitch in a nice suit."

"Old school friends are usually cunts," Pete agreed. "I met with a girl I did A-levels with when I was engaged to Terry, and she spent the whole time trying to get me to invest in a pyramid scheme."

Jack shook his head, mouth forming a bitter line. "Wendy and me was more than that. I saved her life, you know."

Pete decided she was so glad they weren't talking about where they were going, or the mess they were in, that she'd discuss Wendy until the cow came home, propped up its feet, and turned on the telly. "I didn't," she said. "She wasn't exactly eager to chat with me, for obvious reasons."

"That you don't look like you were hit with a lorry full of bad decisions and aging poorly?" Jack snorted.

Pete laughed and fetched him a soft punch on his arm. "You're a terrible slag. She wasn't that bad."

"She used to be me only real friend," Jack said, abruptly sombering again. "After me da fucked off for the last time, Mum was in and out with a different man every week. Wendy used to make these fuck-awful beans on toast and steal lager from the downstairs neighbor, and we'd sit up in her room and have dinner because our parents were all too stoned to feed us."

Pete stayed quiet, glad that the vise grip of Manchester's Black had eased a bit and she could feel the thrum of power again, rather than drowning in it, as the train raced into the country.

"My da was a degenerate scum-coated wanker," Jack said. "But Wendy's was true horror. Put her head through a wall because he didn't like her wearing makeup. Came for our usual beans and chatter, found her on the stoop looking like fucking *Carrie*. I took her to this old tip of a warehouse where me and my mates hung about, and just sat and talked with her all night, about shite I've never told anyone before or since. Just making sure she didn't go to sleep. Walked her home at dawn because she ordered me to, even though I would've rather eaten nails then take her back there."

Pete put her head on Jack's shoulder, much as she imagined Wendy would have. She felt the spark of his talent against hers. There was a time when they had to be careful not even to touch skin to skin, because her talent would drink his down. At least they'd solved that problem.

Jack stroked her hair once, absently. His eyes were miles and decades away. "I wanted to kick the shit out of her da, but he was friends with my mum's Kevin, and it would've gone bad for her mum besides if I'd interfered."

"You did the best you could," Pete said quietly. "You were just a kid, Jack."

"I always told myself I'd be better," he said, vicious against her ear. "That I wouldn't fuck about with a bunch of whores or drink or beat my kids. That I'd be a rock, not a voice you hear on the wind or a tosser who comes around on your birthday, throws money at you and then fucks off again so some other bastard can beat seven shades of Hell out of you and keep your mum so stoned she doesn't even know it's happening. I told myself I'd be better." He gave a shuddery breath, and Pete knew if she looked up she'd see his wet eyes, so she didn't. Jack would never open up again if she witnessed that. "But I'm not," he whispered, voice thick. "I'm shit."

Pete slipped an arm across his chest, so close and warm they might have been at home in bed. "You're a good man," she said. "You're a good man who makes shit choices. That's different than being shit." She slotted her fingers into the shallow spaces in between Jack's ribs, spaces she'd memorized night after night and longed for when she'd been away. "Lily is going to remember you as that man. None of what came before matters to her, so that's all that should matter to you."

Jack said nothing, just breathed in time with the clack of the rails, and Pete started to wonder if she'd enraged him or saddened him beyond speaking. She let out a silent sigh of relief when her mobile buzzed with Ollie's number.

"You never can stay away from trouble, can you?" Ollie said when she picked up.

"I bloody well can, thank you," Pete said. "All I did was ask you to find one man who's not even crooked as far as I know. What's troubling about that?"

"I mean the Smythe bit," Ollie said. "I got your address, and HOLMES kicked back five or six calls to the locals for fights between the Mr. and Mrs." He didn't need to elaborate. They both knew what that meant. "What's happened, Pete?" Ollie said at last. "You're the last person I'd peg to go nostalgic over an old case."

The last case. The last one she'd ever worked for the Met. The one that showed her, irrevocably, that she couldn't hide from the Black inside the mundane. Eventually it would always find her.

"Just give me the address," she snapped. "I know what I'm doing, Ollie."

"Never said you didn't," he said, mild as ever. Pete felt like shit for snarling at him.

"Sorry," she mumbled.

"Here's the rundown," Ollie said. He wasn't one to hold grudges, which Pete figured was why they'd stayed friends for so long. She could be hard to live with on the best of days.

"Looks like the Smythes picked up and moved soon after the Treadwell business. Dear old dad came home from Pentonville and the whole lot buggered off to a little map speck called Overton, in Herefordshire. Sheep and quaint cottages and all that."

"Yeah, heard they moved away from London," Pete said. "I wouldn't blame them, honestly."

"There's something else about Overton you should know," he said. "The families of the three other kids are all living within five miles of each other." He took in Pete's silence and then heaved a deep sigh. "But you already knew that."

"I'd heard the news," Pete said. The thought of coming face to face with the other families—the Killigans, the Leroys, and the Dumbershalls, the children she hadn't been able to save—made her want to stick her head between her knees. "Tell me what you found, though," she said. "I appreciate it, Ollie."

"Property records say they all picked up and moved within a month of each other. Hell, the Dumbershalls and the Leroys live in the two halves of a semi-detached. If you can call it living, poor souls."

"Anything else?" Pete asked. Memories of white eyes and mouths open to scream but producing no sound flooded up at her, and she dug her fingers into her own palm.

"Just a string of backpackers and dog walkers disappeared about three months ago. Locals think it's some kind of Russian mafia deal, sex slaves or whatnot, which gives you an idea of exactly what kind of brain trust you're dealing with out there." Ollie gave a snort. "Probably nothing. It's rough country—people do stupid things or they wander off."

Or they got caught up in the supposed demon summoning Jeremy Crotherton had investigated, before he'd gone missing. "Thanks," Pete said. "Call me if you run across anything else, Ollie."

"You take care," Ollie said, more concern roughening his voice that was usual for his unflappable soul. "You've got a little one now." He rang off and Pete swiped a hand over her face. She wasn't going to cry. Or scream. She was going to hold it together and do her bloody job, because that was what she did. She was cool under pressure. She wasn't some fragile, birdlike thing that fell apart at the slightest hint of trouble.

Jack was staring at her, and when she blinked he spread his hands. "Come on, spit it out. The Met know where this Crotherton bloke fucked off to?"

"Ollie hasn't found anything," Pete said. "All I know is that all of Treadwell's survivors are living down there, and sooner or later I'm going to have to talk to them."

"Well, you don't *have* to," Jack said. "You don't owe those people anything. You saved their kids."

"Not soon enough," Pete whispered. If she'd just believed Jack when he popped back into her life, if she'd just listened from moment one, she could have put

Treadwell out of comission before three lives had been ruined and Margaret Smythe's had nearly been snuffed out.

"You did every fucking thing you could for them," Jack said in a tone that brooked no argument. "And now we'll go down there, find out what soggy pub Crotherton is holed up in, put the demon back where it belongs, and go home. Spend a few days in the country in the bargain. Won't that be lovely?"

Pete felt the weight of the soul cage in her pocket, saw the memory of the children's blank white eyes after Treadwell had taken away everything that made them human. "Yeah," she agreed, feeling the knot of fear twist tighter than ever in her gut. "It'll be fucking wonderful."

12.

The last train to Hereford arrived a few minutes after midnight, and a silent, empty station greeted them. Pete traded a look with Jack. "Got to love God's country," he said. "Everyone rolls up the streets at eight p.m. sharp."

The front of the station was absent of vehicles, either buses or cabs. The street itself was quiet and empty, a light fog spinning under the streetlights like sand suspended in water.

"Shit," she said. "You'd think if Morwenna wanted us here so bad, she could at least have sent us a bloody car."

Jack pointed across the street, where a skinny kid slumped against the fender of an ancient Puegeot. "Our chariot awaits," he said, pulling out his wallet. "Oi," he called to the kid. "How much for a ride?"

He appraised them, sucking on gums high and white from some kind of speed. "For you, pervo? Not enough in the world. For the lady there? Could be free if she's into the kinky stuff."

"I'm into beating the shit out of smart little tossers

with my bare hands," Pete said sweetly, giving him a wide smile. She half hoped the kid would push the issue. She was wound so tightly violence would feel like a relief.

Then she got hold of herself and wondered what the fuck was wrong with her. She didn't lose her mind and beat people up for no good reason. Being here, thinking about the Treadwell case, missing Lily—it was pushing her too far. She pressed her thumbs into the center of her forehead, feeling the whisper of her talent. *Just let me go and we could burn him alive on the spot.*

Sometimes it was like having a serial killer rooming in her head. Once she'd started to really understand her talent, she never questioned why Jack's had turned him into a junkie and nearly driven him to suicide.

The kid regarded her, perhaps rightly thinking she was a madwoman, then shrugged. "Hundred quid."

"I haven't even told you where I want to go," Pete said with a roll of her eyes. She needed to calm down and be steady, reliable copper Pete instead of deranged, magically inclined Pete. "Forty, and I don't let my man here kick your teeth out and feed them back to you."

Jack stood silent and unsmiling. His menacing glare did the trick, because the kid huffed in contempt and threw up his hands. "Fifty, and I ain't carrying your bags."

Pete slung her kit into the cab and got in after it. "Deal. But you better drive fast."

Once out of Hereford, the cabbie drove as if he were being pursued by large, mutant weasels intent on mating with him. Pete thought that if this was what he'd do for fifty quid, she'd hate to see what happened when he was actually motivated.

"What'd you say the name of the town was?" he bellowed over the car's distressed engine and whining transmission.

Pete told him, and he veered onto a B road before stopping abruptly by a sign in the middle of nowhere.

VILLAGE OF OVERTON, the sign proclaimed. POPULATION 271.

"Spooky, innit?" said the kid, smacking his gums. "Not keen on being turned into some fat farmer's bum buddy, so I'll let you out here, I think."

"Are you kidding me?" Jack said. "It's got to be two fucking miles at least into town."

"Man, you ain't heard about the backpackers that went *poof* up here month before this?" said the kid, making a disappearing motion with his fingers. "Not to mention those fuckin' travelers in their tent city. Don't trust gyppos. 'M not going another inch."

"Your attitude is as charming as your breath," Pete told him, thrusting a fifty at the kid and climbing out.

"Thanks, Mum," he said with a grin that was begging to be smacked off his face. He screeched away, nearly before Jack was free of the door, and Jack flipped the bird at the red smears of the car's taillights.

"It'll be all right," Pete said. "Like we really expected anything to be easy on this jaunt?"

"*I'm* not a fuckin' backpacker," Jack grumbled. "I don't swan all over the country on foot."

"Find your balls and let's go," Pete snapped. She could see lights ahead, and even though it was the middle of the night, they were also in the middle of nowhere. People *had* gone missing in recent memory, not to mention Jeremy Crotherton and his theory that a demon was running loose.

Pete walked close to Jack, swinging her eyes from side to side, seeking for anything hiding in the shadows. The moon was high and horned above them, and Pete could see the blue shadows of hills on either side of the road. She'd never been much for the country, preferring the eternal twilight of streetlamps and the buzz of motorways. Too much silence just made her think there was someone out there, watching.

Jack rolled his gaze from one side of the road to the other, and his step was short and hitched. "Waiting for the cannibals to break from the forest and carry us off to make attractive jumpers out of our skin," he said.

"You're acting as if you're twelve," Pete said. "Knock it off."

"I'm not being spooky," Jack insisted. "This fucking place is off. Do you hear anything? Anything at all?"

Pete listened. There was nothing. No dogs, no doors slamming, no car engines. Even the wind was quiet, the air still, as if the earth held its breath. "It's a small place," she said with a shrug. "Not like London."

"There's small villages, and there's boneyards," Jack said. "Last place I was in that was this quiet was a tomb."

Pete reached into her pocket and brushed her baton. Just knowing it was still there let her keep walking.

When they reached Overton proper, the village was empty and silent. The high street consisted of a few blocks of semi-detached homes that had been made into snug storefronts, and a square with a statue in it of a Franciscan in a robe, his staring eyes weeping oxidized tears. A pair of ravens sat on his shoulders, the only movement in the whole square. Not crows—true ravens, like the one in her dream, with bodies as long as Pete's arm and beaks sharp as pikes.

She stopped in the center of the cobblestone street, watching the birds. They paid her no mind, hunching against the chill and blinking their obsidian eyes. If the Hag cared that she and Jack were in the village, she wasn't immediately tipping her hand.

Jack flicked a fag-end in the general direction of the birds. "Still think everything is right and good?"

"Of course not," Pete said. The shadows and reflections on the glass were liquid, and the first real unease stirred, a flutter of her stomach that had nothing to do with the silent town. Nobody being in residence would be a much better outcome than *something* being there.

"Can't do anything about Crotherton until morning," Jack said. "So aside from bunking with the travelers, where are we sleeping?"

Pete had hoped that, as with most villages that attracted hikers and tourists, there'd be an inn or even a shoddy chain hotel, but there was nothing. Everything was dark and silent, and no signs on any of the store-fronts promised lodging.

Pete sighed. "I can only think of one place, and you're not going to like it."

"Luv, I'd sleep cuddled up with a horny skinhead inside a roach-infested box at this point," Jack said, punctuating his words with a wide yawn.

"All right, then," Pete said, telling her mobile to give her a map to the address she'd gotten from Ollie. "Come with me."

The Smythe house was only about half a mile from the square, but it was the most uncomfortable half mile Pete had ever walked. She could feel stares, hear whispers, and sense the rising crescendo of unearthly magic all around them. It was as if they'd tripped an alarm, and now the electric fence was on and charging the air itself to prick her skin.

Jack grimaced and rubbed his forehead. Pete glanced at him. "You going to make it?"

"It's not even sight," Jack said. "Something else. Whole damn place sets me teeth on edge."

"If everything were all right, we wouldn't be here," Pete said. "Think it's some residue from the summoning? Maybe that's what made Crotherton bugger off."

Maybe it's what sent Preston over the edge.

Or maybe she was just tired and far too edgy. She stopped at the correct house number and looked up the walk, not sure what to expect.

The Smythe house looked normal from the street. White plaster, red tile roof, almost like an Italian villa plopped down in the middle of green England. A neat garden with a weathered fence containing late mums and lilies. It was a far cry from the dank council house the Smythes had occupied when Pete had first met Margaret's mum, after Margaret had been kidnapped by Treadwell's agents.

The lights were off, but she pushed through the gate and up the path. The gate springs gave a shriek, deafening in the quiet night. Jack stayed on the street, eyes roaming through the darkness. Just knowing he was behind her gave Pete the nerve to pound on the door.

After a minute of thumping, she started to hope that they weren't home, or had moved, or *anything* that would save her from having to talk to Margaret's parents. But then the lamp flared on above her head, and the door flew open.

"What!" a skinny man in an undershirt and pants barked. "It's one in the fuckin' morning! Did you lose your watch up your arse?"

"Mr. Smythe?" Pete said, purely as a formality. She recognized his craggy face and sad, rapidly retreating gray hairline from the family photos she'd seen in London.

"Who the fuck are you?" he shouted in response. "I told you lot, you wait for the morning like everyone else! Go camp on the green with the other freaks and stay off our personal property!"

Pete didn't bother asking him what he was on about. "Sir, you don't know me, but I worked your daughter's kidnap case. I'm afraid my friend and I have come to

Overton on business and we're in a bit of a spot. Might we come in?" Honestly, she was glad it was Margaret's father and not her gin-soaked, teary-eyed mother. Being shouted at by convicts was familiar ground, one she could navigate.

Mr. Smythe drew back visibly, as if she'd brandished a tire iron at his testicles. "You're a copper?"

"May we come in?" Pete asked again. Let him think she still had a badge, if it made life easier. It wasn't a crime not to correct an assumption.

"Well, this ain't a fuckin' B&B," Mr. Smythe said. "My wife and kid are asleep, and whatever it is can wait until mornin'."

"I'm afraid it can't," Pete said. "I've been asked to look into the disappearances in the area, and there was a mixup at our lodging."

She tried a different tack, giving Mr. Smythe a warm smile. He curled his lip, as if a small dog had pissed on his shoe. "I know it's a terrible imposition, but I and the investigation would certainly benefit from it."

She kept smiling and put her foot over the threshold, closing in on Smythe's personal space. Like any scrawny rat who'd been locked up, he shrank back instinctively, out of blade distance.

Pete stepped inside. The Smythe house smelled the same as their old one—stale cigarettes, overpowering floral cleaner, and the faint tang of rancid takeaway grease. Mr. Smythe gave her a dull glare. "Come in then, I guess," he muttered.

"Thank you so much," Pete said, borrowing the

false cheer her mother often employed when she was trying to cajole Pete and her sister into doing something they didn't want. She turned and gestured to Jack, who hopped up the steps and grinned at Philip Smythe.

"Really appreciate it, sir."

Smythe regarded Jack with a slack jaw, eyes working over every inch of him. "You a copper too?"

"On Her Majesty's secret service," Jack said with a perfectly straight face, and Smythe blinked at him.

"I don't know about this . . ." he started, but a door banged open and Pete watched Norma Smythe came stumbling down the hall, scrubbing at her face. Margaret's mother was wearing a lavender nightgown that stopped far north of what Pete wanted to see, and yesterday's makeup still lingered on her eyelids like bruises.

"The fuck is all this racket?" she muttered, before focusing on Pete. "I know you."

"We've found ourselves in Overton without a place to stay," Pete said, "and your husband was kind enough to offer the spare room."

"Haven't got a fucking spare room," Norma grumbled. "Kid's in it." She fixed her gaze on Pete, and it was less bleary than Pete had hoped. The Norma she knew was an afternoon drinker and considered sobriety an untenable state. "Thought you'd left the Met. Tried to call you at the one-year of you finding my baby, and they said you'd left."

"I'm investigating a private matter," Pete said without missing a beat. "A man named Jeremy Crotherton who's gone missing."

"Crotherton one of them hippie hikers?" Philip said. "Good luck finding him, then. Probably got stoned and pitched down a ravine."

"Mr. Crotherton's . . . family is very concerned," Pete said. She looked back at Norma, trying to come up with a way to make this more palatable, but she caught sight of movement at the top of the stairs and her heart nearly stopped. "Hello, Margaret," she said softly. "How are you, sweetheart?"

"I'm very well, thank you," Margaret said. Her tone was heavy, like she'd downed a fistful of painkillers. "Have you come to see me?"

"I'm sorry, luv, but I'm here for something else," Pete said. "A man named Jeremy Crotherton. You haven't heard anything, have you?"

"Oi," Philip said. "You ain't a copper, so don't talk to my kid. You can sleep on the foldaway, but in the morning I want you gone."

"That's fine," Pete murmured, her eyes still on Margaret. The girl's gaze was wide and unblinking, and Pete could see her vibrating with panic from three meters away.

"Meg, get your arse back in bed," Norma snapped at her daughter. "You've a huge appearance tomorrow."

"What's tomorrow?" Pete kept her tone conversational. The Smythes weren't going to catch on she knew they were full of shit. Not from any betrayal of her eyes or face, anyway. She might not be as good a liar as Jack, but she could fool two greedy, chavvy council rats for a few minutes.

"A meeting," said Norma, lighting a cigarette from a pack on her end table and sucking on it like it dispensed champagne and Vicodin. "Tent meeting, what like they have over in America. You haven't been following the news story?"

"She's been busy putting her nose in other people's lives," said Philip. "You think London cares about the back of beyond?"

"Stop being a twat," Norma shot back. "You were locked up, you didn't see it—whatever else she is, this lady brought my little one back to me." She lunged for Pete and enfolded her in a vodka-scented hug before Pete could dart away. She wondered how quickly you could suffocate against another woman's tits while Norma Smythe mumbled into her ear, "I can never thank you. Never ever thank you enough."

"It's . . . it's all right," Pete said, wriggling free. "Just doing my job and all that."

"My Margaret was so much better when she came back," Norma said. "And the other parents were so lovely about what had happened. When we found all four of these poor children could do the same . . . sort of things, well. We've attracted quite a local following, and tomorrow's our biggest ever. Someday we'll be larger than Glastonbury, Philip reckons."

"You should come," Philip broke in. "See for yourself, then you can call the care workers off our arse. It ain't like we're auctioning off our kids to the highest bidder."

"I'd love to see what you've been up to," Pete said. "Tomorrow, you said?"

"Eight a.m. sharp," Norma said. "But people are already camped on the green to get a good viewing spot."

"Oh, for the great detective inspector, I'll see we get her a front-row seat," Philip said. Something slithered across his face that was malicious and unpleasant, the anticipation of seeing someone he hated in pain.

Pete looked to Jack, who grimaced at the magic that even now ran all over Pete like thorns against her bare skin. "Make it two spots," she said. "We wouldn't miss it."

13.

Pete passed the night next to Jack on the Smythe's spring-infested rollaway bed, pressed into him out of necessity as much as need. It lacked a lot of the glamour it had held when Pete was sixteen, and when she managed to fall asleep, she opened her eyes to find herself standing on a hillside, wearing only her underwear and one of Jack's shirts. Dew coated the soles of her feet, and mist curled low amid lichen-crusted stone walls and a single tree that bent over a cairn of black stones.

She looked behind her and saw her footprints in the long grass, a silvery trail leading back over the hills, presumably toward the village. She didn't know how far she'd come, just that she was here now.

She was only half-surprised to see the raven from her other dream. It lighted on a tree branch and croaked at her. Pete heaved a sigh. "Your mistress can creep around my mind all she likes. Doesn't change my answer."

She took a few steps forward, wet grass brushing her

calves. Cold found her through the thin material of her shirt, and she wrapped her arms around her waist. She wasn't usually cold in dreams.

"That's because this isn't a dream."

She stared at the raven. She'd never heard an agent of the Morrigan speak to her so directly, not inside her mind. "It isn't?"

The raven ruffled its pinion feathers and adjusted its grip on the branch. "You're awake. Does this really feel like a dream?"

Talking bird and all, it *was* substantially less horrible than most of Pete's prophetic dreams. "I don't know."

"You need to leave," said the bird. "Right now."

"Let me guess," Pete said. "You and the Morrigan have your own plans for this place." It would explain the magic wound through this place tightly as the rock met the earth, tightly as the roots of the tree in front of her.

"This place? No. This is not our place," said the raven. "Nor the place of any living thing. Not of gods, or of men. It is a place of death, a place that will lead only to your destruction, Weir."

The raven rotated its head to her, stared into her eyes. "Stop looking for Jeremy Crotherton and stop trying to appease the Prometheans. In the long run, it's not going to matter anyway. Run," it said. "Run and don't look back."

"Says the talking bird," Pete grumbled. "Perched up there in his fancy little tree."

"I can only talk to you in this place," said the raven. "Only here, where it's strongest."

"I fucking hate you types and your talking in circles," Pete said. "Do you know that?"

"It's spreading," said the raven. "And you need to get away from the heart of it before it infects you like . . ."

"Pete!"

The scream cut through the mist, and Pete turned, all at once feeling frozen, damp, and footsore. "Jack? What the fuck is going on?"

He came running, blond hair bobbing through the mist until he was fully in view. "The fuck are you doing?" he gasped, leaning over and bracing on his thighs. He fumbled a cigarette and lit it with the tip of his finger.

Pete looked to the raven, but it had flown. She was alone. "Sleepwalking, I guess," she said.

"You scared me," Jack said, regaining his breath. "I woke up and the window was open and you'd done a runner. We're five fucking miles from the village."

"Seriously?" Pete regarded the hillside with more scrutiny. "I thought I was dreaming . . ."

Jack grasped her by the arms and examined her face. "What happened, luv?"

"I don't know," she said honestly. "But I don't feel well." The longer she stood, the more sick and dizzy she felt, like when she'd had morning sickness with Lily to the power of ten.

This is not a place of gods or of men, the raven said, and Pete looked back at the cairn of stones. The entire place vibrated with power, as if what was in front of her was slightly out of focus. The vague unease she felt in the village had turned itself to full-blown panic.

"Yeah, I can't say I fancy it," Jack said. "I was too worried to really pay attention but now . . ." He flinched. "There's bad mojo running through here."

Pete let him put his jacket around her and his arm in turn, and lead her back to the road. "What time is it?" she said. She felt small, out of place, and sick to her stomach. She'd never sleepwalked, not even as a child. Never woken up like that, alone and vulnerable.

Get it together, Caldecott, she told herself. Strange shite had happened to Preston and Jeremy Crotherton, too. If anything, this meant she could finish the job and get away from the Prometheus Club all the quicker.

"Around seven, I think," Jack said. "Took me a while to find you. Don't worry, we'll still make the Smythes' freak show if we hurry." He looked down at her as they walked, bumpy asphalt poking at Pete's feet, and frowned. "What do you think is going on here, Petunia? Really?"

"You're asking *me*?" Pete had to laugh. "You really must have no fucking idea."

"Nope," Jack said. "Never run into anyplace that felt like this. Not a mass grave, not a sacrificial site. This is new."

"I don't know what's happening," Pete said, as the mist began to burn away under a pale and overworked sunrise. "But I know whatever it is, it can't be good."

14.

Pete might have spent the rest of the day trying to figure out what the fuck was happening, but there was Margaret to think of, and barely time to pull on real clothes and comb her hair before she and Jack were off again, moving toward the village green with a crowd clutching rucksacks and portable chairs, sporting a higher-than-average ratio of natural fibers and New Age bangles. Some were travelers, but some looked like ordinary folk, rumpled and red-eyed and not used to sleeping rough.

Pete didn't tell Jack about the raven, or about what it had said. There was enough going on this morning—later, she could tell him the whole story and see if he had any idea what they might have stumbled into.

The green was just a flat space at the edge of the village, bounded on one side by a series of stone buildings and on the other by rolling open country. A hill fort looked down over the grassy expanse, blocking the light and trapping the mist in a low bowl of shadow and chill.

The crowd congregated under a white tent, the sort used for church fetes or picnics.

A plywood stage had been constructed at the edge of the green, and four small chairs sat across the length. Pete intended to slip in the back of the tent, but Norma Smythe spotted her and dragged her to the front of the crowd, to assorted grumbles from the surrounding hippies.

"Oh, shut it," Jack said. "Smear some more patchouli on your nethers and calm down."

Norma gave him a dirty look, and Pete tried to smooth her over with a smile. "Sorry. We're just a bit tired."

"Stay here," Norma said. "We'll find you when it's over."

Pete looked for Margaret, but when she found her, she was being held tightly by Philip, who gripped her arm as though it were a leash. Margaret had circles under her eyes even deeper than Pete's, and she slumped in her father's grip like a broken toy.

"Shit," Pete muttered. She had to speak to Margaret alone and find out what was going on. She chewed on her lip and tried to look interested in what was happening onstage.

"All right, then. We're starting." Pete tried not to stare when she caught sight of Bridget Killigan's father. The last time she'd seen Dexter, bent over his daughter's hospital bed, he'd looked wrung out but still lively. Now he was gaunt and pale, looking close to keeling over but for the microphone he clutched to hold himself upright. "I'll tell you how this works, then I'll turn this over to Philip," Dexter Killigan said. His voice, even amplified, was a thin shred of what Pete remembered. "You can ask one question. The children will answer. Their answers cannot be disputed or argued over. You may not ask another question." He paused, staring out at the silent massing of people with unfocused eyes. "That's it, then." With a limp gesture, he passed the microphone to Philip and slumped offstage.

"This is great," Jack said against her ear. "When do you think they're going to start falling on the ground and jabbering at snakes?"

"Be quiet," Pete snapped, not even pretending to indulge him. You didn't even have to be observant to sense the wrongness. It was like watching a parade of mental patients try to convince you they were perfectly sane and really *did* hear space aliens transmitting in their fillings. They might have the right words and gestures, but something would be slightly blurred, slightly wrong.

"All right," said Philip Smythe. "Those of you who've been here before, welcome back. Consider letting some new folks take a turn at the front. Also, consider pitching something in the bucket when it comes around, yeah? We're running on your gas."

"Bring on the kids!" someone shouted, and Philip glared into the crowd.

"You put that tongue back in your head. This isn't a carnival sideshow."

"Could have fooled me," Jack grumbled.

"Be quiet and be fuckin' respectful," Philip continued.

"This isn't a trick. This is a gift to us all." He gestured to the back of the stage, where thick plastic hung as a makeshift curtain. "Welcome the kids, please."

As they came out, all Pete could do was stare. Margaret sat as far as she could from the others, folding in on herself. Bridget Killigan came forth, walking as if she were moving underwater, arms spread in front of her. Philip took her arm and guided her to her seat. "There, luv," he said.

Pete's mouth opened, and her air grew short. Bridget Killigan couldn't walk. She couldn't do anything. She was blind and catatonic, a victim of Algernon Treadwell's hungry ghost. He'd drained everything that made her Bridget and left a shell, but he hadn't filled it. He hadn't been after a body, just her strength. Jack had been Treadwell's end goal, and Pete had stopped him, but she hadn't been fast enough. He'd taken three children, three children who should *not* be up and walking around.

Diana Leroy and Patrick Dumbershall walked out together, clutching hands. Patrick, who still had one eye that wasn't completely clouded with cataracts, helped her into her seat before feeling his way to his own.

Jack leaned down and pressed his lips into her hair. "Do you have any idea what the hell is going on?"

"Less than none," Pete said. She was almost afraid to keep watching, but any outburst now would just draw attention, and she didn't think the rapt crowd would take too kindly to that. Self-proclaimed pacifists were the first ones to start throwing rocks at the riot police, that much she knew.

A pudgy woman with purple ribbons woven through her hair and a skirt swirling around her ample bottom stepped up, and Philip hopped off the stage, presenting her the mic. "Go ahead. Ask one question."

The woman focused on the four children. Margaret dropped her gaze, foot kicking at the wood, but the other three stared serenely ahead, white gazes unblinking.

"Will I ever find someone to love me?" the woman asked, her voice wavering.

"Hey, now," Philip said. "Before we hear the answer, let's give this sweet lady a round of applause for being so brave."

The crowd set up an earnest clapping that made Pete want to kick every one of them in the shins.

Bridget Killigan traced her hand against the air. "I see a man, but he will be taken from you before love blossoms. You will remember him, when you are alone."

The woman stared for a moment, and then bowed her head. "Thank you. I know you speak the truth." She crumpled a fiver in her fist and shoved it at Philip before pushing through the crowd and disappearing.

Pete reexamined the whole setup. The tent, the crowd of adoring followers, the patter from Philip . . . it was a confidence scam, but that didn't explain how the children were up and talking. Faith healers relied on spectacle and giving people what they wanted, and Bridget's answer had been the opposite.

Another woman, this one young and slender, sporting rainbow dreadlocks, took the mic, but a man in a nylon windcheater pushed her out of the way. "Excuse me . . ." Philip started, but the bloke shouted. Red-faced, he looked more like a farmer than someone who'd be in line to talk to fortune-tellers.

"Here's the thing," he shouted. "I think this is a load of shit. You lot ain't no better than the gyppos, coming into our town and turning it into a circus. Can't say anything useful. You want us not to run you out, tell me somethin' I can use. Tell me the lotto numbers."

There were murmurs of assent from the back of the tent, where a complement of four other similarly large and ale-bloated men lurked. "Nice to see the local racists are out in force," Pete murmured.

"Eh, it's been a while since I booted one of those in the balls," Jack said. "Don't worry, nothing's going to happen to your girl."

Margaret was visibly shaking at the confrontation, but Diana Leroy cocked her head at the man. "You're not nice," she said, her voice singsong.

"What I thought," the man said. "Fuck off back to your sideshow. Don't want none of your shite around here." He pushed a fat finger into Philip's chest. "And if you don't light out, we'll make *sure* you leave."

"Your wife doesn't know." Diana's voice rang over the yells from the local yobs, and the grumbles from the hippie set. "She doesn't know what you do when you go to Hereford first Saturday of the month."

The punter's lip curled as Pete watched, waiting for

the moment she was going to have to save Philip Smythe from getting his arse handed to him. Maybe then at least he'd be civil to her.

"You're guessin'," the punter sneered. "You're doing that shite from the telly where you guess at me until you get it right."

"Your wife doesn't know about Geoffrey, or that you like to force yourself on boys even younger than him," Diana said. "And she doesn't know you're the one who gave her the clap. But she'll find out, because you're not smart enough to keep your stories straight. One night you'll stumble home drunk, and she'll be waiting for you with your rifle. She's smarter than you think. It'll look like suicide, and you'll never hurt anyone, ever again."

The silence endemic to Overton reigned with a heavy hand. Philip Smythe gave the punter a smug look, folding his arms. "You asked, mate."

The punter dropped the mic and shoved his way through the crowd, violent and churning in his panic. He knocked aside one of his friends and kept going across the green, until he was just a speck.

Pete looked at Jack, feeling cold all over again, down to her bones. "Are they really doing it? Telling the future?" Divination wasn't exact. It was a hard discipline to master, and not a talent that came naturally. You could get snatches, but the future was fluid. The Black could always change. Events were not immutable. Nobody could speak with the accuracy of Diana and Bridget, but they seemed so *certain*. And more importantly, so did their marks.

"I don't think so," Jack said. He rubbed the center of his forehead. "I think they're reading what's already there, not the timestream."

"Mind reading's not a first-year trick either," Pete muttered.

"And what sort of nasty do we know that excels in picking apart your deepest fears for their own amusement?" Jack said, tensing up and staring at the stage with his glacial eyes unblinking.

Pete looked at the children onstage, save Margaret, in a new light. She might not have Jack's vast store of knowledge, but this one was easy. She'd seen it before, firsthand, up close and far too personal. "Oh, fuck," she breathed, turning back to Jack. His face went grim, and he didn't take his eyes off Bridget, Patrick, and Diana.

"'Fraid so, luv. Those kids up there aren't kids. Those are Crotherton's demons."

Part Two

Possession

Hell hath no limits, nor is circumscrib'd
In one self place; for where we are is hell,
And where hell is, must we ever be.
                              —Christopher Marlowe,
                                    Doctor Faustus

15.

Pete stayed perfectly still. No breath passed her lips, and if she could, she would have stilled the blood in her veins. "Are you sure?" That was a silly question. Demon should have been her first guess, given what Morwenna had told her. Besides, what else could make a broken body ambulatory, give voice to a silent tongue and sight to ruined eyes?

Actual demonic possession was rare; because most demons strong enough to possess were strong enough to mold their own human shapes. Pete had never seen a demon in a human body with her own eyes. It was harder than it sounded—you had to wrestle the living into submission, subvert their will, and ride their body like a bucking horse.

Of course, Pete supposed, picking on catatonic children made the whole game a lot easier.

"Sure as I can be," Jack said. "I'm not gonna get close enough to poke and prod them, that's for sure, but I don't know any other nasty that can do what they're doing." He was pale, and small beads of sweat had collected in the hollows of his cheeks and across his upper lip. With his second sight, Jack saw the children for what they really were—hollowed-out bits of flesh containing something that had never been human and never would be.

"All right," Pete said, staying still and quiet and trying not to telegraph alarm with her words or her face. Up on the stage the prophecies went on, the tone grimmer and grimmer. The worse someone's future was, the wider Bridget, Diana, and Patrick grinned and the more poor Margaret looked like she might throw up. "So what do we do now?"

"Got to get them one by one," Jack murmured. "I can't exorcise three bodies at once. I don't even know if they're Named or just travelers."

Pete swallowed hard. Named demons were the 666 leaders of the legions of Hell, the big hard men. If a Named was responsible for this, they were, as the Americans put it, up shit creek. Thinking about trying to exorcise a Named demon made her throat constrict. She felt as if small rocks were embedded in her chest, making her breath burn. "I could touch them. Find out their true names and use them in the exorcism."

"No," Jack hissed, harsh enough that the people around them looked. Pete glared in return until they went back to staring at the stage.

"It's not like we have a lot of other options," she said. "And I know the parents will let me get close enough if I play into their bullshit."

The cash collection basket came by, heavy with coins

and rustling with notes—many of them twenty or fifty pounds. Jack nimbly pocketed a hundred and twenty quid before passing it along to the woman next to him. "Pete, I don't need to tell you what's going to happen if you try to empty out a demon with your talent. The last time you tried, you nearly burned down me flat and both of us with it."

"I don't *want* to," Pete told him, fidgeting at the implied criticism of his words. The Named that she'd accidentally exorcised just after she'd met Jack hadn't been much of a fighter—more of a skulker, really—and even getting rid of him had nearly killed her. "I haven't forgotten that I have a tendency to go apocalyptic when I brush up against demon magic, but I don't see that we have much of a choice. You're never going to have time to set up a proper exorcism—these kids are being watched like hawks."

She wasn't letting a demon worm its way into Margaret Smythe, and it was simple as that. Margaret was the only one who'd survived Treadwell with her mind intact, which was probably why she hadn't been possessed yet. *Yet* being the operative word.

Before Jack could say anything else, Pete started for the stage, moving through the thick knot of people waiting at the mic, until she found Norma Smythe. "So," she said brightly, amazed at herself and how easy it was to sound cheerful. "This is quite a show."

"Yeah," Norma said, relaxing when Pete smiled. Norma Smythe liked attention more than she worried about Pete being untrustworthy. It had been the same

way when Algernon Treadwell had taken Margaret—
she'd been more interested in crying for the telly cameras than she was concerned about Pete finding anything
untoward during her home visit. "Margaret ain't
showed any abilities yet, but since Philip had the idea
to organize this . . ." She dropped her voice conspirato-
rially. "That twat Dexter Killigan might think he's in
charge, but we're the ones who are . . ." she searched for
the word, her heavily made up brow crinkling. "Mone-
tizing it," she said at last. "Philip said we might get on
Tricia if this keeps up. Wouldn't that be a laugh?"

"A huge one," Pete agreed. Norma Smythe went
back to frowning.

"Dexter's not gonna be happy you're poking about."

"Oh, don't fret," Pete said. "Like I told your husband,
I have no authority. I'm just looking into one of the
men who went missing, and I'm very glad I was able to
see how you're all . . . aiding your children's recovery."
The lie burned like acid. When this was over, when
Crotherton's demon was back in Hell and the Prometheans were off her back, it was going to be hard not
to come back to Overton and put the fear of all the
gods into the Smythes.

"You should come to supper!" Norma exclaimed
with a wide, sloppy grin that bespoke a handful of small
white pills. "Mrs. Leroy hosts this big supper after
every festival. Middle-class cunt that she is, tryin' to
show everyone up." Norma pulled out a fag, patted her
too-big blue blazer down for a lighter, and gave a defeated sigh. "Should give this up, anyway. Ain't good

for the kids, and those poor sick ones is so delicate. Not like my baby."

Personally, Pete thought there wasn't much that could put a dent in Diana, Bridget, or Patrick in their present condition. She'd seen a demon take a hit from a lorry and shake it off as if he'd collided with a shopping cart. *That* sort of demon, she knew how to handle. They were like Belial and his ilk. The Prince of Hell was at least rational, interested in making bargains with Pete and Jack that helped him leverage his spot as one of the ruling Triumverate of Hell. Really, it was no worse than dealing with a shady lawyer, albeit one who had the power to incinerate most of London with a flick of his fingers.

This, though—this demon was something other, and she had no idea what she was walking into. If playing nice with these deranged parents for a few more hours was what it took to learn more, then she could be nice.

On the stage, the festival was breaking up. "That's all for today," Philip said. "Remember, you can come by the house—that's 79 Exeter Court—between the hours of noon and four to book a private consultation, and we'll do this all again in three days' time."

The crowd dispersed in remarkably good humor for what they'd just witnessed, talking and laughing. A pair of sturdy-legged women in hiking boots and shorts discussed where to go for lunch as they brushed past Pete.

"Meg!" Norma bellowed. "Get your arse over here!"

Before the girl could move through the crush of

people, someone in the crowd pulled Norma aside, thrusting a handful of money at her and babbling about a private session.

Pete jumped a bit when Margaret touched her arm. "I saw Mr. Crotherton," she said, voice barely above a wind's whisper across the barren green. "Couple of weeks ago, he came by the house." Her voice was slow and muddled, and Pete thought Margaret might actually be drugged. If she wasn't possessed, that would be the easiest way to keep her docile.

"You're sure?" Pete bypassed shock and crouched so she could look at Margaret. She didn't have to crouch as far as she'd had to four years before—Margaret had shot up several inches. If she survived this ordeal, she was going to be tall and pretty as an adult. "Did anything happen?"

Margaret shrugged, a gesture as disaffected as Pete would have expected from a thirteen-year-old girl. "My dad sent him on his way. He hung about for a bit in the garden, waving some kind of compass about."

"Scrying," Pete said, more to herself than Margaret. Scrying for the demon, no doubt. Pete wished she could talk to Crotherton and ask him what he'd found.

"Mum told me not to tell," Margaret said. "But you're a detective inspector, so I reckon it's okay to tell you."

Pete didn't correct her as she saw Norma start to elbow her powder blue bulk back through the crowd. "Margaret," she said quickly. "I'm going to be honest with you—you do know there's something terribly wrong with all of this, yes?"

Margaret's large eyes unexpectedly filled, and she blinked rapidly. "Shit," she said, swiping at her tears. "I hate it, Inspector. I . . ."

"There's my good girl!" Norma Smythe boomed, clutching her arm around Margaret and grasping her shoulder hard enough that the girl gasped. "Don't she look lovely onstage, Miss Caldecott? She loves the attention."

Philip came gliding up, his sharkish grin firmly in place, even though the folds around his eyes said he wanted to give Pete a punch in the teeth. "You and your bloke'll be joining us for supper, I hear?" he said.

"If you'll have us," Pete told said. "I know we didn't get off on the best foot, Mr. Smythe, and for that I apologize."

He smirked at her. Making a copper apologize to him must be some kind of lifelong fantasy for a stain like Philip Smythe, but if it got her what she wanted, Pete would smile and kiss his arse for as long as the day lasted.

"More the merrier," he said at last. "Always thought you were a bit of a bitch during the investigation, but after what you did for our Margaret you're welcome any time." He offered his hand, and Pete shook. His handshake was limp and sweaty, as insincere as his words, but there was no prickle of magic there. Philip Smythe was a dead wire, in more ways than one. Pete thought that after she'd figured out what was going on in Overton, she'd see that Philip made a return visit to Pentonville. A fraud charge from these phony meetings should keep him away from Margaret until she was in university, away from her poisonous parents.

"I can't wait," she told him aloud, and looked over at Jack, fidgeting at the edge of the crowd. He jerked his chin at her, the universal *Let's get the Hell out of here* gesture. If there were any other way, she would have waited, gone in to do a proper exorcism, with tools and spells and the ritual that such a thing commanded.

But she didn't have time, so she was going in blind.

She just hoped it wasn't the last mistake she ever made.

16.

The Leroys' semi-detached brick was a far cry from the Smythes' untidy pile of a house. Mrs. Leroy, a small, nervous woman who didn't keep her hands still for more than three seconds at a stretch, had scrubbed the place within an inch of its life. Even Pete's obsessively tidy father would have called it compulsive.

"Drink?" Philip Smythe gestured at Pete with a bottle of gin when she and Jack stepped over the threshold.

"Thanks, mate," Jack slid up and relieved Philip of the bottle, refilling his dented flask before passing it back. Mrs. Leroy was already shooting them murderous looks, but she pasted on a fake smile when Pete caught her eye.

"I owe you a great thanks for what you did for our Diana," she said.

"Just wish I could have gotten here sooner," Pete said. "It looks like you're holding up well. All of you."

"Mr. Killigan started a support group back in London

so we could all find each other and share our stories," Mrs. Leroy said. "That man, he's a saint. So patient. Helped us so much with our poor child."

"And all of this? The tent and whatnot?" Pete asked. "His idea?"

"Oh heavens, no," Mrs. Leroy said with a laugh that sounded more like a scream. "That was Mr. Smythe's idea. Said we had an obligation to share our girl's gift with the world, and he's right. What Diana can do comes from a higher place."

"An obligation, eh?" Pete said. She eyed Philip Smythe, holding court in the corner with two men she assumed were Mr. Leroy and Patrick Dumbershall's father. They were laughing, grins wide as shark mouths.

"Mrs. Leroy . . ." Pete started, but the woman cut her off.

"Carrie, please."

"Carrie," Pete said. "This isn't easy to ask, but have you noticed anything . . . odd about Diana since all this started?"

Carrie Leroy gave a start, as if Pete had reached over and stuck a pin in her arse. She swiveled her head slowly, smile still in place, clocking the other parents in the room. "Not here," she murmured through clenched teeth. "Meet me in the kitchen."

Then she pitched forward into Pete, knocking her drink down her shirt. "Oh, no!" Carrie exclaimed. "I'm just too clumsy for words. Do come with me, Miss Caldecott, and I'll take that stain out."

Jack gave Pete a look over Margaret Smythe's head. He'd been talking with her the entire time, laughing and showing her sleight of hand tricks with quarters and cigarettes. Margaret was smiling for the first time since Pete had arrived in Overton, slowly and nervously, but she was acting less dopey than she had been in the morning.

If Margaret was with Jack, she was safe for the time being, so Pete let herself be tugged into the kitchen.

"Sorry about your blouse," Carrie Leroy said. "I couldn't . . . I had to . . ." She started to shake, and she buried her face in her hands.

"Hey," Pete said. "It's all right. Really."

"No, it is not," Carrie said. "It hasn't been all right since we came here." She sniffed deeply, then looked Pete in the eye. "You have a spare cigarette?"

"Sorry, no," Pete said. She wondered if there was such a thing as quitter's guilt.

"Out here," Carried said, pushing open the back door. It opened onto an alley barely wide enough for the bins sitting against the brick wall. Carrie lit the butt of a fag from a chipped ceramic dish on the ground and wrapped her arms around herself. "My husband'd knock my teeth in if he caught me smoking."

"I have a theory about what's going on, if you don't mind," Pete said. Carrie Leroy didn't stop her, so she rolled it out.

"Diana isn't the child you remember. She started acting strange not long after you all moved to Overton, and things just got worse. She doesn't act like a child. And when people started disappearing, you suspected things were off the rails, but it wasn't until Jeremy Crotherton poked around that you really knew."

Carrie looked at her askance, one penciled-in eyebrow up. "Those people were just hikers," she said. "Stupid gits. But you're right . . . Diana . . ." She sucked the last life out of the fag, then scraped it out against the back wall of her house.

"You have no idea what it's like," Carrie said. She wasn't shaking now, just cold and flat as an expanse of roadway. "To have your child snatched away from you. But you get used to it, you go on, even when your marriage falls apart and your daughter sits staring out the window day after day even though she can't see." She coughed, deep and rattling, a sound that spoke to damp cellars and too many cigarettes. "You move to the country because your husband worships at the altar of Dexter bloody Killigan, as if that man knows everything. You stay trapped in this shitebox with a husband who can't stand you, and then one morning your child looks up at you and her eyes focus and she says " 'Mummy, I'm hungry.' "

Pete chewed her lip, wishing it was a fag. "You know it's not Diana."

" 'Course I do," Carrie snorted. "I saw her MRIs. I know there's nothing in her brain except dust. Whatever's walking and talking through her skin, it's not my Diana."

"Can I ask you why you didn't leave?" Pete said. "Or

call someone like Jack and me? Hell, you could even have talked to Crotherton when he showed up."

"I don't know who that is," Carrie said, her voice thick with weariness. "And I can't leave or call for help because she *knows*. She and the other two see *everything*. They watch us even when they can't see us. It's like we're prisoners. Prisoners of those things that took our children." Her whole body quivered, and Pete put a hand on Carrie's shoulder to steady her. No prickle of the Black there either. Just a tangle of wrath and sadness that threatened to explode into Pete's mind. She let go after a quick squeeze.

"The only reason they don't know I'm talking to you now is that they're resting," Carrie whispered. "They like saying those horrible things to people, but it takes the fight out of them. It's the only time we get any peace."

Pete looked back at the lit kitchen door. "Where are they?"

"Dexter Killigan keeps them at his place," Carrie said. "He took it the worst. Wanted his girl back so bad he can't see what's become of them. They don't like to be apart, and he does whatever they want. Acts like all of this is fucking business as usual."

Pete remembered the stricken face, cheeks sunken and eyes impossibly dark, of Dexter Killigan beside Bridget's hospital bed. "It'll be all right," she lied. "Jack and I are here to help you."

Carrie sucked in a deep breath and shook her head. "No one can help me now, Miss Caldecott."

"Carol Anne!" Mr. Leroy bellowed from the kitchen. "Where'd you get to? I need a refill!"

"Coming, dearie!" Carrie shouted. "Just running the bin bag outside!" She looked at Pete, eyes wide and animal. "We'd better get back before they realize what we're doing. My husband's too stupid, the Dumbershalls are too terrified, and that chavvy bastard Philip Smythe is too greedy to realize what we've really gotten involved in."

It was quite a scam Philip Smythe had going, Pete thought. Convince the other parents that his own kid had similar abilities. Watch the cash roll in with absolutely no regard for what might really be happening.

"I need you to keep Margaret someplace out of the way," Pete said to Carrie. "Jack and I are going to the Killigans' to look around."

Carrie chewed on her lower lip. "You don't know what they're capable of, Miss Caldecott. They'll be so angry that you've interfered . . ."

"It's all right," Pete told her. "At this point, I guarantee I'm angrier than they are."

17.

The Killigan house sat at the end of a road at the top of the village, tucked among the hills. A wide yard full of trimmed rosebushes put the scent of rotting flowers and manure into the air. The house was shut up tight, windows blindfolded with thick blackout curtains, and a shiny new top-end deadbolt sat in the mildewed wood of the front door.

Jack crouched and examined the lock. "Bad news," he said, grimacing.

Pete sighed. "Hoped you wouldn't say that, given your talent for unlocking locked doors whether they like it or not. Can't you pick it?"

"This thing?" Jack yelped a laugh. "Not on me best day. This is designed to knock out professional thieves. I can't even hex it open. It's got protection charms on it. The whole house does."

Pete regarded the white-painted brick, flaked and chipping like cheap makeup on the tail end of a long night. "So Killigan knows enough to protect his house. More than the others can manage," she said.

"Not exactly A-level work," Jack said. "But they'll do for anything this side of a demon."

"That's the problem," Pete said, regarding the Killigan house as the moon slipped from behind a cloud and made the white hulk glow. "A demon is what Killigan's dealing with."

"About that," Jack said. He sat on the stoop and lit a fag, carefully blowing the smoke away from her. "This Crotherton fella was all hot that demon summoning was going on in the back of beyond, but none of these cunts have the talent the gods gave a stray cat."

"So what are you saying?" Pete said. "They didn't summon the demon, they were just victims? Figured that much out for myself, thanks." She nudged his arm. "I used to be a cop, you know."

"If you do it right, your demon doesn't go fleeing into the extras from *Village of the Damned*," Jack said. "It stays right where you put it and does your bidding, until you fuck up and it eats your face whole. So either whoever summoned this thing fucked up . . ."

"Or this is the summoner's bidding," Pete said. All at once the low-level craving for a fag vanished. She'd seen sorcerers do plenty of sick and twisted shite in her time with Jack, but siccing a demon on kids was a new low.

"I think it's a possiblity we have to consider," Jack said. "What they have to gain by making spooky soothsaying kidlets, I have no fucking idea. But this sort of thing doesn't happen by accident. I think Crotherton was half right, about the summoning. I just think his nose was so far up Morwenna Morgenstern's shapely arse he couldn't look for bits of the bigger picture."

"Oi," Pete said, turning her nudge into a jab. "You're not supposed to look at anyone's arse but mine."

"And yours is definitely tip-top in my book, darling," he said. "This does leave us with the matter of being exactly where Crotherton was before he buggered off— nowhere."

Morwenna wasn't going to like nowhere. Pete was fairly sure she'd have a fit, one that ended with more threats and more shite tossed on Pete's doorstep.

She stood up, regarding the Killigans' door. "Then we go inside. I'm fairly sure Crotherton never got this far."

Jack shrugged. "I'm all for a bit of B and E, luv, but unless you're going to shimmy up the drain pipe like Catwoman, we're out of luck."

Pete sucked in a breath as the wild energy of the Black surged around her. Here, on the outskirts of Overton, it was less tainted and strangled. The farther from town she got, the easier the magic came.

"I have an idea," she said. "But you're not going to like it."

Before Jack could protest or even question, Pete stepped into the Killigans' ragged rose bushes, the thorns grabbing at her jacket, flesh, and hair. Pete levered herself up onto the raised bed next to the front window, then turned her back and smashed her elbow through the glass. The wavy single pane shattered on impact, and Pete felt the charms Dexter Killigan had set about the place grab hold of her.

The magic slithered over her hands, across all of her bare skin. It felt like the slick underbellies of dirt-dwelling things, smelled like leaf rot and mildew. She held on, gripping the frame of the window, small pearls of leftover glass slicing her palm. The hex groaned in pleasure at her blood, and the power covered her, trying to find ingress via her eyes and mouth.

She'd only done this once before, with a hex designed to kill rather than merely shoo away, but back then she'd had the advantage of being a complete bloody idiot with no idea that using her talent to siphon something so powerful could kill her.

Now, she was aware with every atom of her being as the Weir woke up, snarling and hungry, feeding on the slippery marsh magic of the hex. It fed with an alacrity that alarmed even Pete, and she felt the Black flow into her as if she were completely hollow, only a vessel.

Which she would be, if the Weir had its way.

Pete was aware of Jack shouting, but she couldn't understand the words. She pulled the hex to her and refused to let go, even when it began to struggle.

The rush hit as the hex withered and died, the euphoric high of pulling in power not her own. Just as quickly the sick burning developed in Pete's guts, the knowledge that her mere flesh could not contain a carefully woven spell.

She screamed and dropped to her knees, the thorns

cutting at her. The pain brought her back, let her expel the magic of the hex and feel it dissipate. Only frayed ends of the spell were left now, nothing that could hurt them.

When she came back to herself, she was looking up at scaly rainclouds and the glow of the hidden moon. Jack stood over her, hands gripping her coat, face pale as a corpse. "I'm all right," she said. Her voice came out choked and raspy. That fit—she felt as if someone had wrung her neck, shaken her, and dropped her to the ground.

"Are you crazy?" Jack demanded. "I mean, are you completely off your nut? You could have really hurt yourself."

Pete let herself be still for a moment. She ached like she'd run miles, but that was usual. Her scratches stung in the cold, wet air, but other than her cut palm and the redoubled ache in her arm from Mickey Martin's attack, she was in one piece, and that was about the best one could hope for.

"I'm all right," she said again.

"Stupid," Jack said. His expression hurt Pete more than the slight. It was the one he reserved for people he thought beneath him, who weren't clever enough to circumvent anything that hurt or was unpleasant.

"What else are we supposed to do?" Pete asked, standing up. All around her, the rosebushes hung black and ashy, flowers reduced to nubs. The ground itself was dead, the grass and dirt ravaged from the magic that had flowed back into the ground.

Jack glared at her, but he didn't have an answer. Pete waved him off. "Just stand back."

She put her boot against the deadbolt, gauging the distance. She didn't want to kick in the door itself, but the doorjamb. Bust apart the housing of the lock, and even the strongest door wouldn't have anything to hold it shut. The trick was hitting right, and not breaking your foot off in the process.

Pete took a breath, willing herself to stay upright, and drove her boot into the apex of the door and the jamb. The wood splintered, and another kick dislodged the door entirely. Musty air breathed out, air that hadn't touched the outside in months, coated with the faint, sweet odor of decomposition. The hair on the back of Pete's neck, trained by a hundred crime scenes, prickled as she stepped inside.

"Fuck me," Jack said, voice echoing in the empty room. "Smells like something crawled up a bum's arse and died."

Pete shushed him with a gesture. There were times—not many—when she missed her pistol, and this was one of them. Not that bullets were much use against demons. She could punch holes in their host body, but she couldn't kill a demon. Not unless she burned them from the inside out with pure magic, and that could just as easily kill you as them.

Inside the Killigans' home, things were bare and dusty. A few spare pieces of furniture were shoved in one corner of the sitting room. The kitchen held only a table and a single chair, and dishes rimed with spoiled food were piled on every surface. The drone of flies hung heavy in the room, even in the chill of the darkened house.

Trying not to breathe too deeply of the stench, Pete moved on to a back parlor fitted with windows that would usually look over the back lawn and out to the hills. Now they'd been covered in spray paint, hasty frantic marks in a splash of colors that looked like the inside of a particularly bad acid hit.

Pete backed out. "Nobody here."

"There's a cellar," Jack said. The door was thin, barely the width of a person, and when Pete opened it, she saw a ladder leading down into darkness.

"Of course," she grumbled, putting her foot on the first rung.

"Oi," Jack said, and Pete prepared to scream if he tried to stop her, but he only handed over his lighter.

"Thanks," she said softly. Jack could surprise her. He was too stubborn for his own good, taciturn and unreliable and everything she should run from, especially when she had Lily to consider. But there was this side, too. The Jack she'd first met, the Jack she loved, the Jack who'd never leave her.

Dirt met her boots when she reached the bottom of the ladder. It was an old cellar, older than the house above it, from a time when food rotted slowly in the dark, and the dead who passed in winter stayed down there until the ground wasn't frozen any longer.

Pete flicked the lighter wheel and examined her surroundings. There was a small brick arch leading to an antechamber across the dirt space from her, and Pete picked her way toward it. The lighter flickered, and she thought she heard a low sound. Laughter, maybe.

Just keep walking, she told herself. *Not the worst place you've ever been. Not even close.*

Before she reached the support arch that framed the larger cellar, her foot caught on something firm but yielding.

Pete pitched into the dirt with a grunt, the impact knocking most of the fear out of her. What good was she if she went on her arse the moment someone turned out the lights?

She rekindled the lighter and illuminated a canvas-wrapped bundle, crawling with more of the blowflies she'd seen upstairs. Pete drew back the canvas gingerly and winced at what she found, then scrambled up and went to the ladder.

"Jack," she said. "Remember when I said I thought Crotherton hadn't made it here?"

"Yeah?" he said, brows drawing together.

Pete tried to breathe through her mouth, to cut out some of the putrefaction scent rising from the open canvas. "I was wrong," she said. "I just found him."

"Do you need me to come down?" Jack asked. He tried to make the question casual, but she knew that any time there was a dead body, there was the chance of an associated angry ghost, one that would hook on to Jack's sight like a hawk striking a rabbit.

"No," Pete said. "Stay put and keep watch."

She went back to Crotherton, crouching. He was

turning colors, the gentle blooms of green and black mold under his skin telling Pete he'd been moldering in the basement for at least a week.

She felt bad for Jeremy Crotherton, just doing his shit job like any street-level plod. His lips had pulled away from his gums, and even though Pete knew it was just an effect of decomposition, she put the canvas back over his face. She didn't need to think about how his last expression looked like he'd been screaming.

So the hikers had disappeared, then the bird-watching couple, and now Crotherton. Had they been early victims, before the demon had found a perfect host body? Sacrifices required to complete the summoning? Demons were varied as people and required everything from catsup to still-beating hearts as tribute.

Or was she sneaking around a house that wasn't her own with a dead man in the cellar, just asking to be fitted for something she hadn't done by the local coppers?

Honestly, Pete decided, she didn't care. She'd found Crotherton, and now she had to get Margaret Smythe out of here. Morwenna and her little shell game with the Prospero Society could go piss up a rope.

"Have you come to play with us?"

Pete whipped toward the support arch, raising the lighter.

A small white face stared back at her, half-buried in the earth. Bridget Killigan had carved herself an alcove in the cellar wall, and she and Patrick and Diana were pressed into their individual dirt dens, staring at Pete with unblinking eyes.

"I think you've all had enough time to play." Pete advanced toward the three figures, trying to get a better look at them. Maybe if she was lucky, the thing inside the children would be in a chatty mood.

She'd ignore the nauseating fact that she was talking to something living inside the bodies of three children she'd tried and failed to save. Ignore that this was a nightmare she'd had more than once.

This bastard was going to learn Pete Caldecott was made of sterner stuff than falling apart when faced with living nightmares.

Her foot bumped against something else yielding, and she glanced down to see Dexter Killigan lying face down on the cellar floor. A tray lay just north of his outstretched hand, and a shattered plate next to it. Flies had already massed on the raw meat the plate had carried, and maggots wriggled under the lighter's glare.

This time she wasn't surprised at the corpse. The poor sod was likely much happier wherever he was than he had been here, serving the whim of something he had to know wasn't actually his Bridget.

Pete looked back up at the three figures and frowned her most disappointed and motherly frown. "I don't know what kind of fuckwit takes over children's bodies, but it wasn't your smartest move. You're small and fragile. Easily handled."

Bridget laughed. It was low, rough. Her throat distended as she spoke, as if something were trying to claw its way free of her skin. "Jeremy thought so, too. Big boy that he was. He actually tried to exorcise us."

The others laughed, bullfrog throats throbbing, and Pete fought to keep from turning around and running until she was out of air. "I can't do that," Pete said. "But what's waiting for you upstairs sure can."

"The crow-mage doesn't scare us," Bridget snarled. "*You* don't scare us."

Pete stepped over Dexter's body, holding the lighter within snuffing distance of Bridget's face. "You don't scare me either," she said. "So I guess we're even."

"Lies," Patrick hissed, turning the upper half of his body to face Pete. She winced as she heard his vertebrae crack, spine unhinging. Even if she and Jack pulled off an exorcism, these poor kids weren't going to be long for the world. *And maybe that's for the best,* she thought.

"We scare you all right," said Diana. "You used to be the fearless one, but everything scares you now. You think about her every waking moment. Your blood given form. Your Lily."

Bridget started laughing again. "She has dreams about Lily being like us. Dreams about the demons who want to possess her."

Pete didn't usually give in to temper—that was Jack's problem, not hers. She could hold herself together past the point of screaming. But not this time. This time, she wasn't even aware she was moving until she'd dropped the lighter and wrapped her hands around Bridget Killigan's throat in the dark. Until the laughter choked to a stop. Until their talents clashed.

"*Don't you ever,*" Pete snarled, in a voice so grating

and enraged she couldn't believe it sprang from her, "*use your filthy Hell-spawned mouth to say my daughter's name.*"

Not even her voice—Connor's voice, as if he were reaching out to lend her every last ounce of rage she could pour into the words.

Bridget gave a choking gasp, but she was still laughing. "There's your first mistake, Weir," she croaked. "We're not from Hell."

Pete started, but she couldn't have let go if she tried. She was lost in the demon's power, as her talent opened up and drank it down. The Weir was hungry, denied the power of the hex, and now it wasn't letting go until it had its fill.

"Stop . . . stop . . ." Bridget vomited up bile, the green of the bottom of a pond. Pete felt her palms burn, nerves screaming as if she'd thrust them into an oven, but she couldn't let go. Wouldn't let go, until the thing grinning at her from Bridget Killigan's face burned, too.

As the Black surged around them, a tidal wave smashing on rocks, the shape of the thing inside Bridget—the true thing, which gave life and speech to the little girl's body—began to show itself. It was cold and slithering, a thing that dwelled in the dark of the earth, driven by a hunger only sated by wholly consuming its hosts. They would sicken and die, withered husks of what they had been. Bridget was such a host—entirely hollow, left to be filled by this presence, this thing that wormed its way through vast empty expanses Pete only caught a glimpse of, ashy gray earth topped by a sky the color of pus and blood, triple suns oozing endlessly from one side to the other. Three children were enough for the thing and its companions, three of them escaping that miserable place to come here, to this breathing and fertile and verdant place.

Not from Hell.

Not a demon.

Shit, Pete thought, even as Patrick and Diana set up keening screams to go along with Bridget's wail.

"Your name," she bellowed at Bridget. "Tell me your name or I'll burn you out of her!"

"You can't finish us off!" Bridget screamed, though by rights Pete's grip should have crushed her vocal cords. It didn't matter any longer. Bridget Killigan was dead, had probably been dead the moment this crawling, slithering madness had taken up residence in her flesh.

Pete put her face as close as she dared to Bridget's ear, as the Weir howled at the power it drank down.

"Watch me."

"We are not of earth, not of Hell," Bridget hissed back, and Patrick and Diana took up the chant. "Not of the Black, not of magic. We are the nothing, the endless."

Bridget stared at Pete, white eyes bulging and turning slowly crimson as tiny veins popped one by one. "We are the end."

Pete loosened her grip a fraction at that, but the Weir had taken hold now and there was no letting go until it had its fill of this strange power that felt as old as the earth and rock itself. Pete's talent flashed that endless white place, that desperate scrabbling, the emptiness of being completely alone in the universe.

The Weir didn't care what it showed Pete, though. It just wanted power, and Pete heard herself scream as the pain that followed the euphoria rushed up at her and hit like a freight lorry.

All three children screamed along with her, but before Pete could finish draining the thing riding Bridget, heavy arms grabbed her from behind and yanked her away, tossing her into the wall. Earth clods rained down on Pete's head, and she went to her knees, the cloying power of the thing inside Bridget coursing through her. It was like drowning in shallow mud, cold and unyielding and so, so hungry.

She managed to roll and get a look at the shape looming above her, just before Dexter Killigan's boot hit her in the face. Lightning struck inside her skull, and she tasted dirt and blood when she hit the floor.

The power was still there, still scrabbling to be let out, but the more imminent danger helped Pete get a handle on her talent, if only for a few seconds.

"Kill her, Dexter," Diana said, voice flat. "Kick her 'til her brains come out."

Pete rolled away from Dexter, curling around her vital organs, while he loped after her. There was a black indent in the side of his head. Old blood had dried on his cheek and around his eye, and the flesh around the wound had festered to the color of old moss. He was a little fresher than Crotherton, but not by much. Dexter Killigan shouldn't be up and walking around, never mind kicking seven kinds of Hell out of her. *Should* and *were* rarely intersected in the Black, though, so Pete concentrated on not getting beaten to death by a zombie. She could figure out how Dexter Killigan had joined the ranks of the recently alive once she'd gotten out of the cellar.

And once she'd figured out what the thing riding Bridget had been.

Dexter lunged for her again, and Pete grabbed his ankle and yanked as hard as she could. Dexter stumbled off balance, crashing into the dirt wall, and Pete made it to her feet and made a beeline for the ladder. Her skull rang, and everything blurred at the edges as if she were underwater. Splinters bit into her palms, and she felt the wet sting of the blood she was leaving behind.

She screamed again when she crashed into Jack coming down, and he caught her, looking past her at Dexter, the children, and Jeremy Crotherton's shroud, which was starting to twitch and ripple as the corpse within moved of its own accord.

"Don't let them go!" Bridget snarled. "Kill them, Daddy! Kill them for me."

Jack's eyes went wide. "The fuck is all this, then?"

Dexter managed to grab at Pete again, but she knocked him off balance and he went down, scrabbling in the dirt for her legs, snarling and baring his teeth. "Zombie, you bloody idiot. What's it look like?"

"That's not a zombie," Jack said. His eyes were as

wide as a child who's just discovered that Santa Claus *is* real, and he eats brains. "Zombies are bespelled, red thread and voodoo and shit, not . . . *this*."

"Call 'em whatever you want," Pete gasped, kicking at Dexter. "They're the walking fucking dead, and I'd like to get out of here." The steel toe of her boot dislodged Dexter's nose, turning it to the side, but he paid less attention than if a mosquito had bitten him.

Jack grabbed up a brick from the cellar floor and smashed it across Dexter's face. The rotten flesh collapsed, revealing the skull beneath. For somebody who'd been alive less than a day ago, Dexter was going quick. Whatever magic kept him slavering after them like an undead guard dog was rapidly turning him to compost.

Dexter fell back, one of his milky eyes dangling out of the bony socket, and Jack shoved Pete. "Go."

She scaled the ladder and yanked him up after her, adrenaline making him weigh no more than a heavy sack. Pete collapsed, panting, as Dexter moaned and snarled in the cellar, lacking the motor skills to chase them.

After he went quiet, and the blood roaring through her head was the only sound Pete heard, the three children came to the edge of the ladder, turning their faces up, and bared their teeth. Their gums were starting to go black, and they hissed in the language that Pete had heard inside her head when she'd touched Bridget.

"Never seen a demon that can reanimate the dead," Jack panted. "Clever little bastards, aren't they?"

"They're not . . ." Pete started, but before she could

say more Dexter Killigan crested the cellar ledge with a single leap, staggering toward them. He snatched up a carving knife from the block on the countertop and came for Pete.

"Shit!" Jack yelped, yanking her out of the way. Pete still felt muzzy—the smack on the head had definitely slowed her down, and that wasn't acceptable in this situation. She dashed through the kitchen door and shut it, hearing Dexter's body hit the other side. She threw the bolt and stumbled after Jack to the front door.

"This way," Jack panted, pushing her toward the hill. "We can find some cover up here."

"You know how to kill a zombie?" Pete asked. She wanted to vomit, or possibly just lie down on the ground and curl up in a ball, but she kept moving.

"'Course I know how to kill a zombie," Jack growled. "I told you: that back there ain't a fuckin' zombie, any more than I'm a ballet dancer."

Pete tried to catch her breath, beyond the ragged panting that sawed at her lungs. Dexter's kick had knocked the wind from her as well as the sense.

At least the magic she'd pulled down had dissipated a bit. It was still there, vibrating in her, but she wouldn't know how to release it now without killing someone innocent. She was crap at offensive magic, and always had been. The spell-slinging was Jack's thing.

Glass shattered behind her, and Dexter Killigan burst from his home's sunroom window, landing on the grass, finding his feet, and charging after them with his knife. He was fast, faster than they could move, and his lips drew back in a feral grin, the kind Pete had only seen on PCP addicts or the profoundly insane.

"Shit!" Jack said. They ran, but Pete could already see it would have the same effect as trying to outrun a pack of wolves. Sooner or later they'd get tired, and slow, and Killigan was so bloody fast . . .

He was going to catch them, and he was going to kill them unless she came up with a plan.

You know you want to, the Weir cackled. *Burn it down, Petunia. What's the worst that could happen?*

Beside her, Jack caught his foot in a rabbit hole hidden by dry grass and went down, cursing. Pete swayed, but she forced herself to stay up. She braced herself against the muddy ground, watched the blade of the knife, impossibly sharp and shiny for something that had come from the filthy house, grow larger and larger in her vision. She was going to take the knife, either by disarming Dexter or getting him to stab her instead of Jack, but just before he drew back his arm to make the kill shot, a voice rang across the hillside.

"Sciotha!"

Dexter lurched and jerked to one side, falling in a heap as his legs became useless logs. Pete swayed uncertainly, trying to make sense of what had just happened.

Dexter Killigan moaned and squirmed, reaching for his knife and shimmying across the grass toward her like a snake.

Pete let the spell fly before she even realized it had left her lips, the only flashy spell she knew.

"*Aithinne*." Such a simple word, not shouted or cried out but whispered. Still, the Weir heard, and her talent responded. Bright white flames engulfed Dexter Killigan and the grass around him, then rushed in a gout toward the house. Windows shattered and anything not brick went up with a roar of displaced air.

The rose bushes were ash, drifting through the damp air like snow.

Almost as if the land around her, the Black itself, were responding to the inferno, it began to rain.

Pete collapsed to her knees in the mud, her heart thudding. The insidious whisper of her talent was gone, and in its place was just a ragged hole.

In the flames, she saw three small white figures, untouched, emerge from the hulk of the Killigan house and start toward them across the scorched grass. Pete was having a hard time seeing straight through the heat, but she perceived a tall figure in front of her, dressed in a dark coat and holding out his hand. "Now that was damn impressive," he said. "But it's not quite pie-and-a-pint time yet. Let's get out of here before those worms get their hooks into you."

"Yeah," Pete said, ignoring the hand and levering herself to her feet. Just because she'd cast a spell that would normally take four mages and a quart of whiskey to accomplish didn't mean she was going to get sloppy about touching strangers. "Let's go, Jack. I don't want to get near those things again if I can help it."

He didn't answer, and she turned to look at him. *You burned him up*, her traitorous inner voice screamed before she really got a look at him in all the smoke and ash. *You burned up everything, including Jack!*

But he was fine, only still. Jack stared at the man in black, eyes fixed and mouth slightly open, as if the man were more terrifying than anything the three children could do to him. "Is it really you?" he finally rasped. "You're really fucking here after all this time?"

The man in black canted his head, as if the question puzzled him. "Of course it's me, Jackie. Who else would I be?"

"Jack?" Pete said again. The expression on Jack's face had gone from shocked, the only bit of vulnerability she'd ever seen him display in public, to something hard and carved from ice. Pete knew that face, too. It meant things with Jack were about to get ugly.

She shifted away from the man in black, regarding him now through her pounding headache as an interloper. "What's going on here?" she asked. "Who is this bloke, Jack?"

"Petunia," Jack said with a weary sigh, passing a hand across his face. "This is Donovan Winter. My father."

18.

Pete stared at Donovan, unable to think of a single thing to say, while he nodded to her. "Good to meet you. Now can we get the fuck away from the worms before they turn us into more of what your bird here just burnt up?"

That seemed to stir Jack into motion. He got up, though he grunted when he put weight on his ankle.

"Here." Donovan grabbed Jack under one arm. "Double time, boy. Make me proud."

Jack grunted. "Fuck off."

"That's no way to talk to your old man," Donovan said, veering to the side of the hill. Pete percieved a path, nearly overgrown, worn into the skin of the earth. Stones caused her to stumble. Even with short children's legs, it wouldn't take the three things long to close the distance. Panic climbed her throat, burning and sour.

"Just over this ridge," said Donovan. "Come on, luv, you can manage it."

A low stone wall grew out of the mist like the spine of a lizard, and Donovan hopped over it at a set of rotted wooden steps. On the other side, held in the hollow of the valley, Pete saw a collection of small stone buildings, scattered and leaning as if a hand had dropped them on the grass.

Tombs.

Jack balked, breath coming in a rusty wheeze, and Donovan tugged on him. "Now, now. I know it seems crazy, but they're not going to follow us if we can make it to the fence."

"No . . ." Jack mumbled, eyes clouding over. Pete made it to his side as he swayed and started to fall.

"Shit," she grunted as his full weight hit her. "Jack, it's all right. Stay calm."

"What on earth is wrong with him?" Donovan demanded, glaring at Pete as if it were her fault. Behind them, the three figures started down the back side of the hill, Patrick helping Bridget and Diana over the wall. They didn't even have to run. They could take their time, let their prey see them coming.

"He has second sight," Pete said to Donovan. "Cemeteries are bad news for him. He can't tell what's real and what's not."

Jack's breath was shallow, and he clung to Pete, fingers knotted in her shirt, head cradled against her chest. She rubbed the back of his neck, trying to hold back her talent, which clamored to take all of the energy stirred up by Jack's visions and drink it down as it had soaked up Bridget's magic moments before.

"Fuck," Donovan sighed. He took Jack's other arm, easing some of the weight off Pete. "Of course my son is a psychic who can't stomach the dead. Why would this be easy?"

"Your idea to come here," Pete grunted as they dragged Jack inside the rusted, half-fallen iron fence around the graveyard.

"I didn't know he was psychic, did I?" Donovan snapped.

"Maybe if you'd stuck around for more than five minutes, you would," Pete said. Donovan cocked his eyebrow, but he kept quiet as they passed among the headstones into the cool corpse-handed embrace of the mist that clung to Overton like spider silk to skin.

Close in, standing amid the mausoleums and falling-down monuments, Pete saw what had so agitated Jack.

Shapes moved between the tilted gravestones, shimmering as they drifted from place to place, long spectral fingers sinking into the earth before moving away. Some perched on the rooflines of the mausoleums, swaying with each breath of wind and watching the surrounding country with their blank silver eyes.

"Wraiths," Pete breathed. She found she couldn't take her eyes off them.

Donovan smirked. "I see Jackie doesn't just keep you around for your looks."

On the hill above, the three figures slowed, then stopped a dozen yards from the fence, watching Pete with unblinking white eyes. Donovan shoved open the door of the closest mausoleum. A wraith drifted down from the roof, but Donovan hissed at it under his breath, and it drifted away.

"Just a little aversion hex," he said. "Make 'em think we're not all full of soul energy for them to suck up like an espresso."

Pete let Jack down on top of the sarcophagus in the tomb, and he groaned before shutting his eyes and curling in on himself.

"He going to man up, or is this an ongoing thing?" Donovan asked, folding his arms across his raven-colored wool coat.

Pete ran her hand over Jack's forehead, brushing sweaty lines of platinum hair away from his skin. She felt a stab of desperation, that knee-jerk need to do anything to make his pain stop.

Except there was nowhere else to go, nowhere the children wouldn't find them. It was the wraiths or die screaming. "Depends on how long we're here," she said to Donovan. "He can hold it back with the dead, but this is different."

There had to be twenty wraiths in the graveyard, ghosts that went up to eleven. Jack shuddered under her hand, scrabbling at it with his fingers until she laced hers in. "Shh, luv," she soothed. "Just hold on and it'll be over soon."

"Not soon," Donovan said. "We stay here unless we want those wee little monsters to send us the way of dear old dad," Donovan said. "They won't come close enough for the wraiths to drain them, and the wraiths won't go too far from the spirit buffet in the graveyard, so we're all right for the time being."

Pete chewed on her lip. She didn't think "all right"

applied to any facet of the situation, but most of all not to Jack. "He can't stay here."

"Poor little Jackie always did have a delicate constitution," Donovan said. "Thought that boy would turn out more like me. I've looked just like him waking up from a hangover and I soldiered through."

"Listen," Pete said, dropping her voice into Official Copper. "He's an unusually strong psychic, and this place is a nightmare factory, so unless you want him to be catatonic and drooling on himself within the hour we need to find somewhere else."

Donovan grinned at her, which Pete found both infuriating and utterly familiar. It was the same kind of smile Jack had, when he thought he was in control of a situation. "Bossy little thing, aren't you?"

"I appreciate that you helped out with Dexter Killigan," she said. "But that doesn't make you the general."

"I think it does make me the man who saved your arse, seeing as it would be all full of zombie bites by now if I hadn't thrown that little leg-locker hex," Donovan said, grinning even wider. "Though I'd never let that happen. You're far too adorable."

"I had it handled," Pete said. "Need I remind you that I was the one who actually burned that bastard up?"

Donovan pursed his lips. "You know, I'd like you much more if you didn't frown."

"And I fancy I'd like you much more with a mute button," Pete snapped back.

"For the love of all that's fucking sacred," Jack

groaned. "Will the both of you shut it? Me head hurts enough as it is."

Pete crouched at Jack's side, examining him for signs that the sight was eating into his mind, permanently altering the pathways, making him unable to tell the dead from the living.

The mausoleum was dim, the only light coming from the small, smeared window above the sarcophagus, but she could see that Jack's skin had taken on a sick pallor, with spots of red on his cheeks and forehead. His eyes, though, were mostly clear, only rims of white encroaching on the blue. "This is not fucking comfortable," he told Pete. "Help me up."

She got him up and helped him sit on the small rickety bench under the window. His ankle had swollen, and he favored it badly. Pete cursed to herself. You couldn't run with a bum ankle, even if you had a place to run to.

"You all right?" she asked softly, tilting her head at Donovan. Jack's father looked like an older, paler version of his photo, long dark hair replaced by a short salt-and-pepper crop. He still carried himself ramrod straight, though, and still looked, in Pete's estimation, like the world's champion tosser.

"'Course I'm not bloody all right," Jack said. "Are you?" His brows drew together. "That Killigan bastard knocked you pretty bad."

"I'll be fine," Pete said. "He just jostled my head a bit."

"Not her vulnerable area, fortunately for you and I," Donovan said, looking out the door of the tomb before shutting it tight. "I hope she's magnificent in the sack, Jackie, because so far all I've heard is mouth, mouth, mouth."

Jack didn't speak the word of power fully—it was more of a hiss of air and anger—but the hex smacked Donovan like a fly swatter and flung him backward into the wall of the tomb. Mortar and loose dirt rained down around him as he crumpled to the floor.

"Good boy!" Donovan said, clambering back up with a wince. "I see somebody managed to teach you a few tricks."

"You talk to her again and the last trick you learn will be how to swallow your own teeth," Jack said, trying to stand. He didn't make it, and he sank back down hard.

"By all means, let it out," Donovan said. "Got a lot of feelings pent up in that bleached blond head, Jackie? Let me have it, son. Let's get all the daddy issues on the table, since you clearly didn't learn to let bygones be bygones from that hysterical mess of a mother. Knew I never should have left you with her."

"You're right," Jack snarled. "You shouldn't have. But I always assumed you knew you were leaving me in a miserable shithole with a pill-popping teenage mother to be smacked about and forgotten and not fed. Always thought you just didn't give a shit."

Pete stayed quiet, watching Donovan carefully to

make sure he didn't return the hex, ready to leap on him and kill him with her bare hands, if necessary, if he made a move on Jack.

Not just for the threat he posed now. For everything that was on Jack's face as he looked at his father. The resemblance was stronger the more she looked, but Pete thought the eyes were what arrested her the most. Donovan's eyes were Jack's eyes, crystal blue with the same cold depths that could never be plumbed.

"You're a grown man," Donovan said. "So I'm going to skip explaining myself, you're going to skip the day-time talk show crying bit, and we're going to get straight to the apology." He drew himself up. He was broad where Jack was skinny, but their height and build were similar. Pete squeezed Jack's hand as Jack growled something obscene under his breath.

"I'm sorry, Jackie," Donovan said. "I didn't do right by you. But I'm here now and we've got a situation, so what say we both act like the adults we are and fix this mess?"

"I say take the apology and shove it up your arse until it squeaks," Jack shot back. "This working out like you hoped? Do all your families welcome this load of shit? What number am I?"

"First and last," said Donovan. He sat down on the edge of the sarcophagus with a sigh and rubbed a hand over his chin. Pete watched all the arrogance ran out of him like used dishwater. "You're me only son, Jack. Your mum must have told you that."

"She didn't tell me much," Jack said. "'Cept to fuck off down to the corner and get her some more fags."

"I thought she'd be all right," Donovan said, his voice so quiet that it would have been lost if not for the echo of the small stone room. "She was on medication when I left. I thought she could handle it."

"She was always on medication," Jack said. "Neighbor's medication, boyfriend's medication, the type you buy from the hoodies who hang around the car park behind the ASDA. That was sort of the central fucking issue in me childhood, *Dad*."

"You act like you think I wanted it to end up this way," Donovan said. "It's going to sound like a load of shite cliches, but I was young, Jackie. I did a stupid thing."

"'M really not interested in a touching moment replete with swelling violins," Jack said. "So why don't you kick on about whatever it is you really want and then leave me in peace?"

"What's happening in this town?" Pete interrupted. Donovan and Jack could be going in circles all night. "You called them worms, those things at the Killigan house," she said. "Not demons. You know something."

"I know a little," he said. "Mostly what I extrapolated after I found out that poncey cunt Jeremy Crotherton had stuck his nose in it."

Donovan knew Crotherton. That certainly made Pete look at him in a new and not entirely flattering light.

"You and Jeremy were mates, then?" she said. Keeping it casual. Letting Donovan lead. If there was one thing she'd learned about Winter men, it was that they liked to think they were the ones in charge.

"Better question is how *you* knew Jeremy," Donovan said with his snakelike smile. He held her there, pinned to the spot, but Pete swallowed the knot in her throat and lied.

"Just of him. Heard he'd gone missing along with the other folks when we came looking for the demon."

"That the sort of thing you two do for a romantic date, then?" Donovan cut his eyes between Jack, who curled his lip at his father, and Pete, who tried to paste a smile on her face. "Hunt up a demon summoner?"

"Freelance," Pete said. "Local constabulary hired us." She banked on Donovan having the same aversion to anything carrying a badge that his son did, and sure enough he gave a snort of derision.

"Working for civilians, like this was that TV show about the wizard with the talking skull and the twatty name."

"Pays the bills," Jack said. "But I suppose you get your bankroll from our substantial family fortune, right, Dad?"

"You're funny," Donovan said. "Must get that from your mum." He shed his coat, hanging it on one of the hooks meant to hold a vase of flowers, and wandered the permieter of the small room, reading the names engraved on the wall. "No, I make money the old-fashioned way, by taking it from mages who are too lazy to do grunt work like tracking a demon summoner them-selves."

"So who sent you here?" Pete said.

"Crotherton's family," Donovan said casually. "Jer-emy and I were school mates."

"I hope they weren't banking on an open casket," Jack muttered. "Because old Jeremy is passed on with a side of undead, extra crispy."

"I imagine I'll be a bit more delicate when I break the news," Donovan said. "But when I tracked Jeremy here, I realized that this wasn't any ordinary sort of pos-session."

"They're not even demons," Pete said. Jack shot her an alarmed look, eyes widening, but she looked back and begged him with her expression to just play along. *I'll explain later,* she mouthed.

Donovan tapped the closed door. "We'll be safe here for a while. Eventually the rest of the horde is going to realize something's up, but not many have the stones to toe up with a wraith. Once it's dark we can maybe move."

Pete thought of the raven, telling her to run. That this was a dead man's town. It hadn't been wrong. Just her stubborn fault she hadn't listened to it. "I can't hide until dark," she said. "I've got to go and get Mar-garet."

"And who's Margaret?" Donovan said.

"She's the last kid," Pete said. "The only one the worms didn't get their hooks into."

"Then she's dead," Donovan said. "Just like the rest of

them. No help. We want to stay in control of ourselves, not join the walking dead out there, we stay hidden."

"Fuck off," Pete told him, and pushed open the door. Donovan hauled her back by the arm.

"You go out there, I can't protect you," he snarled. He was strong, stronger than Jack by a long way.

"You just showed up, so maybe you don't know," she told him. "But I'm not the one needs protecting."

"I have a hard time believing you're seriously willing to die for some snot-nosed kid that's not even yours," Donovan said. "That's not human nature. 'Least not any I understand."

"There's a lot you don't understand, then," Pete said. Donovan relaxed his grip, giving a sigh.

"I'll come with you, then."

"And leave Jack by himself?" Pete said. "I don't bloody think so."

"If you want to see either of us in one piece again," Jack said, "*please* do not leave me alone with this arsehole."

"I set up protection barriers around the tomb," Donovan said. "They'll hold the wraiths off while we go get your brat."

"Margaret," Pete said. "Her name is Margaret."

"I could not care less what her name is," Donovan said. "But if this'll get you to listen, then so be it." He swept his arm toward the door, black coat flapping like the wing of a dire bird. "After you, Milady."

Pete looked back at Jack, who leaned his head against the stone, swiping at the sweat on his face. It was painfully clear he couldn't stay here much longer, but Margaret was in more immediate danger. Pete just hoped she wasn't making the sort of choice she'd have nightmares about in the years to come.

"While we're young," Donovan said, as Pete hesitated on the steps of the tomb. Watching the wraiths flit among the tombstones was surreal, like watching a group of panthers strolling along Oxford Street.

"That doesn't seem to be a problem for you," Pete muttered. Donovan chuckled, dry as kindling.

"I can see why my boy likes you. That mouth good for anything except clever quips?"

"Keep it up and you'll find out what my foot is good for," Pete told him. "If it's this or silence, then let's agree to shut the fuck up."

They passed the iron fence on the other side from the Killigan house, and Pete found a dirt road winding back toward the village. The mist pressed in, keeping them hidden from all eyes, trailing spectral trails of moisture across Pete's face and hair.

She walked quickly to keep pace with Donovan's lanky city-dweller stride, praying silently that she wouldn't be too late to keep Margaret from become just another white-eyed dead girl.

19.

"So, you and my son," Donovan said, having kept quiet, by Pete's count, for precisely two and a half minutes. "What's happening there?"

Pete concentrated on her footsteps, digging the steel toes of her boots into the mud and gravel as hard as she could, pretending they were Donovan's face. "Why don't you ask him?"

"Not the sort of conversation you have during the first hour you see your kid," Donovan said. "So I'll ask you instead, gorgeous: Are you two sleeping together, or is it an adorable sort of telly-friendly unresolved sexual tension gambit?"

Pete decided that she could see, after less than an hour with Donovan, why Jack's mother had chosen to get stoned out of her mind while they were together. "I've got a better hideously rude non sequitur for you: After thirty-five years, you show up now?" she countered. "What prompted you, exactly? Need a kidney?"

Donovan smirked at her. "Not hardly. I'd wager I'm in better shape than a man who spent half his adult life slamming smack into his bloodstream, even if he is my son."

Pete went quiet at that. She hadn't been sure how much Donovan knew. He didn't seem aware of her talent, or the extent of Jack's, and she was happy to keep it that way.

"It was the sight," Pete said. "The heroin helped keep it manageable. He thought it was the only way."

"Until you came along?" Donovan said. "Love of a good woman and all that rot?"

Pete gave an involuntary snort of mirth. "Not hardly."

The B road merged with the wider road into the village, and Donovan stopped walking, regarding the shifting mists before them.

"You're observant, whatever else you are. Been here for a week and you're right—I do know a little. Not much, but a little."

"They're not demons," Pete said, and Donovan nodded.

"So what are they?" she asked.

He laughed. "If I knew that, I wouldn't still be in this fucking back of beyond shitehole, would I?"

Pete wrapped her arms around herself. The Black stung her again, that odd strangled feeling of wild magic directed into an unnatural channel.

"The magic is all wrong," she said. "It feels like static on a telly, except it's in my head."

Donovan's lip pulled up in a disconcerting imitation of Jack's grin. There wasn't any warmth to the expression, though—unlike Jack's face, looking at Donovan's

was like looking at a great white shark, an apex predator devoid of anything recognizably human.

"I have a feeling if we find out what's causing *that*
bit of ruckus, we'll have solved the whole thing, Watson."

"Not Holmes?" Pete said. She started forward, trust-
ing Donovan at her back. It might be the last mistake
she ever made, but she needed to draw him out so he
would think things were fine when she hit him with her
next verbal punch.

"You seem rather comfortable as the sidekick,"
Donovan said, walking beside her. "Just going by what
I see."

"I do hold Watson's contempt for roundabout
bullshit," Pete said. "So why don't you get down to what
you really want to say to me, Donovan?"

Jack's father lifted one dark eyebrow. "Which would
be?"

"You're not here for Crotherton," Pete said. "You're
here for Jack and the Prospero Society." She glanced at
Donovan over her shoulder, and the slight hitch in his
gait told her she'd been right to voice her suspicions.

"What gave me away?" he asked at last, having the
gall to look amused.

"Oh, let's see," Pete said, ticking her fingers. "Somebody from Jack's past, so we'd feel an instant connection
to you for good or ill. Showing up with perfect timing to
save us from a problem you lot created. Agreeing to help
me with only the most pathetic of token protests."

Donovan shook his head. Droplets of moisture had

collected on the tips of his short hair, and they rolled down his face, giving the impression that even in the chill he was sweating. Or crying. Pete knew better, though. Sociopaths like Donovan Winter never sweated, never felt the prickle of a tear they didn't manufacture themselves.

"I stand corrected," he said. "You are Holmes."

"Left my violin at home," Pete agreed. "But I do all right."

"You got one bit wrong, though," Donovan said. They walked through the green, which was empty and littered with garbage, crumpled sleeping bags, half-collapsed tents, and empty lager bottles. Pete kept her eyes out for any movement in the fog, but found none.

"Oh?" she asked, only half paying attention to Donovan now. Morwenna had better pin a fucking medal on her, or better yet give her a fat stack of cash. Using Jack's own father had been a master stroke on the Prosperians' part. Who better to recruit Jack than the man he hated, yet most wanted to please?

"We didn't do this," Donovan said, sweeping his arm over the empty field. "Crotherton really was here of his own free will, looking for that fat fuck Preston Mayflower. What he found, well . . ." He shrugged. "Who can say? But those things aren't anything I've run across. Not demon, not spell-spawned. It's like they come from someplace where magic doesn't work right, and the longer I'm in Overton the worse it gets."

"So I guess you won't be saving us again if we run into more worms," Pete said.

Donovan shook his head. "You saved yourself back there, missy. I can't throw around the flashy shite like you and my boy. The leg-locker is about the extent of it."

"So you're not the Prospero Society's hard man?" Pete said, feigning disbelief. "Then why send you to talk us in? Haven't you heard Jack and I are dangerous types?"

"From half of the hedge-hexers and kitchen witches in the UK," Donovan said. "But when it comes to human mages, I'm not worried. I'm more of a person to person sort of magic user."

When Pete gave him a blank look, he spread his hands. "I'm a mind-bender, dear. I can make you think you love me, or you hate that bloke over there and want to punch him in the teeth."

"You mindfuck people," Pete said. "All at once, so much about you makes sense, Donovan."

"Came in handy with Jack's mum," Donovan said. "You ever try to convince a bipolar pill addict to calm down and give you the knife *without* magical powers of persuasion?"

"I appreciate you slipping that bit about her being a nutter in there," Pete said. "Make me think you know all about my troubles with Jack and his sight."

Donovan shot her a glare, the first expression she'd seen of his that Pete judged genuine. "I spent a lot of time dealing with smooth talkers when I was a cop," Pete said. "So if there's a recruitment spiel, get to it.

Otherwise, let me find Margaret and you can do whatever it is you came here to do."

"Started out just getting you to come over to our side," Donovan said. "Now, it's finding out what's going on here for the men upstairs."

"I hate secret societies, and I hate sorcerers, and I hate deadbeat parents more than the two of them combined," Pete said, slowing as they reached the populated area of Overton. "So why the fuck, when I've already given the Prometheus Club the finger, would I consent to join Darth Vader and his merry band?"

"Because I've looked into you, Pete, and you don't like to lose," said Donovan. "And when the Morrigan makes her move on the daylight world, that's exactly what the Prometheans will do. They're a Bic lighter in a hurricane. The Prospero Society is smart enough to realize you don't beat the Morrigan by ordering her to stop all this nonsense and go back to her room. They know that you have to play dirty."

He grinned at Pete again, and the shiver it sent up her spine had nothing to do with the chill mist. "I know that about you, too. I know you've flat out made bargains with demons to get your way, Petunia. That's the sort of dirty pool that plays very well among my colleagues."

Pete didn't want to look at him, so she did a quick sweep of the road. It was lined with cars and caravans, and Pete caught a flash of movement from behind a few. The guillible sods who'd come to the tent meeting that morning stumbled forth and glared suspiciously at Pete and Donovan as they passed, unblinking eyes watching them until Pete finally glared back. "What're they waiting for? A written invitation to eat our brains?"

"They can't help it," Donovan said. "It's this place. This village. It works on you, makes you think strange things." He cast a look down at Pete. "You must have noticed it, even only being here overnight. Had any bad dreams?"

Pete returned his gaze steadily. He was fishing, and it didn't take a former copper to see through him. "Slept like a baby," she said. "Besides, prophetic visions are more Jack's territory."

"I know you'll do anything to save him," Donovan said. "That's why eventually you'll say yes to the Prospero Society. To whatever it takes." His words, calm and soft, still cut, and Pete felt the salvo all the way down to her bones. She didn't bother snapping back. Men like Donovan lived for setting you off balance, and she was too sensible to play that game. If he wanted her to get defensive, proclaim her innocence, she wouldn't. Because she wasn't. She *had* made a deal with Belial—not just a Named demon but a Prince of Hell, for fuck's sake—to save Jack from the Morrigan. What she'd resort to next time, to keep Jack or Lily from the Hag's darkness, she had no idea.

But Donovan was right—it would be whatever was necessary.

"How well does the mindfuck trick really work?"

she asked, to turn her thoughts from the dark, raven-filled place where they'd wandered.

"I can't keep all these bastards at bay, if that's what you're asking," said Donovan. "But I can misdirect the ones around the brat long enough for a snatch and grab." He grinned. "Hope those short little legs can move if they have to."

"Worry about your hex, not my legs," Pete said. "Didn't anyone ever tell you chatting up your son's woman is poor form?"

"More than once. Can't say it ever sank in, though," Donovan said.

The Leroys' semi-detached drifted into view, a wind ruffling the mist and drawing back the curtain. Music still drifted from the open front door, but as they drew closer Pete heard the drone of a record stuck on the last five seconds, over and over. She stepped through the door and saw an old-fashioned turntable in the corner. Beer bottles and spilled food covered every surface, and flies clustered thickly, just as they had in the Killigan house.

"This whole place is rotten," Pete murmured, and jumped when she realized Donovan was just behind her.

"Top to bottom," he agreed. "So where's your little friend?"

"Not sure," Pete said. *Please don't be dead, Margaret.* "Carrie?" she called softly, not wanting to risk waking anyone who might be less than friendly. She'd been chased by enough creepy crawlers for one day.

A snore emanated from the sofa. Mr. Dumbershall lay on the cushions, half on and half off. Vomit crusted his face, and the smell of ale was thicker than air. Pete pressed a hand against her nose to avoid retching. She needn't have worried, though, because Donovan gagged, staggering back.

"Fuck me, is he dead?"

"No," Pete said. She forgot that not everyone, mage or no, regarded dead bodies as ditchwater dull. Donovan's wobbly expression did give her a tiny thrill of superiority, though—if he tossed his guts like a first-year rookie, she'd be delighted.

Dumbershall shifted in his sleep and groaned, eyelids twitching. "Just drunk," she told Donovan. Pete wouldn't blame any of them for turning to drink, or worse, when they saw what was happening to their children.

"Suburban bacchanal," said Donovan, surveying the ruins of the gathering, the stained carpet, the mildewed wallpaper. "How sadly typical."

"I'm sure you're used to a better class of bacchanal," said Pete. "So sorry to disappoint." The stairs were narrow, and she kept her foot near the wall to avoid creaks or snaps that would alert anyone conscious to their entry.

"Never was really a Dionysian," said Donovan. "Did attend an orgy once, in Blackpool, and met these twins who . . ."

Pete held up her hand at a small exhalation of air very near her ear, over the squalling music from downstairs. "Did you hear that?"

At the crest of the stairs was a narrow closet, probably a dumbwaiter at one point, now closed off with a cheap folding door. Pete pushed it aside, and found Margaret and Carrie crouched on the floor, half-covered by hanging duvets and linens. Carrie gave a small cry, but Margaret just rocketed forward and grabbed Pete around the waist. "Get me the fuck out of here," she mumbled into Pete's shirt.

Pete nodded, gesturing for Carrie. "Donovan, help her up," she said.

"Gladly," he said, extending a hand and a smile to Carrie. She took his hand and climbed shakily to her feet.

Pete almost thought they'd gotten away, when she saw a shadow at the foot of the stairs, soon joined by a second, standing and waiting, perfectly immobile. In the sitting room, the record player screeched, needle skidding across the vinyl. Next to Pete, Margaret jumped, clinging to her even harder.

"Donovan," Pete whispered. He came to her shoulder, Carrie clinging to him like a burr.

"Yeah, I see 'em," he said. He moved around Pete and called down the stairs. "Hello, gents. No need to get upset. Why don't we all just gather 'round and have a drink and a laugh." His voice was slow and soothing, far from the scratchy rasp Pete had gotten used to. She felt gentle waves of power roll over her, and a sense of well-being stole into her mind. Beside her, Margaret whimpered and shivered.

"What's he doing?"

"Magic, luv," Pete said, as Donovan jerked his head at them. She started down the stairs with Margaret and Carrie. "Don't worry about it," Pete said. "We're getting out of here."

When she pulled abreast of Donovan, he touched her on the shoulder. "I think they'll be in dreamland for a few minutes more," he said. "But let's not hang around to find out, yeah?"

The men, including Mr. Leroy and Mr. Dumbershall, stared into the distance, nodding their heads and smiling as if listening to music only they could hear. Pete herself felt wonderful—of course they'd make it back to the graveyard. Of course things would be all right. Donovan was here, and he had everything taken care of. She couldn't believe, in that moment, that she'd ever doubted him. He was Jack's blood, after all, and she trusted Jack implicitly.

The feeling of bliss and the lightness in her head lasted precisely until the end of the Leroys' walk. Outside, a crowd had gathered, villagers and travelers, including the hippies who'd been asking questions and the big brute who Bridget had chased off.

Everything came crashing down, and a wave of nausea rolled over Pete. Margaret made a small, strangled sound. Carrie gasped and stopped short.

Pete looked back at Donovan, whose face went slack. "Shit," he said softly.

"Took the word out of my mouth," Pete said.

Donovan's breathing was shallow, and he backed up a step, nearly knocking into Pete. "I can't do this many," he murmured. "You and I could run for it, but Mumsy and the brat are deadweight."

He looked Pete in the eye. "A Prospero would leave them."

"Thank fuck for all of us I'm not a coward like you, then," Pete growled. "Now grab hold of your balls and do what you can."

Donovan, hands shaking, drew himself up. Pete felt the Black wriggle around them, as if the skin of the world were a living thing, and the crowd parted, just enough for them to get through single file.

"Move your arse," Donovan said through clenched teeth. "This ain't lasting long."

"You first," Pete told Margaret, pushing the girl ahead of her. Margaret swiveled back, hesitating.

"Miss Carrie?"

"I'll be right behind you," Carrie whispered. Donovan shoved past her and followed Margaret, hustling her by the arm. Pete decided that when they were somewhere without this strange, staring horde of hostile villagers, she was going to give him a good smack. Or possibly a kiss, if he actually managed to keep the crowd from rioting before they reached the graveyard.

The mob had grown exponentially even as they stood in the Leroys' yard, hundreds upon hundreds of vacant-eyed people staring as one at Pete, Donovan, and Margaret. Carrie brought up the rear, shuddering every time she brushed arms with someone in the crowd.

Pete could see the rear of the mass of people, the stragglers wandering down the road toward them as if they'd woken from a dream and were still disoriented, when she heard a low exhalation of breath behind her and the big brute who'd nearly disrupted the gathering turned and fixed his gaze on Carrie Leroy.

"Run," Pete said, but it was already too late. She watched as the brute grabbed Carrie and dragged her down to the ground. The people around him moaned quietly, and then they too turned, staring down at her, lips parted and crimson, dehydrated tongues flicking between their teeth.

Carrie Leroy only got out one scream, as Pete watched, her stomach tumbling into infinity. One scream, as the brute clamped down on her throat and the blood welled up, red and thick and steaming against the cool air.

Pete started back, out of reflex, into the moaning horde, who closed on Carrie with a speed belied by their stupor. Cloth ripped, and with it flesh; teeth flashed and chins became stained with blood. Pete found herself against a wall of warm, moving, heaving bodies, each of them fighting to draw closer to Carrie, where she lay on the ground, thrashing and croaking out the last breaths of her life. No matter how Pete hit at them, how many she threw aside, there was another body in front of her, and she felt hands rake through her hair and teeth snap against her fingers.

"Miss Caldecott!" Margaret grabbed her by the arms and hauled her backward, her strength greater than what Pete would have expected from a skinny teenage girl.

"No!" Pete screamed, and she was shocked at how loudly her voice resonated off the houses around them. "I can't just leave her there!"

Margaret's face was streaked with grime and tears, but she tugged harder at Pete. "Nothing to do for her now," she said, barely audible through her sobs. "Please, Pete. Please just come."

Pete saw that their avenue was rapidly closing, and she turned and followed Margaret. Because the girl was right—there was nothing else she could do.

Donovan stopped a dozen yards ahead and gestured at them wildly. "The fuck you doing? Trying to fight off a mob with your bare hands? Get to running!"

Behind them, the bulk of the crowd still clustered around Carrie's body, but the outliers had focused their attention on Pete and were moving after her. Pete grabbed tightly to Margaret's hand. "Don't look behind you," she said. "Don't look anywhere but straight ahead, and don't stop running until I tell you."

Margaret was fast, and she didn't have a problem keeping pace with Pete and Donovan. Pete ran until she felt like her lungs would explode, but her distance and stride were definitely easier since she'd kicked fags. Maybe all that nonsense in zombie movies had something to it. If only she could solve this problem by putting a few bullets in the skulls of the undead and calling it a job well done.

The graveyard was uphill from the village, and Donovan started to flag before they'd gotten halfway. The villagers, on the other hand, had only gained speed, and they were moaning and crying now, their voices echoing off the surrounding hills, creating a drone of hunger and pain that was all Pete could hear besides her own thudding heart.

When Donovan stumbled and fell, Pete fought the urge to shout at him and instead let go of Margaret's hand. "Keep running," she said. "Straight into the graveyard, and into the biggest tomb. Jack's there. He'll take care of you."

Margaret hesitated, and Pete gave her a none too gentle shove. The time for coddling was long past. "Go!" she shouted. "Fast as you can!"

She ran back to Donovan, giving the lead villager a shove backward and causing him to tumble while she pulled Jack's father up with her other arm. "Move," she snarled at him. "If you die out here before Jack gets to kick you in the teeth for all those miserable years you weren't around, I'll find a necromancer to raise you up and kick your arse myself."

Donovan ran, panting, his face a dangerous shade of cardiac-arrest crimson. "Bossy little bitch on top of it all. Hate to tell you this, luv, but you're a tailor-made Prospero."

Pete felt hands snatch at her hair and the back of her jacket, but then they were through the graveyard fence and the crowd clustered outside, moaning and pawing at one another as they fought not to get pushed through the iron. One of the wraiths drifted over, its mouth opening into a fathomless maw, and quicker than a hawk strike, it snatched one of the punters from the front of the crowed, wrapping him in silvery tendrils. The rest of the crowd drew back.

The punter thrashed and screamed until he went still, skin taking on a blue cast and frost growing on his eyebrows and in his hair. A black shape writhed inside the wraith's silvery body, then disspated like ink in water.

Pete looked next to her, to where Donovan stood, eyes intent and lips moving. "Power of persuasion, luv," he said, and turned to head for the mausoleum.

Pete watched the figures fade into the mist until a wraith brushed by her, and she hurried after Donovan.

20.

Inside the mausoleum, Margaret crouched next to Jack, brushing hair back from his forehead. "I think he's sick," she told Pete when she came in.

"He'll live." Donovan slumped, sucking in a deep breath. "And so will you, thanks to us. Hope you're grateful."

"Will you shut your gob for ten seconds?" Pete said, crouching beside Margaret. "You all right, luv?"

Margaret nodded. Her face was streaked with dirt, the river tracks of tears cutting through, but she took a deep breath, wrapping her arms around her knees. "I'm all right. I feel bad for poor Miss Carrie, though. She only ever tried to help me, ever since my da brought us to this stupid place."

"I do, too," Pete said, stroking Margaret's hair. "I'm so sorry you had to see that, luv."

Margaret shrugged. "It's all right. I'm with you lot now."

Pete wondered what exactly the Smythes had done to their daughter in the intervening years to make her this flat and closed off. She'd want to murder them a lot more if she didn't think the mob outside would take care of the pair soon enough. Not that mindless living zombie would be a great leap for either Philip or Norma Smythe.

Pete stripped off her jacket and wrapped it around Margaret, who sank into it with a sigh. "Thanks. It's so cold here. Never gets any warmer."

"Stay put, luv, all right?" Pete said, guiding her to the small prayer bench under the stained glass window. "Don't go outside, whatever you do."

"You kidding?" Margaret said. "I'm not going anywhere with those things about."

"Smart girl," Pete said, patting her leg. She looked back at Jack, still prone on the ground. Donovan was bent from the waist, looking him over.

"So far, I can't say I'm very impressed," he said. "Your reputation is a lot worse than your reality, son."

"Up yours," Jack grumbled, and Donovan chuckled, the round low sound echoing in the tomb.

"That's more like it," he said. "That's the Jack Winter I was expecting to meet." He poked at Jack with his toe. "You could stand to have a little more spine, Jackie. Maybe that's my fault, leaving you to be raised by your mum."

Jack's cheeks colored, and he started to lever himself up, but fell back with a groan, pressing his hands over his eyes.

"I never wanted to leave you," Donovan said, "but I was foolish. I thought you had my blood, and you'd manage to grow some stones on your own. Guess I was wrong."

Pete felt her stomach clench, a sensation that was all too familiar to her. It felt good to have a target for her rage, though. She could gather all the pain and confusion and fear of the past few days and turn it on Donovan. She grabbed him by the arm and jerked him away from Jack. "Outside," she snapped when he started to protest. "No more spewing your crap in front of Jack."

Donovan followed her out, stumbling slightly when she pulled him down the steps. "My son might be into the kinky stuff, but don't think I won't smack you if you get too touchy-feely."

"I would love to see you try that with me," Pete told him. "I'll tell you right now, I'm not Jack's mum. I hit back."

Donovan rocked back on his heels. "Oh, calm your self-righteous little soul. I never raised my hand to Hannah. I'm not in the habit of knocking women around. Or abandoning my children, though I don't expect you to believe me."

"Good, because I think that's a load of bollocks," Pete said. "You admitted to me your entire talent is based around lying. Got to tell you, Donovan—I'm not your biggest fan."

He spat an impatient sigh and then pressed his hands together, as if she were a small child who was being willfully obtuse. "I don't have to explain myself, but would it help you to know I tried to take Jack with me when I had to leave Manchester and Hannah pitched such a fit I backed off? She threatened to have the council round, and then the police. And I wasn't exactly on the straight and narrow back then. Would I have been any use to Jack in prison?"

"Here's a thought—you could have stayed put and fucking raised your kid," Pete said. "But that's hard work and I get the feeling you're allergic."

"I told you, I was stupid," Donovan said. "I was doing a lot of work back then for a gangster named Harold Combs—Hatchet Harry, to his mates—and being the pet mind-bender of a man who chopped people's thumbs off for fun had gotten me into hot water. There were threats."

"Imagine that," Pete said. She folded her arms, but at least Donovan wasn't trying to shine her on with his talent. He looked tired, as if the words put a weight on him with each sentence he spoke.

"Before you come at me again with those terrier teeth, by the time I made it back to Manchester Jackie had lit out, and the next I heard, he was in shit up to his arse with the *Fiach Dubh*. Now, you might have the juice to toe up against the crow brothers, but I'd learned my lesson. Jack was fine, and he didn't need me."

"He wasn't fine," Pete said softly. She thought about the first time she'd seen Jack after he'd vanished on her when she was sixteen, thirty pounds lighter, hollow eyed, haunted. "He was killing himself as fast as he could."

How much of that could Donovan had prevented, if he'd just shown up? How many nights spent sleeping in doorways, how many doses of skag, how many years of a black hole inside her where Jack should be?

"I can't change the past," Donovan said. "Not even the gods themselves can do that. But now we're all in trouble, and for once I can be on my son's side when he needs me. I'm sorry you don't like my methods, but I'm doing what I can."

Pete felt the fight drain out of her. The rage swirled away like the mist around them, drifted up among the wraiths and was lost. "Don't think I don't know that you tried to lay the sodding mojo on me back there," she said as a parting shot. "And don't think this has changed my opinion of you. I think you're a piece of shit, and I'll be watching you every second until we get out of this horrid place."

"Fair enough," Donovan said. "You think what you like, dearie."

"I always do," Pete said, and they glared at each other for a moment until she decided she'd played the hard act enough and dropped her arms down, sitting on the steps of the tomb. "So what now? You've been here, what's your bright idea for getting past the zombie horde?"

"They're not . . ." Donovan started, but Pete flipped up her hand.

"Whatever. Talk."

Donovan heaved a sigh and sat next to her, patting his pockets. "Got a cigarette?"

Pete shook her head. "I'm off them since I had the baby."

He sighed and rubbed his forehead. "Too good and pure for words, aren't you?"

"Talk," Pete reminded him. Around them, the wraiths flitted, clustering over an old corner of the graveyard. Several of them converged on one grave, and Pete sighed as she saw a flash of silver spirit energy and felt rather than heard a spectral scream rake over her mind. Another poor ghost, caught up in the feeding frenzy.

"This isn't normal," Donovan said. "You felt it in the village, how the Black stops flowing. All of this, with the wraiths and the creepy village and Hell, even the fog." He swatted at a tendril of mist. "Do you know where we are?"

"Herefordshire," Pete said. "Village of Overton."

Donovan nodded. "Too right. And just over the border in Wales is where a lot of the airy-fairy types think Camelot used to lie."

"You are joking?" Pete said. "I mean, Camelot? That's a story." Morwenna's idiotic story about the Merlin and the thousand-year cycle came back to her, but what were the odds that was anything except a load of crap, designed to make Pete more willing to work with her?

"You may have heard another story," Donovan said. "Of a lady in the lake who gave a mage unimaginable power, the power to live for a thousand years, to return when the end of the world was near."

"Second verse, same as the first," Pete said. "Have you got a theory about what's going on *here,* at this moment, or do you want to spin me the same tale as

Morwenna Morgenstern did back at the Prometheus Club?"

"Herefordshire is riddled with holy wells," Donovan said. "Pilgrims been coming since the lion-baiting days to drink from the water. Curative properties and all that." He leaned forward, eyes bright with a fever light. Droplets of moisture hung from his skin, and he couldn't keep his hands still. "But there's another sort of lake that occurs, in the fabric of the Black. I think you've felt it before, when you and my boy ran up against Abbadon. All that old boy wanted was Hell on earth, but the principle is the same—a tear, a void in the Black leading to another place."

Pete thought of the white place, the bleeding sky, the feeling of endless nothing that was worse than any torture Belial and all his legions in Hell could dream up.

"That's your theory?" she said. "We've run into the magic porthole to nowhere?"

"I think we've run into what could give a mage the power to unite the Black, at least for a short time," Donovan said. "Power so thick it's corrupting everything in range. But that's only my theory, and I can't check it with the higher ups."

"And why not?" Pete said. "Afraid they'll think you're as far around the bend as I do?" She didn't trust Donovan, but she couldn't come up with a better explanation for the creeping wrongness that was spreading across the hills and through the people of Overton.

"No," Donovan said, ducking his head sheepishly,

not meeting Pete's eyes. "I can't check in because I can't leave."

Pete felt as if the air were touching her bare skin, all at once, all over her body. The deep sort of cold she only felt when making contact with something from the Land of the Dead shot through her, deep down and straight to her core. "What do you mean, can't?" she whispered.

"I mean I walk to where the motorway should be, and I find myself back here," Donovan said. "I try to make a call, and my mobile battery goes dead. I've walked tens of miles away from this bloody village and I always end up right back here. It's the void, wherever the worms come from—it's fucking with the Black, and once you're in it you don't get out."

Pete felt panic rising on a tide of bile in her throat and swallowed hard to keep from screaming. "There's got to be something you haven't tried."

"I've tried locator spells, scrying—hell, I even broke into the pub and tried to dial out collect. I'm stuck. It's all chaos and rude magic writhing around this place from the tear. Imagine what'll happen if it spreads. It'll infect the earth. Infect the spirit of anyone nearby. Allow all sorts of dark-dwelling monsters like the worms to run free." Donovan rubbed a hand over his face, dislodging the mist. "It poisons everything, and it will just keep coming. Preston must have stumbled onto it, and that idiot Crotherton couldn't see that they weren't dealing with a demon but with something like Purgatory itself, the way Dante understood it."

"That's a lot of shit and you know it."

Pete and Donovan both whirled and gaped at Jack, standing unsteadily in the door of the tomb, supporting himself against the jamb on one side and a hand on Margaret's shoulder on the other.

"Jack!" Pete went to him and examined him, even though he tried to wave her off.

"Don't fuss," he said. "I'm fine."

"You look like a pile of entrails shat out on a sidewalk," Pete told him. "But I'm just glad you're awake. Try to stay that way."

"I hardly think I made up something that's happening in front of your eyes for my own amusement, boy," Donovan said. "I'm only telling you based on what I've seen."

"Voids of magic that grant you eternal life and power?" Jack grumbled. "Yeah, tell me another."

"How long exactly were you eavesdropping?" Donovan demanded. Pete felt a smile twitch over her face.

"Long enough," Jack said. "Just because you're stuck doesn't mean we have to hang around here." He looked at Pete. "We did what Morgenstern wanted. Now we're leaving. Aren't we, Margaret?"

Margaret looked between Pete and Jack with wide eyes, and Pete soothed her with a hand. "Don't put her in the middle of your fight with Donovan, Jack."

Jack's jaw knotted up, and his hands twitched. "Donovan, is it? Haven't you two gotten cozy."

"Enough," Pete said. "You know it's not like that, so stop trying to pick a fight with me. You're going to stay with Margaret, and I'm going to try to find a way to get in touch with Morwenna."

She grabbed Donovan's arm and drew him close. "You need to say to Jack what you said to me. And don't start anything while I'm gone."

"Your wish is my command, my dear," he purred, and Pete shoved him away before she could get any of Donovan's slime on her.

"No," Jack said, causing Pete to pause in mid-stride.

"What d'you mean, no?" she said.

"No, you're not running out there by yourself," Jack said. He pointed at his father. "Go with her."

Judging by his expression, Donovan was at least as surprised as Pete at his son's pronouncement. "I don't think she'll have me, Jackie," he said. "She's only got eyes for you, and being the hero of the hour."

"Fuck off," Pete said. It wouldn't be such a bad idea to have another body around. At least Donovan could keep the villagers off her arse long enough to figure out how to get in touch with Morwenna. "You better keep up," she told Donovan. "If you fall behind, that's where you're staying."

"Mercenary and cold, just like I like my women," Donovan said. "Lead the way then, Ice Princess. I'll follow you anywhere."

21.

Pete decided to skirt the village, staying to the side streets, and she walked in silence with Donovan until they reached the police call box she'd spotted on her way into Overton. It felt like months ago. Had it really been less than three days since she'd come to this place?

A dial tone buzzed encouragingly in her ear when she picked up, and she used her old code from the Met to bypass the direct line and dial out. Whatever was fouling the lines in town had missed the rickety call box. Morwenna picked up before the phone had even completed one ring.

"I trust you're calling with good news, Petunia."

Pete cast a look at Donovan and forced a smile into her voice. "Would I be calling with bad, Morwenna?"

Donovan lunged forward at the mention of Morwenna's name, but Pete knocked him back with the force of her glare. *Trust me,* she mouthed, though at this moment she couldn't care less what happened to Jack's father. He was in bed with black magic, and he deserved what he got. Much as she resented calling in the cavalry, she wasn't leaving Margaret and Jack to be consumed by the infection spreading through the village.

"That depends on if you're going to tell me you found Crotherton," Morwenna said.

"Oh," Pete said, gripping the phone at the memory of the Killigans' basement. "I found him, all right. There's much more, Morwenna—"

"And the Prospero Society's agent?" Morwenna snapped. Pete sighed.

"Right next to me," she said.

"Excellent. We'll be there shortly," Morwenna said.

"I don't think you understand . . ." Pete started again, but Morwenna cut her off.

"You can explain it all to me in person. Now go to the village square and wait for me with the Prospero Society's agent. And Pete?"

Pete gave up on warning Morwenna. If she and the Prometheans wanted to rush in blind, that was their problem. "Yes, Morwenna?" she said with exaggerated politeness.

"He better be there," she said. "If you tip him off, it's your arse."

Morwenna hung up, leaving the phone buzzing once again in Pete's ear. Donovan was staring at her, face red and hands quivering with rage.

"You," he spat. "You treacherous little bitch. You dimed me out."

Pete spread her hands. "How else exactly am I supposed to get her here, Donovan? Like it or not, the Prometheans are probably the only ones who can get us away from here. You two can duke it out all you like when she arrives. It's no skin off my nose either way."

She pointed back down the road. "I need you to go get Jack and Margaret and meet me in the village square. You better hurry, too—if you're not about when Morwenna shows up, I'd say it's time we bought a cottage and settled down in Overton to enjoy the zombie apocalypse."

"I did *not* agree to this," he snarled. "I told you the Prometheans don't care about you one way or the other, but you didn't want to listen." He spread his hands. "I'll get Jack to you, but then I've got to light out. You brought Morwenna down on us, you take your chances. I'm sorry—I didn't want to, but you pushed me."

"But you did," Pete said, surprised at how calm she sounded, given how slagged off Donovan looked. "You didn't want to abandon Jack, but you did. Didn't want to get him involved in this, but he is. Your son needs you and you're running. You're in this for yourself, Donovan. That's obvious. So if you want to save your arse, stop with the indignation and do as I say. Morwenna is the only one strong enough to stop this spell."

He stared at her, eyes burning, mouth working with too many curses to actually articulate. Then he stomped to the center of the road and threw up his hands. "Fine! I'll meet you back in the square. If you haven't been chewed to bits by then."

Without another word, Donovan turned and stormed off. Pete started to walk back to the village as well, but she caught the raven gliding across her vision like a flicking across the sun. As quickly as it came, it was gone, but Pete wrapped her arms around herself and jogged the rest of the way, keeping her eye out for wayward villagers. Many lay on the pavement and in their gardens as bloated corpses, not moving. A few reached lamely for her as she jogged past, but they were sluggish in daylight, even the diffuse, gray light of the half-day that dawned on Overton.

The square was as deserted as when she'd first arrived in the village, and Pete sat on the edge of the St. Francis statue, keeping the bronze monk's feet at her back. She had a good view from the small hump of earth, and she watched white shapes wander to and fro in the fog.

No sign of the worms, for now, but at least two of them were still out there. The thought of touching them again, of seeing that place of nothing from which they came, made Pete want to scream.

She sat, perfectly still and quiet, counting off the seconds in her head, and that worked for a few minutes, before her eyes started roaming again and her nerves started pinging. The pull of the void was stronger than it had been even this morning.

How long before it spread beyond Overton? How long before it reached Manchester, Leeds, Newcastle, London?

Movement stalled her wondering, and Pete was almost thankful for it. It wasn't the slow rolling gait of a spirit-poisoned villager, and it wasn't the quick flicker of a raven. This was a deliberate gesture, and as a slim figure appeared in the door of the inn across the square, it grinned and beckoned to her.

Pete's stomach plummeted. She'd know the trim suit, the dark hair, and the permanent sneer anywhere. Of all the fucking things in existence, this was the one bastard who could make her day even worse.

Still, she got up and walked, because to ignore him would invite even worse consequences.

"Hello, Petunia," Belial said when she was close enough. "Thought it was about time you and I had a heart-to-heart."

22.

"Look at you," Pete said, staying out of reach of Belial's black nails and shark's teeth. "Swanning about England, and nobody even had to summon you. You've come up in the world, Belial."

"I don't mean to brag," he purred as the door of the inn shut behind Pete, "but I am a prince now."

"Forgive me if I don't go weak in the knees," Pete said. The front room of the inn was like every other sad pub in every other tiny village she'd ever seen—a few sticky tables, video poker, and dusty signs advertising lager on the walls. "I've got more pressing matters to deal with than you."

Belial's eyebrows went up. He could pass for a man, if you didn't look too closely. Black hair, black eyes, pale skin, and a funeral suit. The thin man who held out his hand and offered you bargains beyond your wildest dreams—all he wanted in exchange was everything.

But Pete had encountered him far too often to feel

the swell of terror that should accompany confronting a Prince of Hell.

"You're rather less pleasant than the last time we met," he said. "I don't know as I like it."

"Then fuck off and leave me alone," Pete said. "I don't owe you anything this time. We're square—we got rid of Abbadon and you cleared my note. Mine and Jack's. I believe the phrase 'Never darken my doorway again' might have been used."

Belila inhaled, narrow nostrils flaring. "Did it ever occur to you that I simply missed you, Petunia?"

"Bollocks," Pete said. "Spit it out, Belial."

He grinned at her, tongue flicking between his pointed teeth. "I do see what you mean by pressing matters. What sort of place have we come to? Something about the way the air tastes . . . I haven't gotten a whiff of magic this black for a thousand years."

"Your guess is as good as mine," Pete sighed. "Something about a void in the Black leading to an in-between place like nothing anyone has ever seen, unlimited power, big bad evil, blah blah blah."

Belial clicked his black nails on the tabletop. "Soul well," he purred. "Well, well. That *is* worth rolling out of bed for."

"You've dealt with these things?" Pete asked. Absurdly, she felt relief. What had it come to when Belial, once the specter of her nightmares, made her feel safer?

"No," Belial said, and laughed. "I look stupid? I stay the fuck out of the in-between, Pete. It's the place for lost souls, lost things. I'm a creature of Hell. They'd love to pick my bones clean over there."

"The worms," Pete said, fishing to see if Belial actually knew anything or if he was just fucking with her head, which was probably the demon's favorite hobby after showing up where he wasn't wanted and ruining her day.

"That's cute," he said. "That you give them little nicknames. They're *Ba'tsubuota b'ad la d'anasha*."

"Bless you," Pete said, curling her lip in what she felt was a fair impression of Jack. "Need a tissue?"

"That's the closest I can get in a human language, you insufferable brat," Belial said. "Aramaic—literally, a thing that is not a man. The antithesis of a living person. Nothingness. In Hell, we call them the Undone— pieces of a human soul that got lost either coming or going, and ended up in the nothingness that lies between everything."

He sat back and folded his arms, regarding Pete. "If a piece of their place is spilling into the daylight world, you've got your delicate little hands full. Touching Purgatory throws everything off kilter."

"I know all that," Pete said. "Out of balance, unnatural, et cetera."

"Not just unnatural," Belial said. He cocked his head at her. "You don't know anything at all, you realize that? You're so blissfully ignorant that sometimes it hurts my back teeth."

"Fuck off," Pete said. "I'm not in the mood for witty banter with you of all people."

"But I'm not a person." Belial grinned. "Not by a long shot." He cracked his knuckles. "Sweet little Petunia, I came here to chat with you about another matter entirely, but this is far more interesting."

"Just tell me," Pete sighed. You could never shut a demon up—they loved the sound of their own voices more than any creature Pete had ever encountered. "And if you have any advice for shutting this leak down and getting rid of the zombies in the bargain, I'm all ears."

"Did you say bargain?" Belial gave a low growl and Pete hitched back reflexively. "My favorite word, dear Petunia. You know that."

"Forget it," Pete said. "I'll clean up this mess on my own, just like always."

"Ah, yes," Belial said. "Always so ready to rush into the fire, aren't you, Petunia? Always so ready to die a bloody, heroic, pointless death. It's not an attractive habit, you know. I much prefer your Jack's inclination toward inveterate cowardice. He's going to far outlive you if this keeps up." His red tongue flicked again. "Tell me, do you think he'll fare well as a single daddy?"

"Fuck you," Pete snapped. "You had a few inches with me, but that's it. Get lost. I didn't summon you, so just go away and bother some other poor sod."

She got up and stormed back outside, slamming the door after her. Her heart was thudding and her breath was short, as if she'd just run a long, long way.

After far too short a time for Pete to feel any semblance of calm, the door creaked open again. Belial's thin white hand, tipped with black nails, extended a blank pack of cigarettes and shook it. "Not very smart," he said as Pete grabbed one and lit it, inhaling viciously. "Taking favors from a demon."

"You've never done a favor for me in your life," Pete retorted. "You just keep me around because it amuses you to see me suffer."

Belial tsked. "That right there proves you don't get it. You and I have a far more beneficial relationship, Pete, and you know it. Now do you want to hear why I traipsed up from the Pit or not?"

The fag tasted sour, like burnt rubber on the back of her tongue. Her throat wasn't used to the harshness, and whatever noxious unfiltered thing Belial was smoking made her gag. She threw it down and stamped on it. "What you said back there, about me needing to be a hero. Isn't true. I just want to stay alive and keep Jack and Lily safe. I just want to get out of here and go home."

"Then hear me out," Belial said. "And instead of kicking and screaming against what's happening, use your head. Unlike the crow-mage, you do have a brain. 'S why I've always preferred dealing with you."

Pete shivered at the thought that she was the preferred company of a demon. How sick was that? "Don't see why," she said. "Jack's got far more to offer."

"And he gives it so easily," Belial scoffed. "What's the saying—never engage in a battle of wits with an unarmed opponent? Jack has his uses, Petunia, but when it comes to the bargain I know if I can get over on you, I'm doing my job."

"Is your job today to annoy the piss out of me?" Pete said. "Because you're blabbing circles and not saying anything useful."

"Demons exist to keep humans in check," Belial said. "To feed on their baser impulses. We're the carrion eaters of the Black, Petunia. We keep sin, stupidity, and evil from spreading too far. I thought you'd have figured that out by now."

"You have ten seconds before I well and truly leave," Pete said. "You got something useful to tell me about how to get rid of this void in the Black?"

"Think about it, Petunia." Belial's voice was dark and silky as the mist, and his fag smoke smelled like crematory ash.

"Think about what?" she sighed.

"Everything," Belial said. "Your whole sad little human life."

"Right, then," Pete said. "I've had my quota of riddles for, well, ever, so I'm done now, thank you."

"You act like everything that happens is some mystical hand of fate," said Belial, and the playful tone was gone from his voice. It was harsh and commanding, befitting a Prince of Hell. "Like all you're trying to do is make the world safe for the queen to sit in Buckingham Palace, the punters to drink in the pubs, and that sad waste of skin Jack Winter to stumble from one disaster to the next." Belial held up his hands to preempt Pete's wringing his neck, or so she supposed. "How many times can you save him before you accept that you're a bigger piece of this than Jack ever was, Pete?"

He turned his black, black eyes on Pete, and she stopped breathing. The demon was arresting, even in his human form, enough to stop a person's heart for a split second.

"You're the last of your kind," Belial whispered, reaching out to brush his pointed nails down Pete's cheek. Mere contact triggered visions in her, of vast plains of shimmering sand covered with crucifixtions like pins in a pinboard, of a vast city with triple smokestacks spewing waste from crematory furnaces into the sky, of the bone fields that stretched on forever, bleached white skulls of the dead staring endlessly into the bloodred skies of Hell.

"So I've heard," Pete murmured, sick and dizzy on the glimpse of the demon's psyche her talent triggered.

"The last of your kind, and you fight and you fight to stop what's coming, but you can't avoid it, Petunia," Belial said. "You can only take your place, the one you like to pretend doesn't exist." He moved his hand away and smiled at her, thin and entirely too knowing. "But it does. Nergal tried and the Morrigan tried and Abbadon himself tried to use you, and it. But it wasn't theirs to begin, was it? It's always belonged to you. The last Weir, the one who will stand at the eye of the storm when it finally comes."

Pete could barely get the words out, her throat raw and swollen as if she'd been screaming for hours. "What storm? What are you talking about?"

"The end." Belial shrugged. "Demons are pragmatic, Pete. Worlds rise, worlds fall. Things end. And all of this, what's happened here in this nasty little village, the old gods stirring, the bleeding of the Black into everything else, it's all a signal that the countdown has started flipping over. I'm not upset by it, but I am bemused that you refuse to see the truth."

Pete glared up at the demon. "I'm sure you'll tell me, so out with it."

"The truth is that you have always been the beginning of the end," Belial said. "The one who'll finally bring wrath and ruin to the Black. You can pretend every one of these things is coincidence, that you're an ignorant pawn, that you don't understand your talent, but you're lying to yourself." Belial lit another cigarette, drew long and hard, and exhaled a cloud of blue-tinged smoke. "The truth is, you were always meant to end up right here, Pete. The moment you were born, everything you've done since, has all led to right here. And you are the beginning of the end of all things. You always have been, and when it happens, all you can really do is be ready."

He put out his cigarette and straightened his tie. "So the only advice I have for you is don't stop it. Don't fight it. Let Purgatory spread. And be ready to rise to your rightful place in the aftermath."

He craned his neck and grinned at Pete as she felt her cheeks grow hot with rage. "I really came here to talk to you about Jack, but it looks as if your little rescue party has arrived, and as I have no truck with demon hunters, I'm going to make myself scarce."

"Wait!" Pete shouted, grabbing for him and finding only smoke. "What about Jack?"

"If you survive this, we'll talk again," Belial said. "I did like this world, but there's no stopping it now. Good-bye, Pete."

Before she could blink, he was gone, leaving only the tinge of cigarettes and black magic behind.

"Fucking demons," Pete hissed, as Donovan, Jack, and Margaret appeared from one street, while Morwenna's fleet of black cars appeared from the other, screeching to a stop in the square.

Pete looked between them, then took a deep breath of cold air that burned her lungs all the way down. Caught in the middle, and no help for it.

As usual.

23.

Morwenna stepped from her black Mercedes, trailed by Victor, and clacked across the square on her heels to Pete. "Is that him?" she asked, pointing at Donovan.

"That's him," Pete confirmed. Morwenna started to brush her aside, but Pete put her hand on Morwenna's shoulder.

"There's just a few things we need to get straight," Pete said.

Morwenna looked at Pete's hand as if it had turned into a spider. "I *beg* your pardon?"

"We did what you asked," Pete said. She cast a look back at Jack and Donovan. Jack stood with Margaret, keeping himself between the Prometheans and the girl. Donovan fidgeted next to them, shooting Pete a glare that she felt could have melted her on the spot.

"And I'm glad I was able to put my faith in you," Morwenna said, trying to shove past Pete again.

"That's not it," Pete said. "Before you go after Donovan, I want your promise that nothing will happen to Jack or Margaret, or Lily. That you'll get us all out of here."

Morwenna gave her a condescending smile. "We're not mobsters, Pete. We'll take care of this."

Pete gripped Morwenna's suit jacket, the soft wool prickling under her fingers. "Promise me," she said. "None of us alone can break the hold this place has, so you promise me you'll get us out of here, or he's going to run, and I'm going to help him. Then you'll never know how far the Prospero Society has gotten into your ranks, and you'll still have a soul well spreading all over the UK."

Victor started to move for her, to separate Pete from Morwenna, but Morwenna waved him off. "Fine," she told Pete. "You have my word. Now get out of my bloody way."

Pete lifted her hand from Morwenna and retreated to stand with Jack and Margaret. "I think we're all right now," she said to Jack under her breath. "Donovan's not going to let himself be taken, so get ready to duck."

"Miss Caldecott," Margaret said, tapping her. Pete shushed her.

"It'll be all right, luv. Just stand by me."

"And that's my cue," Donovan said. "It's been fun, but I'm off."

"What a shock," Jack mumbled as Morwenna and Victor drew closer, forming a loose line to keep Donovan from rushing them. Pete thought that was a supreme display of overconfidence—she would have brought a lot more men.

"Jackie, believe me when I say that this isn't how

I wanted to end things," Donovan said. "Now I'd best be going. You take care, boy."

Pete braced herself. There was going to be a shitstorm when Donovan ran, but Morwenna had to take them out of here. She simply had to. Pete didn't allow herself to worry that Morwenna might be vindictive enough to go back on her word. Or might figure out Donovan escaping was part of Pete's plan. At least Margaret would be safe. She was innocent. Morwenna had to see that.

"Miss Caldecott!" Margaret hissed urgently, grabbing at her arm. Pete turned.

"I said it'll be fine, Margaret. You'll be on your way back to Manchester soon enough."

"That woman is dangerous," Margaret whispered.

"Miss Morgenstern leaves something to be desired in personality," Pete said. "But she's not a bad sort, Margaret. Calm down."

"*No*," Margaret hissed. "I *know* her."

Pete blinked. The cold was back, curling around the base of her spine. Morwenna was less than ten steps away. Pete crouched, looking at Margaret's thin face, her eyes almost impossibly large with fear.

"How do you know Morwenna?" she said quietly. "Tell me exactly."

"I saw her," Margaret mumbled. "When that Crotherton bloke came round, she was with him. She waited in the car, but I saw her. She was staring up at my window."

Pete felt a stone drop into her guts, the weight of knowing she'd been wrong smashing into her like a lorry. Wrong, stupid, and decieved.

"Pete . . ." Jack said, and when she looked up he had his hands raised, fingers spread as if he were waving to her.

"Stand up," Donovan told her. "Don't make me force Jackie to harm himself, because that'd be a real heartbreak on my part."

Donovan wasn't just chattering—Pete looked at his fist and saw a slim black pistol there. "I guess when your only hex is so limp, that's necessary, yeah?" she said.

"It does the trick," Donovan said, giving Jack a gentle prod. "Stand still, Jackie. This isn't going to get ugly if I can help it."

Pete straightened up slowly, keeping her movements easy and calm. She put one hand on Margaret's shoulder and stretched the other out to Donovan. "There's no need for that."

"There's a very great need," Morwenna said. She folded her arms, the smug curl of her lip just begging to be smacked out of existence. "We're not going to rough you up, Pete, but you are slippery. So forgive the harsh treatment."

Get it under control, the part of her that sounded like Connor snarled. *Stop staring and start thinking.*

"Got to hand it to you, Morwenna," Pete said out loud. "Getting Donovan to flip—that was pretty tricky."

"Oh," Morwenna said, patting Jack down with efficient movements, "not at all."

Jack grinned at her, showing all his teeth. "Little higher and to the left, luv."

Morwenna sent him a disgusted look and then stood, brushing off her hands. "Spare me, Mr. Winter. You're not nearly as charming as you think."

"A Prospero goon in your pocket," Pete persisted. "It's like you didn't need me at all." There was a lot about this she didn't understand, but the machinations of the Prometheans didn't interest her. All that mattered was that she'd been set up, and their ride out of Overton had vanished.

"Pete, Pete," Morwenna sighed, performing the same patdown on Pete as she had on Jack. "There is no Prospero Society. That was just to get you out here."

It felt like a punch. Of course—she should have seen it from the very start. One secret mage clubhouse strained credulity; two was a stupid plot from a bad movie.

"Sorry," Donovan said with a shrug. "They needed someone to play the villain, and let's face it—for you two, I fit the bill."

Morwenna stood up again. "Who better than Jack's estranged father to get you on the right track?"

"I know that Crotherton's not the point of all this, then." Pete seized on the chance to slot in the missing pieces. Morwenna wasn't a Dr. Doom type, but she was chatty, and anything Pete could learn would help them get out of this mess.

"It's very simple," Morwenna said. "You're a wild card, Petunia, wherever you go. You never listen to anyone but yourself, and in this case I knew you'd find me what Preston killed himself to avoid giving up. But only if I told you not to—only if I sent you here with some utterly mundane task that you'd rebel against."

Pete felt her teeth grind. "You used me to find the soul well." She resented being tricked—being used was beyond the pale.

"Will use," Morwenna said. "None of us can stand to be in close proximity. The only reason we're not already shambling is because we're all mages. But none of us are Weirs." There was the smile again, cold and satisfied. Morwenna thought she was very smart indeed.

"Well, you're shite out of luck, then," Pete said. "Because I don't know where it is. So do your worst, because that won't change anything."

"Fine by me," Morwenna said. "You've been nothing but a pain in my ass since the day I realized we needed you and Jack to pull this off."

"Pull what off?" Jack scoffed. "The soul well ain't going to make you immortal, luv. It's going to drain you dry and fill you up with something blank and evil and that'll be the end of you."

"If I want ignorant prattle, I can get it from the telly," Morwenna snapped. "I don't need the live show. And if you'd stuck with *anything* long enough to learn about the Black, Mr. Winter, you'd know that the soul well *can* grant power to the mage who knows the proper ritual steps, which I do."

"So that line about Jack being the Merlin?" Pete said. "Just something to string me along?"

"I fully believe Mr. Winter is the Merlin," Morwenna

said, as Jack's eyes went wide. "It's just a shame he'll never get a chance to realize his potential. There's no room for mavericks or loose ends in what's coming, and sadly you're both."

Pete shook her head again, drawing Margaret closer to her. "We're not helping you."

"I understand you want safety for this child," Morwenna said. "And for your own. If you don't help, I can guarantee they'll die screaming."

Margaret flinched under Pete's hand, and Pete had to admit Morwenna had thought up an answer for every angle.

She thought about the raven, when she'd woken up from the dream. *This is a place of death. Run and never look back.*

"I don't know how to get back there," she admitted. "My talent got drawn in, not me. I woke up and I was there."

"Not a problem," Morwenna said. "Donovan, might I borrow you for a moment?"

Victor took up Donovan's position behind Jack, while Donovan approached Pete. "Don't worry, luv," he said. "This'll only hurt for a minute."

Pete tried to shy away, tried to pull back, but Donovan caught her, his powers sweeping away her own talent like so much flotsam under a flood. His talent drowned Pete, and when she opened her eyes, everything had vanished.

24,

Pete saw nothing but the mist, the slivery shapes of the wraiths darting through it like fish above a reef. Her feet were bare, and she dug her fingers into the graveyard earth to see if she was awake. Pebbles dug into her flesh and dirt crept under her nails.

The graveyard was empty, and she was colder than the air would suggest. So maybe not dreaming, but not awake, either. The mausoleum was tumbled down, covered in black lichen, and the village beyond, what she could see, was ravaged by fire and time. Tendrils of smoke, the same gunmetal color as the sky, wafted upward like the tentacles of some great creature, reaching for the last vestiges of light sinking in the west.

This time, there wouldn't be any sudden awakening at her destination. This time, Pete followed the flight of the ravens, dark ink blots on the dirty paper of the sky, and walked. The gravel bit into her feet. She was dressed only in her sleep clothes, one of Jack's T-shirts, underwear, and little else, same as last time.

The landscape wasn't entirely unexpected. She'd seen a lot of strange things, and a slice of the in-between bleeding into the real would could bring visions of the future. Or the possible future. Or just her own fears.

She decided to keep her head down as she passed a pile of bodies—the villagers, now naked and bloated with a week's worth of rot, rivulets of black and green working their way under the skin where veins used to lie.

It wasn't real, she reminded herself. It was just power acting on her frail human neurons, her fear center, electricity dancing through her cerebral cortex. It wasn't a real future, it was just Donovan shredding through her memories and making her see things.

Pete tried to push back, to see things as they really were, but her vision skewed and pain cut her from head to toe.

Donovan's power felt like a net of barbs over her talent and consciousness, and Pete knew that pushing harder would only make her catatonic. There wasn't much she could do when a mind-control spell had its hooks in her. And now, Donovan wanted her to show him the soul well, the place her talent had been so drawn to she'd walked there in her sleep.

She had to play along or see Margaret and Lily and everyone she cared about hurt. So Pete pressed on through the memories, tainted by the proximity of the soul well, showing her all the things she feared most.

It felt like eternity, the walk over rocky paths and

rough-grassed hills that cut at her feet and snatched at her ankles. She'd begun to despair of ever seeing the spot, but she kept walking, kept following the ravens. They stopped occasionally, to perch on the corpse of a dead cow or peck at the eyeball of a fallen villager, but they moved west. Always west.

The power in the earth swelled and groaned, a thrumming like buried cables that Pete could discern through the soles of her feet. The sound reached her ears like the entire world was breathing, sleeping, but not for long. When she came over the hill and saw the twisted tree and the pile of stones, she felt almost an anticlimax, as if the strangest part of the journey were over.

I told you to go away, the raven croaked at her. *Why did you not heed?* It stretched its neck and wings, staring at her with its stone eyes.

"I'm not the Morrigan's bitch," Pete said. "You don't get to order me about."

The raven opened its beak wide, and Pete thought if it were a person, it would laugh in her face. *The Morrigan's desires and those of your allies will never match, Weir,* it said. *My lady makes no secret of what she wants.*

"War, apocalypse, and Jack leading the way," Pete snapped. "I know exactly what she wants. And by the way, these aren't my allies. This dream state I'm in right now was forced on me."

And why do you think what men and demons want is so very different? said the raven. *What has given you*

*the illusion that you and the other humans have dispa-
rate desires? You are all grasping for a little more life,
a little more power.*

"I don't want power the way Morwenna Morgenstern means to get it," Pete told the raven, itching to
pick up one of the rocks from the cairn and whip it at
bird's smug black bulk. "I'm not a psychopath."

*When the day comes that Jack stands at the head of
the Hag's army, Morwenna Morgenstern will be prepared,* said the raven. *Not you. Does that not trouble
you?*

"I don't want immortality," Pete said. "I don't give a
toss about anything except shutting up the soul well,
keeping this infection from spreading, and keeping my
family out of harm's way."

That's all? The raven sounded genuinely puzzled.
Not even the faintest thought of immortality?

"Nothing lives forever," Pete told it. "Not me, not
Morwenna. Not even the Hag."

Then I wish you well, the raven said, *since I couldn't
sway you. The Hag will see you if you attempt to close
the well or to stall the reckoning a little longer. She sees
everything.*

Pete wrapped her arms around herself. Standing
here, the power of the soul well leaking into her mind,
she felt small and frail. She *was* small and frail, in the
face of this thing. Humans in the Black didn't last long.
They were specks compared to the lifespan of a Fae, or
a demon, or a thing like the Morrigan.

But she was here now, and she needed to wake up

before Donovan's zeal to see what she saw blew out the circuits of her mind for good.

The stones piled in a cairn over the well were sharp, lava glass, nothing that could be dug out of the earth of Herefordshire. Pete stretched out her fingers, touched them, and felt the feedback of power. She sensed a vast space, full of white vapors, gibbous bodies, sharp edges. Emptiness, more complete than anything she'd experienced. And always, a screaming. Echoing endlessly, because the place was as infinite as the pain it induced.

Biting down on her lip, Pete closed her fist around the rock and gave a sharp tug. There was no pain for a long moment, even though blood flowed freely. Then she heard voices. She felt someone shaking her and the sharp, hot sting of broken skin on her fingers.

"Come on, luv, wake up!" Jack's rough hands slapped her lightly on the cheek. "What did you do to her?" he demanded.

"I told you, she'll be all right," Donovan said. "No worse than taking a couple of sleeping pills."

"This is *clearly* not the same thing," Jack snarled.

"Instead of second-guessing me, why don't you say thank you?" Donovan growled. "We got what we needed without any bloodshed. Your little tartlet came through."

Morwenna gave a slight twitch of her head. "I wish you wouldn't make it so theatrical, Donovan. Eyes rolling back in the head and all."

Margaret stared at her as well, and Pete guessed she'd been babbling like some kind of streetcorner nutter. "I'm sorry, luv," she said quietly, "but it's for the best.

Need to keep you safe, don't I?" She turned on Morwenna, putting steel in her voice even though her head throbbed so from Donovan's invasion that she was seeing double. "A bargain's a bargain. Get her out of here, now."

"I'm sorry," Morwenna said with a shrug. "But as I'm sure you've guessed, deception is a necessary part of this endeavor. We can't have any witnesses to what we're attempting."

She gestured to Victor. "Please dispose of the girl. The rest of you, fan out through the village. Start looking for what Preston took from me."

"No!" Margaret cried, jumping behind Pete. Jack gave a snarl.

"This is what you're about, you slag? Murdering kids?"

"I'm about saving England," Morwenna snapped. "What do you think will happen if the soul well is not controlled? If it is not channeled into a mage? It will spread, Jack, and what's happened in Overton will look like a low-budget zombie film compared to what's coming."

Pete felt the whirling in her head redouble. The immediate panic of Morwenna's order lapped up against the sinking in her gut when she realized that the soul cage was still in her jacket pocket. In the jacket that Margaret was currently wearing.

"Victor!" Morwenna snapped as a complement of Prometheans started down the side streets of the village. "Are you deaf?"

Victor drew back, frowning. "I don't kill children. I'm not an assassin."

"You are precisely what I tell you to be, Victor," she hissed. "Nothing more, nothing less."

Margaret started to shake behind Pete, and Jack moved in, gripping her arm. "Pete . . ." he said, low. "Do something."

"What the fuck am *I* supposed to do?" she hissed as Morwenna went to Victor and shook him by the lapels of his expensive suit.

"Do as I say!" she shouted. "She's one girl! Take care of it."

Victor drew back, wresting himself from her grip. "No. It's not going to happen, Morwenna. Find someone else."

"Idiot," she spat at Victor, then turned on her heel toward Pete and Jack. "Donovan," Morwenna snapped, and Pete's heart skipped in time with the sound of him checking the chamber on his pistol.

"Sorry, Jackie," he said. "We all do things we don't want to because we must."

"For the greater good?" Jack growled at his father. "Or just because you've bought into the lies this bitch has fed you?"

"I'm beginning to sense that you can't or won't see the bigger picture," Donovan said. He aimed the pistol between Margaret's eyes, and the girl let out a strangled little cry that Pete mirrored involuntarily.

From the corner of her eye, Pete saw the shadow descend, gliding above the rooftops before it turned on the breeze and bore directly toward her. She ducked at the last second, pulling Margaret with her as the raven fell on Donovan, black wings frenzied as it raked and pecked at his face.

Donovan screamed, and in the sky Pete saw a dozen dark shadows, the rest of the ravens she'd seen in the village, watching over the people and the graveyard.

Pete took the opportunity. She hooked Donovan's leg with her foot and shoved, sending him tumbling into the loamy earth. The ravens covered him, black and shiny, rippling backs like oily water. One looked Pete in the eye.

Go. Find the edge of the village.

"What about Jack and Margaret?" she asked.

Jack is the Morrigan's favored son, the raven said. *He and the girl have the same protection offered to you. Now* run.

"Bitch," Donovan gasped from the ground, but Pete ran without looking back. She couldn't care less what sort of fate befell Donovan.

"Go," she snapped at Margaret as more and more ravens descended, alighting on Morwenna and Victor as well, spreading out to follow the other agents of the Prometheus Club, who shouted and ran for cover as the fog filled up with black bodies and the birds' guttural cries.

Jack paused at the edge of the square, watching the rippling mass of birds that covered Donovan. Pete grabbed his arm and yanked, not being gentle. "Don't tell me this is the time you pick to get sentimental," she said.

"No," Jack said after a heartbeat. "Fuck 'im."

They ran, all three, and Pete didn't look back again until the low cottages of Overton were out of sight in the fog.

Part Three

Wasteland

*There's not much more to be said
It's the top of the end.*
                              —Bob Dylan

25.

After they all ran until Margaret's short legs and Jack's abused lungs couldn't take it any more, Pete found a small cottage tucked into the hills, locked up long enough that leaves had piled against the front door and moss had grown on the sills.

"Thank Christ for posh twats and their vacation cottages," she said, peering in the window.

"Odd person to thank," Jack said. He was still breathing hard and heavy, and Pete didn't know if it was from the running or the burden of Donovan stabbing him in the kidney when his back was turned.

"Let's get inside," she said, as mumbles and moans echoed through the fog. "Hills are lousy with folks gone George Romero."

Jack got the door open with a few words, and Pete locked it again when they were all inside and slid the ancient sofa in front of it. She pulled a chair close to the fireplace and put Margaret in it, wrapping a blanket around her thin shoulders. "You all right, luv?"

She shook her head without a word, and Pete sighed.

Stupid question. Margaret might never be all right again.

Jack opened the damper and piled some wood in the grate, muttering "*Aithinne*" to get it going.

"Thought we were fucking dead," Margaret said at last.

"Not yet," Pete said, trying to paste on a cheerful face. Margaret's baleful expression told her she'd failed miserably.

"Can't say I'm surprised every last one of those Prometheus Club cunts was holding out on us," Jack said. "But I do think a fucking-over as deep and thorough as this one is pretty impressive. Once they manage to harness the soul well, we might as well just throw open the door and welcome the apocalypse."

"I thought you said that ritual was bunk," Pete said, casting a meaningful look at Margaret.

"'Course it's not bunk," Jack said. "That Morgenstern bitch knows what she's doing, much as I hate to pay her any kind of compliment. All she needs to get things kicking off is that soul cage."

"Speaking of," Pete said, feeling in the pocket of her jacket. "I'm so sorry I made you responsible for this, Margaret. I never meant to."

In the low firelight the soul cage danced, as if the interior were alive and moving, trying to find any egress to the larger world. "Who d'you think it is?" Pete said, turning it in her hands.

"Crotherton, probably," Jack said. "He seems like a patsy type, all Dudley Do-Right and noble."

"Preston gave me this," Pete said. "Out of everyone, he trusted me, and I walked right back into Morwenna's grasp and practically gift-wrapped the thing for her."

"All that tells you is that he had shite for brains," Jack said. "Probably so buggered from being close to the soul well he didn't know his own name."

"He tried to warn me," Pete said. The soul cage's energy writhed, turning colors under her grasp. She imagined poor Jeremy Crotherton, just looking for his friend, getting a whack on the head and a horrific end as worm food in that awful cellar. Add the indignity of having Morwenna Morgenstern suck out his soul, and it was a crap day all around.

"And you didn't listen because he came across as a crazy fuck," Jack said. "Blame isn't needed at this late stage, Pete. A plan would be nice, though."

Pete found a blanket for herself and wrapped up in it, inhaling the musty odor of mothballs and damp. "You want me to plan a full frontal assault on a bunch of mages who've already got us beat? I can do it, but it's not going to end any way except with us dead."

"Doesn't matter," Margaret muttered. In the low light, Pete saw that dirt streaked on her face and her T-shirt was torn, things she'd missed in the frantic escape. "We're dead anyway."

"Luv, don't talk that way," Pete sighed. "Jack and I are going to find a way to get you out of here."

"And go where?" Margaret whispered. Pete saw a shadow flick in front of the windows, and away. A shiver ran through Margaret, though the cottage was almost stuffy as the fire blazed. "My parents are out there. All the people are out there. We're the last normal ones. Where'm I supposed to go?"

"She's got a point," Jack muttered. "We're either target practice for the Prommies or worm food. I don't exactly relish either choice."

"You want a plan, you could try being the least bit helpful," Pete snapped. "I'm not the one who's been running with mages his entire life. What happens if Morwenna gets hold of the soul cage she made?"

Jack sighed, but he played along. "Likely she's channeling the power of Purgatory through her, giving herself regular old Hulk powers like that stupid, stupid story about the Merlin. And you need a soul to do that— something agonized, in enough pain to lure in the things capable of taking up residence in you and lending you the sort of power Morwenna is after." He poked at the fire. "Mage soul is the only kind that will do, and the more pain Crotherton was in when he died, the better it'll work."

"So very well, then," Pete said, thinking of the stricken terror frozen on Crotherton's face when she'd found his body in the cellar.

"Like gangbusters," Jack agreed. "She wants to be top of the heap, and if we give her that thing she will be."

Pete looked from Jack to Margaret. She thought of their friends in London. Lily. Everything she knew, engulfed in this endless fog. Every face that was familiar, white-eyed with a worm looking out. Or worse, simply shambling about, chewing on the neighbors and waiting to die.

"Fine," she told Jack. "I couldn't care less if Morwenna gets what she wants out of this."

He blinked at her, and Pete spread her hands. "Do you? Let the Prometheans and the old gods fight it out. I don't care. I care about us surviving until the next sunrise." She hefted the soul cage and gave Jack a smile. It wasn't much of one, wan and exhausted as she was, but she did try. "This is the last bargaining chip we have. Morwenna gets us away from here, she can have it and then we're done with her and I no longer give a fuck what her plan is."

"They're not going to do anything in the dark," Jack pointed out. "Give you a few hours to realize this is a bad fucking plan."

"It's the only one I've got," Pete said. "We're not going to beat her, Jack. Maybe a year ago I'd have been inclined to try, but things are different now."

She prayed he wouldn't argue with her anymore. She was too tired to keep trying to convince Jack that the attack plan wasn't always the best plan.

"Never thought I'd see the day when fucking Prometheans beat me," he grumbled.

"In the morning we'll make the exchange," Pete said. "And we'll be alive, Jack. That's the best deal I can think of. Only your pride is keeping you from seeing that."

"I'm tired," he snapped, and stretched out on the floor, rolling away from her.

Pete watched the fire for a long time, trying to believe the lie she'd told Jack, and Margaret, and herself, and not having any luck.

26.

When what passed for morning crept through the fog, and the villagers had retreated to whatever dank holes they crawled into to hide from the daylight, Pete, Jack, and Margaret walked the path Pete'd followed twice now, one asleep and once in memory.

The black rocks poked up all around them, but Pete saw tire tracks in the grass now, and a cluster of figures at the top of the hill.

Silver shapes flitted about, too, a pale counterpoint to the ravens that perched in a loose ring on rocks and twisted trees, and the occasional bloated corpse.

"Shit," Jack muttered, scrubbing his thumb across his forehead. "He's brought those fucking monsters with him."

"Let me handle this," Pete murmured. "Keep Margaret safe. That's your job."

"Pete . . ." he started, but she cut him off with a look, and then raised her voice toward the Prometheans.

"Oi!" she shouted from what she judged to be a safe

distance. The wraiths turned to her as one, and their fangs glowed in the mist.

"If you want your precious little rock back, you're going to call off your low-rent Dementors and speak to me, Donovan!" Pete bellowed.

Faster than she'd give his a man his age credit for moving, he appeared from the clot of the ground, trailed hotly by Morwenna. They slowed, and the wraiths withdrew as he got close to Pete. Donovan sneered through the scratches and bandages on his face. "You're like a cockroach, aren't you?"

Pete pulled the soul cage from her pocket. "I believe you're looking for this."

Donovan's eyes lit up, and he snatched for the soul cage, but Pete whipped it out of reach. "Ah-ah. You promise us safe passage out of here—a *real* promise, this time, and then we'll talk."

"How about I let my friends here drink you dry and take it from your corpse?" Donovan snapped.

Pete dropped the soul cage to the ground and positioned her boot over it. "I'll smash this thing to bits before they even get a drop."

Morwenna gave an involuntary cry, and Pete pinned her with her worst glare. "I want out of here, Morwenna. I didn't ask to be any part of this, and I'm done. You do what you want with the soul cage, but before you get it, you do what I say for once."

Morwenna pursed her lips, as if all this were a minor annoyance. Donovan, on the other hand, looked ready to pop.

"I'm going to clean your mind out, you little bitch," he snarled. "Give it over, or the last thing you'll remember will be your daughter dying in your arms, over and over again."

"You so much as breathe on her and I'll kill you," Jack snarled. "I was ready to let you go—not forgive you, but at least get on with me life—but you just made my shit list all over again, boyo." He toed up to Donovan, and Pete realized with a start that Jack was taller than his father, by a good few inches, and when he was angry he blew Donovan out of the water in terms of the hard man act. "I would like nothing better than to wring the life from your carcass by inches for every miserable fucking day of me life since you left but especially for this one, so *please*—fucking talk to my wife again."

"Enough!" Morwenna shouted. She extended her hand to Pete. "I'll take you out of here after I finish the ritual."

"Not good enough." Pete shook her head. "Now or never."

"Then I might as well just have Victor shoot you—if he has the *stones*," she tossed at Victor over her shoulder, "because I'm not leaving until I get what I came for. You can either leave with me at that time or not at all."

Pete felt a grimace of pure irritation at how thoroughly Morwenna could take control of a situation, but she moved her boot. Donovan swooped in and scooped up the soul cage, shoving her back so she would have gone on her arse in the mud if Jack hadn't been there to catch her.

Morwenna nodded. "Good. Victor, take them up the hill and keep them quiet while we do what needs doing."

Victor prodded all three of them into a loose knot at the edge of the black rocks. Pete watched the cairn rise from the mist. The pull was so strong she could feel it like a second heartbeat, and it was clear Morwenna was wallowing in it like a pig in a sty as she placed the soul cage at the apex of the black rocks.

Most rituals weren't all chanting and incense, wearing robes and scribing ancient symbols. All you really needed for a ritual was a little chalk, some talent, and an intent.

The Prometheans moved into a circle, leaving Morwenna at the center. Donovan smirked at Pete over his shoulder.

"Can't say I ever pegged you as a quitter, sweetheart," he told her. "Disappointing. But then again, most of what Jackie's chosen to do with his life is disappointing."

Pete stayed quiet. Her stomach flipped, and she wondered how long she had, this close to the soul well, before she became another one of the shambling villagers. She wondered what had become of the hikers and the birdwatchers who'd come too close to this place. Worms? Or did they simply go mad and fall down a ravine somewhere to die?

"To the oldest of the old ones, to the things before men and the time before time," Morwenna said. For the first time since Pete had met her, she spoke reverently and quietly, none of her usual arrogance in her posture.

"We bring you this gift," Morwenna said, voice just above a whisper. "The soul of a mage, to do with as you will."

She reached out and started to place her hand on the soul well. Pete looked at Jack. She had to time it just right, so no one had a chance to react.

"You know how you said letting her win was a bad idea?" she whispered to Jack.

He stared at her. Beyond him, Pete saw white shapes encroaching through the mist—worms, called back by the energy she could feel rising around her even now, strong enough to drown everyone in its path.

"For once, you were right," Pete said, and shoved Donovan hard, knocking him aside.

"I am open to receive you!" Morwenna cried. "Come to me with all the power of the Merlin!"

Donovan grabbed for Pete, but she dove toward Morwenna and knocked the woman out of the way, closing her own fist over the soul cage.

All at once, the rising energy disappeared. Everything stopped, sound and breath and air. Pete thought she heard Margaret scream, and then she was in the void, inside the soul well, and the white nothingness had consumed her.

27.

The raven alighted on a tree above Pete. It was gray and long dead, just a husk barely able to support the bird's weight.

I did tell you, it said.

"I'm not letting Morwenna use this place," Pete said. "She'll cover England in worms and zombies, and she'll think she's doing it for the greater good. So I'm shutting the well."

No . . . the raven started. *You don't know what could happen . . .*

The soul well wasn't a physical drop, not really. It rushed up at her, a vortex of mist, full of shapes and screams. She was on a white plane with a gray tree, nowhere, among the stars. She was spread out across a thousand light years and compressed down to a single point, all at once.

"The worst thing that can happen is that I die," she said. "But this thing started, and it's got to have an end."

It started because of what the crow-mage did, the

raven sighed. *It will not end, not simply because you want it to.*

"There's one sure way I know to drain power out of a place," she told the raven.

No! The bird let out a distressed cry. *You know that will be the end of you . . .*

"Then I'll end," Pete said. "I told you, nothing lives forever."

When she'd made the decision to lie to Jack the night before, to stop Morwenna, the shadow had been in the back of her mind, the whisper that it might come to this. But she couldn't hesitate. As much as Belial might insist otherwise, she couldn't do anything else. Couldn't risk her daughter growing up in a world ruled by the white nothing.

Or by Morwenna Morgenstern.

If she did this, if she gave in to the howling energies around her, that would be that. The end, a period as final as her father's lung cancer or a bullet fired from a gun.

If she did this, Lily would never know her. Jack would never be the same.

But if their world was this, the white place full of nothing but wasteland and misery, then it wouldn't matter anyway. If she did this, her daughter would grow up in a world that allowed light and good dreams next to all the shadows and black magic swirling around her. Jack would get to remember her as strong, standing beside him, rather than wrung out, spent, and given up.

So she didn't hesitate, but instead stepped forward until even the tiny white slice of world faded away, and there was nothing but her, alone in the in-between.

It was nothing like the last time she'd visited, when she'd tried to hold Jack's soul back from crossing into the Land of the Dead. She stood in front of the flat where her family had lived when she was a tiny kid, and everything looked very normal.

A shape opened the door and stepped out, and Pete saw the elegant woman in black, feathers for hair and obsidian eyes.

"You again," the Morrigan sighed. "Can't get rid of you, can I?" She grinned, blood dribbling from her pointed teeth. "Besides, I thought you belonged to my sister."

"The Hecate washed her hands of me," Pete said. "Wouldn't do what she wanted."

"She's mercurial, that one," said the Morrigan. "What a marvelous word, *mercurial*. Like mercury. Ever-changing, never still. Much like me."

"Not the word I'd use," said Pete.

The Morrigan laughed. "Here you are, trapped in Purgatory, faced with the gods, and you've still got a mouth." She moved to Pete and stroked her cheek. "How rare you are, Pete."

"I'm not trying to trifle with you," Pete said. "I'm trying to shut the door that's been opened from here to the daylight world."

"Yeah," the Morrigan said. "And I come here, at

great personal risk, to tell you there's only one way to do that."

"I already know the price," Pete sighed. "I'm not afraid of dying."

The Morrigan shook her head. "You're afraid of leaving him behind, though. Your Jack." She made a spiteful sound. "You're not the one he's meant for, Petunia. I am. And I'll have him, make no mistake."

"Then why not just let me die, any number of times you could have?" Pete snarled. "Why keep fucking up my life, instead of just ending it? You've made it clear you have that power." She jabbed her finger into the Morrigan's chest. All her fear was gone now. When she had decided this was the end of the line, her fear had released her.

Nothing the Morrigan could do now would make anything worse.

"If I killed you, Jack would never help me," the Morrigan said. "He'd spend eternity in Hell first, and you know it." She spread her arms and feathers bloomed, wings forming from her fingers. Her eyes turned yellow, and the feathers spread over the rest of her body, covering her face as it elongated. "But if you're lost in a noble fight I help you with, only to just barely let victory slip away, then Jack owes me his allegiance. And I'll have it, Pete. Make no mistake."

"I know all I have to do is channel the soul well. Let the Weir take it," Pete said. "You're not going to tell me anything I don't know."

"Is that what you think? How simple a creature you are," the Morrigan said, laughing. Her feathers rustled, and her eyes narrowed in pleasure.

Pete set her jaw. "Tell me, then, since you're so keen to see me fail."

"You can't close a well by channeling it," the Morrigan said. "There's more power in Purgatory than a hundred Weirs could absorb in a lifetime, never mind that woman who started this mess. No, you've crossed over with that sacrificial soul, and now you have to find a way back. Pull the well after you and collapse it."

She grinned, and the blood rivulets on her chin gleamed crimson in the harsh white light of this empty place. "But you won't make it. No one who enters Purgatory makes an exit. That's why they call it Purgatory, Petunia. I'm afraid, as your dear Jack put it, that you're worm food."

The Morrigan spread her wings. "And now, he's all mine. Enjoy eternity, Petunia. It's going to be a much easier road now that you're not standing in it."

Pete's hand flashed out, before she even really thought about what a horrible, suicidal idea it was, and latched on to the Morrigan's arm. "You're wrong about one thing," she said.

The Morrigan gave a crow's cry, struggling.

"One thing did make it out of here at least once," Pete said. "You."

She opened her talent, with no hesitation, let the power of the goddess she held flow into her. "Maybe I don't have to drain Purgatory," Pete hissed in the Morrigan's ear, so close their bodies shared a heartbeat. "Maybe I just have to drain you."

"Bitch!" the Morrigan screamed, but Pete was beyond caring. The power was vast and cold, the power of death carried across every war, every plague, every place from the beginning, when death had taken root in bloody soil and spread its pall across the world.

Her body convulsed, the pain warning Pete that wherever her physical form was, she was burning from the inside out. The pain worked as an anchor, keeping her focused as the magic flowed from the Morrigan to her, more and more even as the Morrigan screamed and took flight with Pete still wrapping her in a tight embrace.

As they fell through Purgatory, Pete saw the place for what it was as her talent amplified her connection to the Black—not a block of flats but a blank place, a place of stone and ash dropping endlessly into a screaming void absent of stars, the cold of space encroaching. White things wriggled in the darkness like maggots in rot, reaching for her, so close that Pete knew that in another few seconds, she'd have been consumed by the worms and the Morrigan would have had Jack all to herself.

"You keep this up and you die!" the Morrigan screamed. "I'll have your soul, and it will be tormented in my army for eternity!"

Pete watched the Morrigan's inhuman gold eyes as they fell, never blinking. "You didn't believe me," she said, "but I was telling the truth. I'm not afraid of you.

Or death. I'm afraid of leaving the world to people like the Prometheans. I'm afraid of letting Jack down, and I'm afraid my daughter will forget me."

She dug her fingernails into the Morrigan's flesh, and at the touch of the goddess's blood, Pete's vision was filled only with magic, only with the power that was pouring into her so quickly it was a wonder she wasn't turning to ash.

"But you, Hag?" she hissed. "You don't scare me one fucking bit."

The Morrigan screeched, a sound so inhuman it echoed off everything in Purgatory, and then the white flashed away and Pete heard other sounds, sounds of the world she knew.

"Pete?" Jack's voice echoed as if from a tunnel. Like breaking the surface of a frozen pond, her eyes flew open and she saw a spotty gray sky, clouds drifting, felt a thumping on her chest like a hammer.

"Fuck off!" she shouted at Jack, who stopped using his clubbed fists to pump at her chest. "What the Hell are you doing?"

"CPR," he panted. "You stopped breathing."

"You're doing it all wrong," Pete said. The pain wasn't from the CPR, though. It was the power, burning her from the inside. The Morrigan was gone, but an eternity of power harvested from the dead still rode Pete's mind. Her vision blurred, her heart stuttered, and she felt her muscles go rigid and spastic with convulsions.

All at once Jack disappeared, shoved bodily out of

the way by Donovan, and Morwenna was bending over her.

"She channeled it right into her," Morwenna breathed. "I can't believe it. Donovan, we can still do it. She's got enough juice to light up Manchester."

"Hurry up," he said. "And Victor, will you please fucking keep control of my son? He almost smashed her ribcage to bits."

Morwenna grabbed Pete's face between her thumb and forefinger, squeezing hard enough to carve half-moons into Pete's flesh. "I don't care what happens to her body, Donovan. I just want what's riding it. Winter's far too much of a weakling to carry this kind of power. It's evident that I'll be taking up the mantle of the Merlin. Look how the power responds to me."

She placed her fingers on Pete's forehead and inhaled. "Give the power to me, old ones," she murmured. "I await you, your worthy servant, worthy of the gift first given one hundred generations past."

It was as if someone had placed a magnet against her. Pete felt all the power rush to the surface of her mind and travel through the pathways of her neurons toward Morwenna's voice. In the woman's clenched fist she saw the soul cage, still coaxing the vast energies of the emptiness toward the pain and suffering of the mage soul inside.

Well, she thought absently. *At least I'm not going to die in the mud. Might even make it to a hospital if I'm lucky.*

Beyond the roaring of the Morrigan's magic, she

heard a scream. At first she thought it was Margaret, but it was Morwenna, mouth open wide as it would go, a grotesque red slash of rage and disbelief.

The power left Pete as abruptly as it had come, and she fell back into the mud, that hit-by-a-lorry feeling worse than ever.

Beyond the circle of mages, Margaret gave a small shudder, a jolt, and then passed her hands over her face.

"What the fuck just happened?" she asked Jack.

"It's her," Victor said, his voice soft and full of awe. "The magic chose her."

"No!" Morwenna screamed, starting for Margaret. "It's mine! I made the offering! I said the words! I'm the one who bloody stepped up when it counted!"

Victor put an arm out and stopped her as easily as you'd stop a small child throwing a fit. "I'm sorry, Morwenna," he said. "But she's the Merlin. The Weir's energies chose her."

One by one, the mages of the Prometheus Club turned to Margaret, some staring with blantant hostility, others with curiosity.

"Guess that explains why you're not a worm, luv," Jack said, squeezing Margaret on the shoulder.

"Please accept my apology," Victor said, extending his hand to Margaret. "And consider this a formal offer to take your seat at the head of the Prometheus Club."

"Don't do it," Jack said instantly. "Worse than school. Make you wear an ugly suit like his. Install a stick up your arse on your eighteenth birthday."

Margaret just blinked, looking at her hands. "I feel

weird," she said, sticking herself to Jack like a burr. "I just want to go back to Manchester."

Morwenna dropped to her knees in the mud. Pete watched tears streak down her crimson face as sobs racked her body. "I've given my whole life," she said. "I've given everything. Everything I had and more. Don't I deserve something? Anything?"

Pete managed to pull herself into a sitting position, which hurt but wasn't impossible. She tried standing and found that wasn't bad, either.

"Donovan," Morwenna pleaded, grabbing at Donovan's hand. "You stood with me when everyone thought I was insane to try to become the new Merlin. You know it can't be this . . . this . . . *brat!*"

Donovan looked at Morwenna, then at Margaret, and gave a shrug. "Sorry, luv," he said. "Tough break."

Morwenna leaped at his back faster than seemed possible for a sobbing woman in a tight skirt, and Pete shouted. "Donovan, look out!"

Morwenna grabbed for the gun in Donovan's waistband, but he knocked her back into the mud. Morwenna raised her hand and started to speak a word of power, but Donovan whistled, sharp and high, before she could get it out.

Pete saw the shapes advance through the fog, cutting it like sharks in water, and she ran to Jack, pulling both him and Margaret into a crouch and covering the girl's eyes.

Only she had the vantage to see what happened.

The wraiths flew at Morwenna, drawn by the energy

Pete could feel crackling across her skin and pulsing through her blood. Donovan's talent was in full force, and the wraiths found easy prey as Morwenna struggled to get up from the mud. She barely made a sound, could only moan and quiver a bit as the wraiths drank her dry.

Victor and the other mages watched dispassionately, not blinking, Victor's expression a flat slate of nothing.

"We can go," Pete said, releasing her hold on Jack and Margaret. It was hard to let go of Jack, but she made herself do it. "The well's closed. It shouldn't be affecting our senses any longer."

"No," Jack said, harsh as the sound Morwenna had made. "We're making sure she's dead."

They watched as the wraiths drank, then drifted away, sated, at Donovan's bidding. Pete tugged on Jack. "We really need to go."

"You're not going anywhere," Donovan intoned. "The Merlin comes with us." He stuck out his arm to Margaret. "Come, child."

Margaret stepped back, shaking her head wildly. "Get away from me. I don't know you."

"Either we take the Merlin, or I leave your bodies for the ravens," Donovan snarled. "Those are your options."

He fixed Jack with a look of utter contempt. "I had hoped you'd take up your seat, boy, but now I'm almost glad I'll be disposing of you. You're nothing but a disappointment, Jack, in every way possible."

Jack started to reply, but Pete all at once knew she'd had enough of Donovan Winter. Enough to last her a lifetime, and then some.

She set herself and hit him, in the soft spot just under his cheek. Donovan's head snapped around as the sound of the punch echoed back from the hillside.

Donovan dropped, mud splashing all over him, bruise already in full bloom. "You've seen what I can do," Pete told him, keeping her eyes on the rest of the Prometheans. "You lot so much as send a stray thought my way again and you know what'll happen. I can light every last one of you ablaze with a finger snap, so I suggest you use those few brain cells you have, Donovan, and stay out of our lives from now on."

She glared around at the rest of the staring faces. "Anybody else got a problem with leaving the Weir to her business?"

Nobody did.

She took Margaret's hand and started to walk away, but Jack stopped.

"Oh, and Dad," he said, as Donovan struggled to get to his feet. "You can slag me off all you want, but as far as disappointing you goes . . ." He grinned at Donovan, and it was the Jack grin Pete knew, not the pale imitation his father used. "I can't remember when I've been more fucking proud of meself. You ever come near me family again, I'll fucking kill you."

He turned his back and said to Pete, "Let's go, luv. I've had me fill of the country."

"That makes two of us," Pete grumbled. "I've got so much mud on me, I may never leave greater London again."

As they descended the hill and found one of the Prometheans' parked cars to take, Pete realized she could see again. The fog had lifted from Overton. The black cairn marking the soul well was knocked over, and the tree had withered down to a twisted stump.

The sky was clear.

The ravens had gone.

28.

It was a simple enough matter to convince the care workers in Manchester to let Pete take custody of Margaret, at least temporarily. The Smythes didn't have any relatives, and Pete was a responsible sort who actually *wanted* to take control of a belligerent thirteen-year-old. The care worker practically threw the paperwork at her with a bow on it.

When they were on the train back to London, Margaret dozing, Pete put her head on Jack's shoulder and finally let her eyes close. "How are you?" she asked softly.

He sucked in a breath, and then she felt his arm slide around her, fingers squeezing hard enough to leave a mark. "How d'you think I am?"

"Feeling like shite, probably," Pete murmured. "Same as me."

"Too right," Jack sighed. "This was a Hell of a week, Petunia, I won't lie. 'M as bloody and battered as I ever have been."

"I'm sorry I lied to you," Pete said, so softly she didn't know if Jack heard her over the roar of the train.

He was quiet for a moment, and then she felt his chest expand with a sigh. "If you'd told me you were planning to channel the soul well, I'd've done something boneheaded to stop you."

"You had to know I wouldn't just lie down for someone like Morwenna," Pete said.

"Yeah," Jack agreed. "But you did right not telling me, and I can admit that."

"I hated it," Pete confessed, feeling a hot prickle in her eyes and willing them to stay dry. "The thought of never seeing you or Lily again. But I hated the thought of us living in a place like that more."

"I think about it sometimes," Jack said. "One or the other of us not making it. I'm not like you, Pete. I can't even consider it."

Pete found his hand and squeezed it. Jack wasn't one to rush in on a white horse. She'd made peace with that long ago, and it was fine. She could be the hero, and he could be the rock. It'd be a nice change for once. "You would. If it was me or Lily. You have. You're the bravest man I know, Jack Winter, and that'll never change."

"You think that's it?" Jack said. "That the Prometheans'll listen and stay away?"

"I don't know," Pete said, not wanting to voice what she did know. She'd merely hit pause on what was coming, not ended it. The Morrigan was more intent than ever on having Jack for her own. The Black was irreparably broken, and the appearance of the soul well was only the first major crack in the walls between worlds.

"I don't even bloody care at this point." Jack put his arm around her, holding her to him. "I'm sorry," he said. "About Donovan and all of that. You think you don't give a fuck about those people, and then they show up and they slice you right to the fucking core, like you were six years old again. To think for a few seconds there I actually considered forgiving that cunt . . ."

Pete stopped him, shaking her head. "Jack, your parents were horrid, awful, selfish people, and Donovan made the choice to mess with black magic and try to grab a little more power rather than do right by his son," she said. "Don't fucking apologize for him."

He laughed, rough and regretful. "We'll do better. Especially now that it seems we've got two."

"We will," Pete agreed. "I mean, how hard could it possibly be to do better than my crazy mum and your homicidal dad?"

Jack kissed the top of her head. "You always know exactly what to say to a bloke."

"It's my superpower," Pete said. She nestled into Jack's chest again. "It all worked out," she said. "I mean, as well as it ever does for us."

Jack stared out the train window, and Pete followed his gaze. The sky was gray and peaceful, as if the world held its breath, above the spires and down into the deepest core of the earth, where the dead lay silent.

A deception, but one she could let Jack live with, at least until the end of the train line.

He drifted off after a time, leaving Pete alone with the memories of what she'd seen on the hill, under the black cairn.

I'll have him in the end, the Morrigan whispered in her ear, and Pete knew, deep down in the place where she knew things beyond thought or reason, and discerned the veracity in the old gods' words with her talent, that the Hag spoke the truth.

And that she was going to have to figure out how to prove the Morrigan wrong.

Epilogue

That is not dead which can eternal lie,
And with strange aeons even death may die
                                    —H. P. Lovecraft

29.

Victoria Station was the most welcome sight Pete had ever set eyes on. Full of people and movement, just normal people going about their day, the place was un-believeably soothing. She had missed the crowds of her city, and the ebb and flow of the Black that, while not comfortable, was at least familiar.

Jack was phoning Lawrence to meet them with Lily when Pete became aware of another presence, like a shadow falling across her face.

"Save the day again, did you?" Belial said. "You're getting to be a proper little superhero, Petunia."

Jack started as he saw the demon standing between them all at once, his slim form slotting neatly into the space. "Fuck," he said. "I hate it when you do that."

"Leave," Pete said. "I told you we were done talking."

"Oh, what we talked about holds truer than ever," said Belial. "But lovely as you are, Petunia, I never did get to the point of my little visit in Overton. That bit concerns your knight in shining hair bleach."

"You two talked? In Overton?" Jack's eyes narrowed,

and Pete couldn't tell if he was angrier with Belial or her.

"I was going to tell you," she said. "But it did kick off just a bit right after I saw him." She just thanked her lucky stars that Margaret was getting food at one of the cafes that lined the main concourse, and she didn't have to see Belial in the flesh. No child needed that in their nightmares.

Jack shot Belial the bird. "Fuck off," he said, with only a hint of annoyance. Belial was terrifying, but he was also oddly irritating when he was right there, in your face, talking his usual line of shit. Pete empathized with Jack's urge to swat the demon off him like a chatty house fly.

"Aren't you even interested to hear what would bring me up from the comforts of Hell to speak with you? Because let's face it, Jack, you're not a font of witty conversation on your best day."

"No," Jack grumbled, shutting his eyes again. "Or, fuck off."

Belial tsked and turned his gaze on Pete. "How about you, luv? You're interested, aren't you? You know that I know what I'm talking about."

"If we listen, will you leave us alone?" Pete sighed. Belial cracked his knuckles and grinned at them.

"So it turns out being a Prince of Hell isn't all torturing underlings with pliers and massages from nubile succubi," said Belial. "Turns out, there's a bit of a scuffle down in the Pit at the moment."

"What a shock," Jack grumbled. "Treacherous cunts turning on one another. Amazing turn of events."

"Why should we care if somebody is marching with placards against you?" Pete asked Belial.

"Because this particular treacherous cunt doesn't just have his eye on Hell," Belial said. "Ambitious little fucker wants the whole pie."

"Like any one demon could rule the Black," Jack muttered. "Most of you can't even manage to get off your arses and leave Hell."

"Not the Black," Belial said, and for the first time his voice was a cold blade against Pete's neck that sent an involuntary shudder through her. "The whole world. Daylight, dead side, probably even the in-between. All of it." He stood and straightened his tie. "I'm not about to let him upset my apple cart. And having the crow-mage on my side would ensure that."

Jack snorted a laugh. "Yeah, me work with you voluntarily? What'd be in it for me?"

Pete saw the irritation flick across Belial's face, a weirdly human expression that made her slightly sick to her stomach. "You may not care beyond your next pint and wank," said Belial. "But you're going to have to live in the aftermath."

"Same question," Jack said. "I don't owe you shite, mate. Quite the other way around, after I did you that favor with Abbadon."

"You know what's coming," said Belial, and Pete felt the Black vibrate all around them, saw shadows quake at the corner of her vision as the demon's power washed over her. "You both know. The end, Jack. The full stop, the period at the end of the sentence. The Morrigan will march across the burnt face of the world, and you'll be the dead man riding at the head of her army. It's inevitable, and you've always known it."

"Fuck off," Jack said, but his voice was barely a whisper. Pete wrapped her arms around herself as Belial's shadow lengthened and the temperature dropped.

"I can offer you a way out," Belial said. "You help me, I'll help you get out from under the Hag's claws."

"You think we're stupid?" Pete blurted. "If you really knew how to help Jack out with the Morrigan why didn't you dangle it before?"

Belial shrugged. "I never needed you before, Petunia. Was you lot who needed me." He worried his ruby cufflinks with his black claws. "It's a good bargain, crow-mage. It's one of the best bargains I've ever made, and I've been making them a very long time."

"So," Jack said slowly. He'd sat up, and his crystal eyes were fixed on the demon's obsidian ones. "Let me get this straight. I go to Hell, I help you put a boot up this demon's arse, and you help me get the Morrigan off my back once and for all?"

"Yes," Belial said.

"Bullshit," Jack snapped. "I know you. You're a tricky bastard, and you'd never make a deal if there wasn't some third angle working in the back."

"There is *no* angle," Belial retorted. "I want to bargain. What about that is so hard to believe?"

All at once, Pete recognized the emotion on the demon's face. The fact that there was an emotion to be seen was startling enough, but even more alarming was that it was fear. Demons didn't feel fear. Even when Abbadon had escaped and Belial's responsibility was to bring him back, he hadn't shown fear.

"It's already happened, hasn't it?" she asked. "You're on the outs."

Belial flared his nostrils. "The other Princes and I aren't on the best of terms," he said. "But I still rule. I am still one of the Triumverate."

Pete looked to Jack. "He's scared enough to play straight with you," she said.

Jack sighed. Pete silently willed him to take the bargain. She'd never thought it would come to this, hoping for a bargain with a spawn of the pit, but if it would get Jack out from under the yoke of the Morrigan, then almost anything would be worth it.

"All right," he said to Belial at last. "You've got me."

"Us," Pete said. Belial flicked his eyes to her.

"Excuse me?"

Pete stood to face him. When Belial was in his human form, she was nearly as tall as the demon. "You want Jack, you get me, too," she said. "I'm not leaving him with you again."

Belial sniffed, as if she were a teenager clinging to her boyfriend's arm. "Fine," he said. "Two is as good as one, I suppose. And you, you little harbinger of doom . . ." He reached out and flicked his fingers across her cheek, before Jack's growl dissuaded him. "How could I resist?"

The demon walked a few feet away, then glared over his shoulder. "Well?" he said. "What are we waiting for?"

Pete picked up her bag. "Margaret," she called. "You wait right here, luv, and Lawrence will be 'round to get you in just a moment."

"Pete . . ." Margaret said, face crinkling with concern.

"I'll be back before you know it," Pete said.

She turned to walk with Jack and squeezed his hand with her free one. He didn't say anything, but he squeezed in return.

They followed the demon, Pete's heart in her throat, until all she could hear was the beating of it, and the scream of the train whistle as it rumbled from the station, leaving her and Jack behind.

"Kittredge knows how to create a believable world, and her fans will enjoy the mix of magic and city grit." —*Publishers Weekly*

Look for these other novels in the
Black London series from

CAITLIN KITTREDGE

Devil's Business
Bone Gods
Demon Bound
Street Magic

…and don't miss Kittredge's Nocturne City series

Daemon's Mark
Witch Craft
Second Skin
Pure Blood
Night Life

Available from St. Martin's Paperbacks

AY 2 8 2017
AUG 0 9 2018